BOOK ONE OF THE NARBONNE INHERITANCE

The Viscount's Daughter

PHYLLIS HALL HAISLIP

ɘ୬ ୬ɘ

WAKEFIELD BOOKS

For Otis

And for my many young readers
who are now adults. I treasure your enthusiasm and support.

Acknowledgements

Special thanks to thank my writing partners, Laurin Wittig and Kathy Huffman. Their contribution to the success of my book is immeasurable as is that of my husband, Otis, who sends me off five days a week to write.

Jeannine Johnson Maia read an early draft of *The Viscount's Daughter*. Her insightful comments were a big help to me as the book progressed, as were her careful edits when the book was finished. I would also like to thank Russ and Peg Hall who read the book and offered suggestions. I appreciated the kinds words of reader Professor Lee Alexander. As always, Laurin Wittig has been my greatest help and inspiration with everything from computer problems to professional advice.

I would also like to thank my copy editor, Cindy Valler, and my cover designer, Ravven. I'm grateful for their high professional standards and attention to detail. I am indebted to readers Thayer Cory and Cindy Callaway for valuable input.

I would be remiss not to thank those historians who have shared their expertise with me: Bennett D. Hill, Richard Emory, and Joseph F. O'Callaghan. I am especially grateful for the encouragement of my friend and mentor, Professor Walter Wakefield.

Books by Phyllis Haislip

Lottie's Courage, a Contraband Slave's Story, Winner of the Beacon of Freedom Award

Anybody's Hero, the Battle of Old Men and Young Boys

Divided Loyalties, A Revolutionary War Fifer's Story

Lili's Gift, A Civil War Healer's Story

Between the Lines, A Revolutionary War Slave's Journey to Freedom, winner of the Edith Thompson Award for Juvenile Fiction

The Time Magus, A Time-Travel Adventure

Marching in Time, The Colonial Williamsburg Fife and Drum Corps

A novel based on the life of Ermengarde of Narbonne
1126?-1196

Prologue

Fraga, Hispania, 1134

VISCOUNT AYMERI OF NARBONNE GAZED across the dusty plain, his vassal, Peter of Minerve, by his side. Less than a Roman mile away, a Moorish army massed for another attack on their small band of crusaders. "We're surrounded and outnumbered," Aymeri said. "I doubt I'll live to see the evening star."

Minerve wiped the sweat from his brow. "King Alfonso plans to break through a weak spot in the enemy line. It just may work."

Aymeri took the measure of the hundreds of camels and countless turbaned horsemen arrayed against them, and then shook his head. "I have a last request to make of you, *mon ami.*"

Minerve frowned. "With God's grace, we will break through the battle line, escape, and fight another day."

Aymeri bit his lip. "I appreciate your confidence. In truth, I never imagined it might come to this."

"Who would have thought Moors from southern Hispania would come to the aid of Fraga with such an impressive force? Our siege has turned into a debacle."

"And we are but fish caught in a net. If I don't make it back to Narbonne, will you swear to do everything in your power to make sure my daughters don't fall under the control of Toulouse? He has long coveted Narbonne."

"But surely you will survive this day."

Aymeri locked eyes with Minerve and needed to say no more.

Minerve went down on one knee, and then held out his sword to swear a sacred oath. "With God as my witness, if I survive this day, I will honor your request."

Aymeri clapped his friend on the back with his gauntleted hand. *"Merci, mon ami*, I can ask for no more. May God grant us victory." He mounted his destrier, a great agile warhorse, and then put down the visor of his helmet. His heart pounded. A man-at-arms handed him his lance.

Aymeri and Minerve fell in behind the red-and-gold-striped banner of King Alfonso of Aragon, the Battler. When he lowered it, they would charge. Aymeri hastily counted the force that would try to break through the enemy lines. Of the seven hundred knights who had begun the siege, only sixty were left. Sixty knights against the huge army of Moors. Rivulets of sweat ran down his face and back. He whispered a prayer to the warrior saint, "Saint Michael, deliver us in battle."

THE VISCOUNT'S DAUGHTER

Aymeri held his horse to a walk, advancing with the other knights as they waited for the king's signal. The sun glinted off the mail and bright banners of the crusaders. The only sounds were the clanking of their armor and the jingle of their horses' trappings. Far overhead, vultures circled lazily in the cloudless sky.

The king lowered his standard, and Aymeri spurred his destrier. A great cloud of dust rose, warhorses' hooves thudded, and his yelling joined that of the other knights as they gathered speed. A wave of mounted Moors, in their red and blue robes and white turbans, charged toward them from the enemy line.

Aymeri crashed into an advancing Moor. His lance shattered on the overlapping ellipses of the hard Moorish shield. The man holding it careened backward. Aymeri drew his sword, flailing at the swarm of infidels, who came at him from every side with their deadly curved swords. He parried assailants to left and right, dimly realizing the apparent weakness in the Moors' battle line was only a ruse. The enemy had been poised to encircle them and now swarmed around the crusaders like angry bees from a disturbed hive.

Beside him, a Moor skewered Minerve. He tumbled from his horse, his white surcoat spattered with blood. Aymeri spurred to his aid. A sudden onrush of Moors prevented him from reaching his friend. He didn't see his own attacker, but heard the ear-shattering sound of metal against metal as an enemy sword crushed his helmet. A veil of blood blinded him, and before he reached the ground, he saw no more. His last thought was of his daughter, Ermengarde, still a small child, but now heiress to the rich Viscounty of Narbonne. How he regretted leaving her and her sister alone in the world.

Anduze ●

Nîmes ●

● Toulouse

Béziers ●

Carcassonne ●
Narbonne ●

Middle Sea
(Mediterranean Sea)

In the early years of the twelfth century, there was no national state of France as we know it today. The king of the Franks in far-off Paris could not control his wealthy and powerful vassals in the south. Ermengarde's viscounty was a collection of fiefs or holdings and rights, rather than a territory with a defined boundary.

Chapter 1

Toulouse, 1142

ERMENGARDE'S EYES NARROWED IN DISMAY as she entered the gloomy great hall. Peter of Minerve was deep in conversation with her guardian, Alfonse Jordan, Count of Toulouse. In his fashionable, worsted, orange-and-brown surcoat and pointed-toed shoes, no one would have guessed that Minerve had arrived at the Château Comtal only that morning.

She made a point of not looking at them as they sat, with their heads together, at a trestle table at the far end of the hall. Instead she studied the flags and pennons, displaying the maroon and gold twelve-pointed cross of Toulouse, that hung along the centuries-old, stone walls of the hall and from the heavy oak beams arching above it. These heraldic decorations proclaimed louder than any town crier the power and importance of the counts of Toulouse.

Skirting two tables of hearth knights—Toulouse's personal entourage—and men-at-arms, she joined the other women. Each afternoon they gathered near the fire to sew, gossip, and be seen.

Ermengarde sat on the cushioned settle next to her younger sister and picked up her embroidery. The new hair coif was for Ermessende, affectionately called Missee, and would have tiny, blue flowers on it. Missee sewed expertly, but her eyesight was too poor for close work, and to save her sister from squinting, Ermengarde routinely did all their fine embroidery. The fire, always lit in the morning, had gone out, and the hall was growing cold. Ermengarde's chilled hands were awkward as she threaded the needle and then snipped the thread with the little scissors hanging from her girdle.

Jordana, Toulouse's haughty daughter, knitted her dark eyebrows together. "Tell us, Ermengarde, what you learned today from your handsome tutor."

Ermengarde tried to ignore Jordana, whose tongue was as sharp as her angular features. She'd long resented Ermengarde because she was the wealthy heiress to the Viscounty of Narbonne. However, Jordana hadn't been vindictive until her father had asked Ermengarde to marry him and she refused. Now, she was often the target of Jordana's caustic innuendos.

"Well?" Jordana demanded.

"We worked on chess strategy today."

Jordana's mean-spirited laugh echoed through the hall. "I bet that's not the only game you two play."

Missee's earnest heart-shaped face creased into a frown. "You know Ermengarde has always loved learning."

Ermengarde gave her sister a gentle nudge with the toe of her leather slipper. She shouldn't have risen to Jordana's baiting.

Jordana snorted. "That's not all she loves."

Ermengarde swallowed to control her anger, but she could no longer remain silent. "*Pour l'amour de Dieu*, you listen too much to the tales of love spun by the troubadours, Jordana."

"Deny you care for him," she persisted, eyes glittering.

Ermengarde felt her face redden. Jordana had gone too far this time. "I'm not in love with Father Damian. He's only my tutor. He's well spoken and courteous, traits many of the uncouth hearth knights and men-at-arms, who frequent the great hall, would do well to emulate." Her response was more defensive than she would have wished. She had been drawn into an exchange despite her best intentions.

Jordana smirked. "If I spent as many hours a week as you do with an attractive young man, I'd use the time more profitably than you seem to."

The little hairs on the back of Ermengarde's neck prickled. "I'm sure you would," she said archly.

Minerve strode purposely across the cavernous great hall. Sleeping dogs scattered and goshawks, tethered to their perches, wildly flapped their wings, putting an end to their conversation. He approached, and Ermengarde sensed, with a feeling of dread, why he had come to Toulouse.

"Lady Ermengarde, I'd like to speak with you alone," he said.

She studied his lined face with its jutting chin, sharp nose, and unseeing, milky, left eye that he had lost at the battle of Fraga. He had visited her infrequently in the years she had been in Toulouse, but she was predisposed to like and trust him because he'd been her father's vassal and friend. Now, she wasn't so sure. He'd spent the entire morning, it seemed, ingratiating himself to Toulouse. Possibly, his unseeing eye made her uneasy, or it could be his penchant for finery, so unusual for a lesser noble of limited means.

"Privacy? In the Château Comtal?" She raised her eyebrows. "One would be as likely to find gold in a pig's trough." The other women, listening to the exchange, tittered at her remark. "Perhaps we could walk on the curtain wall. The day's fair, and no one will bother us there."

She put down her sewing and touched her sister's hand. "Missee, I'll return soon."

Ermengarde took her mantle, the color of blue cornflowers, from a peg by the door. She loved blue, and its bright presence among the other dull mantles always lifted her spirits. She fastened it with the ancient silver brooch her father had once given to her mother. With its ornate key intertwined with grape vines, the brooch bore the symbol of the Viscounty of Narbonne, her inheritance, the only real home she'd ever known. They made their way along the dank corridor to the winding stairs that led to the curtain wall.

The dark stairway gave way to the sunshine and clear sky of the afternoon. A kite circled above them, calling his shrill phee-phew. For a few moments, they wordlessly looked out at the sprawling city of Toulouse, with its rose-colored stone buildings and orange tiled roofs, surrounded by stout walls. Toulouse never ceased to fascinate Ermengarde. It was the largest and most powerful city in the lands of the southern Franks, and some people said its ruler, the count, would one day control all the territories between Barcelona and Paris. A smoky smell hung in the air, and she craned her neck to see its source. A thin smudge of smoke rose in the distance. Someone outside of the city burned leaves or a field.

Minerve cleared his throat. "Lady Ermessende is well on her way to becoming a great beauty."

Where was this leading? "A beauty yes, but like her mother, she's frail, like a tiny bird."

"A beauty like her sister."

Against her will, a flush heated Ermengarde's cheeks. "You forget that Missee's only my half sister."

"I knew both your mothers and both were lovely like their daughters." Minerve seemed lost in thought for a moment. "Would you mind if I sit? My old bones grow weary."

"Please do. Although I'll not accept you are growing old." Two could play at the game of flattery.

Minerve settled himself on one of the gap-toothed openings on the ramparts. Ermengarde sat across from him on the sun-warmed stones, folding her hands in her lap so the wide sleeves of her emerald-green gown covered them. "What is it, Minerve? What is so important we need to discuss it alone? I have no secrets from Missee or anyone else in the castle."

Minerve coughed and then looked directly at her with his one good eye. "Toulouse asked me here to speak with you about his offer of marriage."

"I know you have my best interests at heart." She paused, wondering again, as she said it, if he really did have her best interests at heart. "My answer is still no. I don't want to marry him. He cares not a whit for me. He only wants my inheritance."

Minerve seemed unfazed by her refusal. "He already calls himself Duke of Narbonne. Your patrimony is one of the pieces he needs to strengthen his hold on the lands of the southern Franks. For more than eight years now, you have been Toulouse's ward. *Certes*, he has acted honorably toward you."

Ermengarde's heart plummeted. She could hardly believe what he had just said. "Honorably? How can you say that when he has been despoiling my patrimony these many years? He has collected rents and tolls where none are traditionally due. He has refused to allow the heirs of my vassals to inherit their estates, sending instead the returns from these lands to his coffers. He has raped my lands and now will not be content until he has me, too."

"Lady Ermengarde, you must remember it is the overlord's prerogative to enjoy the fruits of his ward's estates. It is the price one pays for the security of wardship."

"Enjoy is one thing, despoil is another. I am no more than a pawn in Toulouse's chess game. A pawn that must be eliminated."

"Who has told you this? Surely someone has been filling your head with exaggerations and lies."

Ermengarde could sit still no longer. She stood and, shading her eyes from the bright sun, looked out on the Via Aquitania, the Roman road that connected her city of Narbonne to the city of Toulouse. A peddler with a full sack of goods, a young girl leading a cow, and a heavily laden wain, a farm wagon, approached from the direction of Narbonne. The cow stopped and bellowed. The girl yanked on its rope, and the pair continued on their way. A leper walked along in the other direction, sounding his bell to warn people away. Two small boys emerged from a ditch and pelted him with stones. She took a deep breath and then turned back to Minerve. "I may be inexperienced and have little knowledge of the world, but I'm not stupid. Everyone in the Château Comtal knows Toulouse is in league with the Archbishop of Narbonne, and together they have laid claim to what is legally mine."

Minerve joined her. "You're young, and you shouldn't bother with such matters. They're not women's concerns."

Young? Not women's concerns? Blood rushed to Ermengarde's face. How could he be so patronizing? She was almost seventeen years old, and many girls her age had been already married for two or three years. "I am making them my concerns. You forget that my father made me his heir."

"No, I haven't forgotten your father or that he made you his heir, Ermengarde. It's just that marriage to Toulouse would serve both your interests. And it's unheard of for an heiress to reject whatever marriage her lord arranges for her."

"I fail to see how it would serve my interests to marry Toulouse. He will control my lands, and I won't even warm his bed. He already has his scheming whore, Mahalt, to do that."

Minerve took her hand in his rough one. "You've become unnecessarily upset. Sit down. Since you are determined to be blunt, I'll be blunt, too."

She pulled her hand free and sat. As she did so, one of the castle guards, a young man with a misshapen nose and an under bite, lingered on his rounds with his ears stretched, trying to overhear their conversation. The guard obviously hoped for a tidbit he could dangle before his cohorts tonight in the great hall or, worse still, use to curry favor with Toulouse. Wolves. She had dreamed last night she was surrounded by wolves.

Minerve sat beside her, letting out a sigh of exasperation. With a slight nod of her head, Ermengarde indicated the guard, straining to hear their conversation, and Minerve lowered his voice. "Every powerful lord has a mistress or two. And if you find him so objectionable, as you clearly do, not having to pay the marriage debt could make the marriage more amenable to you."

A whiff of manure rose from the paved bailey, and Ermengarde glanced down to see stable boys shoveling it into a two-wheeled cart. A buxom laundry maid, with her sleeves rolled up and wisps of curly hair escaping from her coif, stopped to chat with one of the grooms supervising the work. Seeing she was being watched, the maid picked up her laundry basket and, giving the groom a saucy smile, left. Ermengarde clenched her fist. She had hardly even spoken to Toulouse and never flirted with a young man. Now, Minerve urged her to marry a man three times her age, a man she disliked and distrusted.

Minerve stared at his hands, and she had the distinct feeling he was making a decision. He towered over her, giving her no room to do aught but stay where she was. "You must listen to reason. If you refuse to marry Toulouse, he'll continue to despoil your lands. You will be his ward until you are beyond marriageable age. Then he will claim you refused a reasonable offer of marriage and send you to a convent. You are a sensible girl, mature beyond your years. Toulouse wants you to understand your alternatives."

"I'm sensible enough to understand he has been anxiously waiting for his wife to die so he can remarry. What kind of man wishes for the death of the mother of his children? And there have been rumors."

Minerve frowned. "You surely don't believe Toulouse had any part in hastening his wife's death?"

"It's said she may have been poisoned with something that Moors use, something having no taste or color."

"I've heard the rumors, too, and even that Mahalt administered the poison." Minerve shook his head. "Idle gossip. Nothing more."

"Perhaps Toulouse didn't poison his wife. I will grant you that. But at the very least, he made no effort to hide his whore or his bastards, keeping them here in the castle for years where his poor, sick wife saw them every day. That was nothing but cruel."

Below them, the creaky wain, filled with ironbound wine casks, lumbered into the bailey, scattering copper-colored maran hens in front of it and setting the hunting hounds barking. She stared down at her brooch with its grapevines, wondering if the fat kegs were from her viscounty.

Minerve sat again. "Ermengarde, Toulouse is a politician. And he must do what is politically expedient, independent of his personal wishes. And so must you."

"I understand that if he were to follow his personal wishes, he'd marry that whore, Mahalt."

Minerve ran a hand through his wispy hair and pursed his lips. "King Louis VII is weak and can't control his vassals. He trained as a monk, not as a warrior. Toulouse is carving out a kingdom for himself, one equal to that of King Louis. You will be countess and, possibly one day, queen of a kingdom of the southern Franks."

Ermengarde's eyes filled with tears of frustration. "If my father wished me to be Toulouse's ward, is it possible he may have hoped I would marry his son, Raymond, born the year Father left for Hispania?"

Minerve's brow furrowed, and he was silent for a long moment. "When I returned from Hispania, you and your sister were already here. Toulouse assured me he had an agreement with your father."

"And you believed him?"

"He showed me a document."

"Did you read it?"

Minerve's face flushed. "I'm not much at reading. But I recognized your father's signature."

"Missee and I were taken from Narbonne by force."

"By force? Your memories are most probably confused. What you thought of as force was probably only the removal of you and your sister from Narbonne, a separation perhaps from a favorite nursemaid."

The memory of the screams of Ermengarde's nurse, followed by the brutal clubbing of one of the men-at-arms who had tried to intervene, flashed into her mind. "I remember being carried from the palace kicking and screaming."

Minerve's face grew stony. "You were just a child. You're still young and a woman. I can't expect you to understand the political realities of the situation. This discussion is getting us nowhere. Your choices come down to marriage to Toulouse or the cloister." His face was as solemn as his words. He paused for a long moment. "Can I tell Toulouse you have consented?"

Ermengarde swallowed the bile that rose in her throat. "No, you may not. I must speak to my confessor first." She was playing for time. If her marriage to Toulouse was inevitable, she hoped to delay it as long as possible.

THE VISCOUNT'S DAUGHTER

Minerve walked to the head of the stairs, paused, and faced her. "Speak with whomever you wish, but Toulouse is anxious to wed and will not be denied. He's expecting your answer by the morrow." He spoke evenly, but his words were a command, not a request. With a lingering look that Ermengarde couldn't read, he disappeared down the stairs.

* * *

Toulouse studied the Templar knight, seated across from him in his private solar, the anteroom to his bedchamber. The solar was a small, ill-appointed room, with no fireplace and only one high narrow window. The Templar sat uneasily on a carved, oak chair with a faded cushion, as if both chair and cushion were unnecessary luxuries. The Templars were warrior monks, who had been founded to protect Jerusalem and the holy sites where Christ had lived. As a result, the Templar's skin was dark from the bright sun of Outremer, and his body taut from fighting. He wore the spotless surcoat of the Templars with its distinctive red cross. Toulouse noted with approval the bulging muscles evident under the Templar's mail.

"Would you like wine?" Toulouse asked, picking up a jug and filling a cup, but hesitating before filling the second one.

"Thank you," the Templar said. "The journey has been long and dry."

Toulouse filled the second cup and then handed one to the Templar. "Ranulf, did the Grand Master explain why you've been sent here?"

Ranulf shook his head. "He said only that you had plans of interest to our order."

Toulouse ran a hand through his thinning hair and then took a drink of wine. "There is much I need to explain to you."

The Templar steepled his hands. "I'm familiar with the exploits of Raymond of Saint Gilles, your father, in Outremer and your family's hold on the County of Tripoli."

Yes, that was to be expected. "But did you know my father turned down the kingship of Jerusalem?"

"I heard he was a man of such great religious zeal that he refused to rule in a city where Christ had suffered."

"Piety didn't prevent Godfrey of Bouillon from becoming king of Jerusalem." Toulouse paused for effect. "I intend to make up for my father's failure to establish a kingdom. A strong ruler here in the south could end the continual warfare of the nobles, bringing peace and prosperity to the region."

The Templar leaned forward. "What would the role of the Templars be in your new kingdom of Franks?"

"The Templars would keep the peace."

Ranulf sat back in the chair, the hint of smile on his thin lips. "And the Templars would render ineffective the bishops and archbishops who, like the petty nobles in the area, are jealously guarding their power and prerogatives. But what about King Louis le Jeune? *Certes*, he'll object to you establishing your own kingdom when he is your overlord and styles himself king of all the Franks."

"King Louis and I have already clashed. He sought to claim Toulouse on behalf of his wife, Eleanor of Aquitaine. He laid siege to my city a year ago and left with his tail between his legs. I'm confident any attempts he might make to foil my plans will come to naught. He's not a strong leader."

Toulouse reached for a parchment on the scarred table. He unrolled it and then spread it out before the Templar. "The Trencavel brothers control Béziers, Carcassonne, and Nîmes." He pointed to the areas on the map. "I've allied myself with Raymond of Béziers, and that is tantamount to neutralizing the other brothers. They generally stick together." He pointed to Montpellier. "Viscount William may be a problem. I supported his town consulate when they rose against him. Their rebellion failed, but I still have supporters there." Toulouse's finger rested on Narbonne, and he tapped the site with his finger. "The most important port is Narbonne, and I've been controlling the city with the cooperation of the archbishop on behalf of my ward, the heiress to the city, Viscountess Ermengarde. The only problem is that she has reached a marriageable age and has refused to marry me." He took his finger off the map and leaned back in his chair.

"And why is that?" the Templar asked, stretching out his legs and crossing his ankles.

Toulouse drained his wine cup. "I can't understand the girl's reluctance. It's after all my prerogative to choose a husband for her. Her refusal is without precedence, especially since I've been generous to her. I've given both her and her sister fine horses and, at Christmas, they both got handsome purses to buy whatever baubles women like. God's teeth, I've even honored her wish for more book learning. I'm not exaggerating when I say that there are few women in the lands of the Franks who wouldn't jump at my offer of marriage."

Ranulf's thin lips were set in a narrow line. "One reason I became a Templar was so that I wouldn't have to deal with the foolishness of women. I know little of such matters, but mayhap, if your ward is so difficult, you'd do better to place her in a convent."

Toulouse snorted. "I've called in Minerve. He was a friend of her father's. He'll talk some sense into her."

The Templar took an apple from the wooden bowl on the table and then turned it over and over in his hand. "Who is this Minerve? I've not heard of him."

"You are new to the area or you would know he's a shadow man, a peacock. When I summoned him, like one of my hounds he jumped at the chance to lick my hand."

The Templar frowned. "So why did you summon him if he's worthless?" He put the apple back in the bowl.

"Vain, but not entirely worthless, if he can sway Ermengarde. He fought with her father, Viscount Aymeri, at the Battle of Fraga.

"I've heard of the battle. There apparently were few survivors."

"The Moors assembled a huge force to relieve the besieged city of Fraga. Ten crusaders escaped through the infidel lines with King Alfonso. The others died. Minerve was seriously wounded." Toulouse laughed scornfully. "Then, as now, he was fond of fancy dress. The Moors, seeing his expensive surcoat, probably thought he was an important noble and could command a fat ransom. So they captured him and kept him alive. But the Moors hadn't heard the last of King Alfonso The king met with reinforcements and attacked the Moors as they loaded ships with prisoners and freed them. The Moors had one shipload full of the heads of fallen knights. That's a detail few forget. Minerve eventually recovered enough to return to his viscounty near Narbonne."

"That's quite a tale," the Templar said. "And your ward's father died?"

Toulouse was thoughtful for a moment. "Yes. His head most assuredly was one of the ones on the boat. I never got along with Aymeri. He was a thorn in my side. His daughter seems to have inherited his contrariness. But she will marry me, and the marriage will secure not only Narbonne, but also will ensure an alliance with Barcelona. Her father was half-brother to the Count of Barcelona, and any success I have in establishing a kingdom will depend on friendly relations with Barcelona."

* * *

Viscount Bernard of Anduze gazed at the 216 steps in front of him that led to the shrine of the Black Virgin of Rocamadour. The day was warm, but not hot, with a light breeze. The coarse, woolen tunic of his pilgrim robe was scratchy, and he couldn't seem to get comfortable wearing it. His heart wasn't in the role a deathbed vow had forced him to assume. The anniversary of his wife's death was this week, and he had promised to visit the shrine and have masses said in her memory. From there he would go to Saint Sernin in Toulouse to have more masses said. Like many others, his wife, Petronilla, with her mother and sisters, had made the pilgrimage to Rocamadour and then to Saint Sernin twenty years before when their marriage was barren. Not very enthused about the pilgrimage, he'd not gone with them. Yet their son and his heir had been born the next year.

Anduze had made the journey from Sandeyren Castle on horseback, and he had stabled his horse behind the best looking of the inns in the village. The sacred site was on a rocky plateau, high above. Many pilgrims ascended the steps on their knees as an act of penance. He didn't know whether or not his wife had climbed the stairs on her knees. But it didn't matter now. He regretted his unhappy marriage, but that was only one of his regrets. Anduze took a deep breath and began climbing. It was enough of a penance to be here without wearing out his knees.

He soon was breathing heavily. He slowed to wipe the sweat from his forehead, regretting that he had left the traditional, broad-brimmed, pilgrim hat in the inn. He spent a lot of time outdoors and was muscular and fit, but he wasn't used to climbing so many stairs. On the steps behind and above him, the pilgrims mumbled the familiar Latin of the *Ave* and *Pater Noster*. Their prayers and the chirping of a few bugs in the sparse vegetation alongside the steps were the only sounds other than his breathing.

THE VISCOUNT'S DAUGHTER

Halfway to the top, in a wide space in the path, Anduze stopped to catch his breath. His knees and legs ached from the unaccustomed climb. The village of Rocamadour lay far below with its scattering of tiled-roofed houses and inns and beyond it, rich fields and vineyards. A yellow and black butterfly landed with a flutter on his tunic. He stood perfectly still watching the butterfly until it flitted to one of the tiny, pink flowers growing from a crevice in the cliff side. As much as he found this climbing burdensome, he dreaded going on to Toulouse. Hatred for the Count of Toulouse had kept him from visiting the city for nearly a score of years. He touched the disfiguring scar on his face that Toulouse had given him and bit the inside of his lip.

Fortunately, the Viscounty of Anduze was far enough from Toulouse that it hadn't been necessary for him to become involved in the affairs of the contentious, southern nobles. He was not known in Toulouse, so he had no fear of being recognized. Yet the prospect of being in the proximity of the man who had blighted his life was unsettling.

Anduze had long ago accepted the responsibility for his failure, but he had never been able to come to terms with Toulouse's part in events that still haunted him. His old friend, Nicholas, had counseled him that life was long and sooner or later, he would be able to even the score with Toulouse. Perhaps Nicholas was right and going to Toulouse was the first step in making that happen.

The murmured prayers of pilgrims below him on the steps came closer. He needed to keep moving. Wiping the sweat again from his forehead, he resumed climbing.

Chapter 2

USUALLY A SERVANT ACCOMPANIED ERMENGARDE whenever she left the Château Comtal and went into the city. But today was market day, and she was quite sure she'd be safe without an escort. In any case, she didn't want anyone with big ears accompanying her. She had told Minerve she needed to speak with her confessor, but instead she intended to seek out Damian, her tutor. He was a scholar and would know about canon law, those strictures by which the church was governed. He might know of some legality that could help her avoid the marriage to Toulouse. Besides, she had come to value his opinion above all others.

Ermengarde passed through the bailey, paying no attention to the servants going about their tasks. Two of Toulouse's men-at-arms, sweating in their quilted tunics, guarded the massive stone entryway. They never stopped her from leaving the castle, but today their very presence seemed threatening. They could insist she not leave the castle without an escort. She took a deep breath and walked confidently by them into the city.

A cart filled with grain rumbled by on the cobblestone street. Peasants noisily hawked scrawny chickens, hares, eggs, apples, pomegranates, fat cabbages, and bunches of onions they had brought from the countryside for market day. Holding up her long gown Ermengarde stepped carefully avoiding fresh clumps of animal dung. The smells of offal mingled with those of fresh-baked bread and savory meat pies.

"Lady," one vendor called, "for you, a special price on my finest chestnuts."

She breathed in the rich smell of the chestnuts, roasting on a small brazier, but gave the man a dismissive nod and walked briskly on, savoring her freedom, however temporary. A well-dressed knight, whose dark blue surcoat was embellished with white v-shaped stripes, grinned at her mischievously. She felt color rise in her cheeks, and she looked away. He was powerfully built, and she almost wished he would put her on his horse and carry her away, away from the impasse that loomed before her like a storm cloud.

A crowd watched a dwarf juggling wooden balls in front of ruins. Did her city have Roman ruins, too? She couldn't call any to mind since she'd paid no attention to such things as a child.

The Basilica of Saint Sernin, the impressive red-brick pilgrim church, rose before her in all its magnificence. The basilica had two main entrances. She entered through the *Porte des Comtes,* near where the counts of Toulouse were buried, with its colorfully painted sculptures of Lazarus and the rich man in the tympanum. As Ermengarde passed through the doorway, she couldn't help but wish her would-be husband lay among his ancestors. She waited for her eyes to become accustomed to the dim interior. Light came through the stained-glass windows and cast patterns on the smooth stone floor. The soaring arches above her made her think of God and heaven. Perhaps God, through his church, could help her now. Or was God, too, in league with the Count of Toulouse?

Dirty and haggard pilgrims, on their way to the shrine of Saint James at Compostela in Hispania, milled about the walkway around the main altar that had been especially built to allow access to the chapels and the sacred saints' relics. She envied them their freedom, their pilgrimage. On impulse, she knelt at the first of the chapels radiating from the nave. "Saint James," she prayed, "if you deliver me from this dreadful marriage, I promise to aid the princes who are driving the Moors from Hispania." She hadn't intended to make a vow to Christ's apostle. But Saint James was known as the Moor slayer, and it seemed right since her father had died fighting in the Reconquista in Hispania.

Ermengarde made her way to a side door that led from the basilica to the hospital. Damian helped out there each day after nones, the time when the cathedral canon said their afternoon prayers. The hospital was a long, narrow, open room. Rows of cots lined the walls, filled with the city's sick and dying and with pilgrims who had become ill on the way to Compostela.

The awful smells of urine and pus affronted her nostrils. Her gaze fell upon a man with blotchy pustules on his face. He moaned weakly, reaching out his hand as she passed. A deformed man, leaning on a crude crutch, hobbled toward the door. One would need a heart of stone not to be moved by the plight of the patients. Tears filled her eyes. It flashed through her mind that her tears were not for them, but for herself. The hospital was a stark reminder of the transitory nature of life, her life. She didn't want to spend whatever brief time she had on earth married to Toulouse.

At one end of the hospital room was a lovely little chapel where a statue of the Virgin in Majesty gazed down upon the sick. Near the chapel, Ermengarde spotted Damian with his fringe of blond hair. As always when she saw him, her heart leapt. He sat on a stool next to one of the patients. His head was lowered, and his lips moved in prayer. She hung back, waiting for him to finish. He finished the prayer and made the sign of the cross over the prostrate man.

When he looked up and spotted her, surprise showed on his face. He hurried to her side. "Lady Ermengarde, what brings you here?" His tone was anxious. She wasn't sure if it was out of concern for her or surprise she had sought him out.

"Father Damian." She paused and swallowed before continuing. "I need to speak with you."

"What has happened? I assume it can't wait, or you would have sent a message for me to attend you."

"No, it couldn't wait. You're the only scholar I know."

Damian frowned. "I'll walk with you back to the Château Comtal. We can talk on the way."

They left the hospital, and Ermengarde's dark mood lifted a little as they walked through the pulsing life of the busy streets. They had gone only a little way when he asked, "What has upset you?"

She hesitated, glancing into his eyes. "I'm not sure I can talk about it here in the middle of the street."

Damian gave her a reassuring smile. "I've learned that things do not look half as serious in the sunlight as they do when we are alone in the dark."

"No matter when or where I look at things, I don't like what I see. Today I met with Minerve, an old friend of my father. I'm being pressured to marry Toulouse."

Damian clasped his hands behind his back, but kept walking. "I've heard that maidens are sometimes reluctant to assume the marriage state."

Two little boys with dirt on their faces ran right in front of them, chasing a mangy dog. Ermengarde didn't know what she expected Damian to say, but his seeming indifference to her plight shocked her like the sudden appearance of a head on a pike. She stopped walking and turned to look at him. "I have nothing against marriage. 'Tis just marriage to Toulouse that I find unacceptable."

Damian didn't look at her; instead he watched the boys and the dog disappear into one of the narrow side streets. "If you are surprised by Toulouse's proposal, I am not. If he had not been saving you for himself, he probably would have married you off as soon as you reached puberty. I shouldn't have to tell you, it's a good match. Toulouse is the richest and most powerful man in the region, more powerful than his king."

Oh, no, not him, too. Ermengarde swallowed hard.

They threaded their way around wilted cabbage leaves and turnip tops, refuse from a market stall. "I don't want to discuss Toulouse," she said. "Rather, I want to understand the position of the church. Doesn't canon law mandate that marriage must be a free choice?"

"Church law does regulate marriage, and yes, it must be a free choice. But you have responsibilities to your vassals and a position to maintain."

Hearing Damian talk so dispassionately about her life, her future, made her heart ache. She gave him a questioning look. Could he also be in league with Toulouse? "I want to decide whom I'll marry, not have it decided for me," she blurted out.

"My dear child, that is not your destiny. Your destiny is in the hands of your overlord. And he wants to marry you and join your lands to his."

"I am not a child," she protested.

They came to a cook shop with a line of patrons waiting to be served. They skirted the line and as they did so, she had a whiff of the greasy meat stew. Her stomach churned.

Damian continued. "I explained to you the precarious position of your viscounty. And marriage to Toulouse will safeguard both you and your holdings."

Amid a surge of emotions she didn't fully understand, Ermengarde struggled to think clearly. Before Damian had become her tutor, she'd thought all men were like the rowdy, uncouth knights and men-at-arms who frequented the Château Comtal. He'd introduced her to philosophy, history, and geography, whole worlds previously beyond her ken. She'd studied diligently to please the tall canon with his amber eyes, clean nails, and ready smile, and expected he'd have seen her as more than just marriageable goods.

They paused in their walk for a moment to let a heavily laden grain wain pass. Damian was only telling her what she already knew. Yet it still hurt to hear him say it. She didn't know what she expected from him, but it wasn't his well-reasoned response. Tear sprung to her eyes. "Toulouse doesn't want me. He only wants my lands."

"Toulouse isn't the only one who wants your lands. As an heiress, you are a valuable asset."

A fat cleric in the black robe of a canon attached to the cathedral approached from the other direction. Damian spoke to him, and Ermengarde nodded politely. For a moment, it looked like the canon was going to engage Damian in conversation. When he kept walking, she sighed in relief. It was hard enough to keep her wits about her without having to engage in pleasantries on the street. "Will the marriage be valid if I'm all but forced into it?"

"You don't have to marry. The convent is always an alternative."

Ermengarde knew little of nuns, but from what she had seen, their lives were restricted, often mean. Certainly as a noblewoman, she could live in one of the finer nunneries, but she had no interest in the religious life with its rules, prayers, and privations. She took a deep breath. "How can you say I am making a free choice if the only other choice I have is a living death as a nun without a vocation?"

"Marriage or convent? In either case, he will have your lands."

Her mouth fell open. "Won't they go to my sister if I enter a convent?"

"If they do pass to Lady Ermessende, Toulouse will marry her to get them."

Ermengarde gasped at the thought of frail, gentle Missee married to Toulouse. She was often ill, and if forced to marry him, she might not survive. If Toulouse or his mistresses had already gotten rid of one sickly wife, wouldn't Missee be in mortal danger?

The Château Comtal, built of rough bricks and large square stones dating back to Roman times, loomed before them. With its high ramparts and sturdy defensive towers, its presence was imposing, threatening. Two flags displaying Toulouse's blazon, one on each side of the doorway, flapped in the afternoon breeze. Her voice quavered. "Don't you care what happens to me?"

Damian's face revealed no emotion. "Lady Ermengarde, it is because I have your best interests at heart that I am recommending you marry Toulouse."

Ermengarde recoiled at the coldness of his reply. "But, Father Damian." She paused. "If I marry Toulouse my lessons with you will come to an end."

Damian's usually sensitive face was impassive, as if she were a complete stranger instead of the pupil he had tutored for the last eighteen months. "For someone of your age and sex, you have a great deal of ability. It's too bad you cannot continue your lessons."

This was the nearest he had ever come to complimenting her, but the coldness of his words hurt.

They neared the gate into the bailey of the Château Comtal. The same two stalwart men-at-arms she had seen earlier paid no attention to their approach. Their walk was over, and Damian hadn't given her the only answers she wanted to hear.

He hesitated, lowering his voice to almost a whisper. "There's one more thing to consider. If you prove difficult, it's possible Toulouse could claim you had lost your reason and commit you to a nunnery."

Ermengarde put her hand to her mouth, fighting back a wave of nausea. Clearly, Toulouse would stop at nothing to get her lands. "Lost my reason?"

"I've never believed it, but some people think too much education deleterious to a woman. That her mind can easily become unhinged. And you have been studying with me."

"Do you really think people would accept such a claim if Toulouse made one?"

Damian shook his head, his face stern. "Don't underestimate him, Lady Ermengarde. He's capable of anything."

"Father Damian, thank you for your frankness." She struggled to maintain her composure. She abruptly turned from him and hastened though the gate before he could see the tears of anger and frustration she was no longer able to contain.

Ermengarde hastily dried her eyes before entering the great hall. Missee separated herself from the knot of gentlewomen near the fireplace. A servant was lighting the fire with a taper. The afternoon light had waned, and the women had put away their embroidery. They were playing tables, a dice game Ermengarde particularly detested, because unlike chess, it depended on chance, not on skill.

"What did Minerve want?" Missee asked too loudly. "You've been gone a long time."

Ermengarde drew her aside, wishing Missee were older than her twelve years. Ermengarde hadn't shared with her the ugly rumors she'd heard from the servants in the kitchen about Toulouse. No servant girl was safe, they said; and he particularly liked them young. Ermengarde lowered her voice. "Minerve has urged me to marry Toulouse."

"I think you should marry him," Missee whispered. She cast an uneasy glance over her shoulder at the women by the fire. Ignoring their game, they were straining to overhear the conversation. "Marriage, any marriage would be better than being nearly prisoners of the count. Besides, a wedding would be exciting."

Ermengarde drew her sister further away. "How can you say that? You know how I feel about Toulouse."

"I'm sorry. It's just that everybody thinks you should marry him."

34

THE VISCOUNT'S DAUGHTER

Missee shivered, and Ermengarde put an arm around her sister's thin shoulders. "You'd better return to the fireside before you catch a chill. If Toulouse wasn't so stingy with firewood, I might like him better. I'm going back to the curtain wall. I've much to think about."

The breeze was beginning to pick up on the ramparts, and Ermengarde pulled her mantle more closely about her. The bells at Saint Sernin tolled in the distance, calling the canons to vespers, their late afternoon prayers. The other churches, taking their cue from Saint Sernin, began their melodic peals. She paced to the end of the wall, passing the guard who had lingered nearby earlier. She glared at him as she hurried by, her thoughts in turmoil. Minerve, Damian, and even Missee had urged her to marry Toulouse. She made another circuit of the ramparts before settling to sit in the sun. Its late afternoon warmth failed to dispel the chill that settled over her like a shroud. It hadn't occurred to her before her talk with Damian that if she didn't marry Toulouse, Missee might be forced to do so. She couldn't let that happen.

Her thoughts turned to one of her earliest memories.

Her parents' bedchamber was crowded, close, the windows shut against the rain. She stood off to one side near the coffer containing the basin and towels used to wash her new sister, Ermessende.

The heavy oak door had opened, and her father strode into the room, his spurs clanking on the stone floor. His surcoat was muddy, and he wore his mail. He went to her stepmother and kissed her. They exchanged a few quiet words. Then he picked up Ermessende, held her out and studied her for a long moment before giving her a welcoming kiss of peace on both cheeks. He looked around. "Where's Ermengarde?" he asked.

Her stomach had roiled. She hadn't seen Father for a long time, and she took a hesitant step closer to the big curtained bed. "Ah, there you are," he said. "Come and hold your sister Ermessende."

Her legs quivering, she approached the bed, looking at her father's knees, visible beneath his surcoat. She'd stared up at the small pink face almost hidden in the swaddling. He held out Ermessende for her to take.

Ermengarde held out her arms. The red-faced midwife, made bold by her importance this day, protested. "My lord, I fear the child isn't old enough to hold her sister."

"Nonsense," their father said. "Ermengarde is four. She's strong. She'll take care of her." He leaned close, smelling of horses and sweat, and deposited Ermessende in her outstretched arms.

And she'd been taking care of her sister ever since. Her love for Missee gave her no choice. She had to marry Toulouse.

If this were a game of chess, right now she had only one move. But that didn't mean the game was over. She sat up straighter. She would use her new status as Countess of Toulouse to find allies, understand Toulouse's weaknesses, and figure out a plan to regain her viscounty. In spite of the forces aligned against her, someday she'd be her own person, control her fate.

A turtledove landed on the battlement and startled her. Ermengarde wasn't sure how long she'd been deep in thought. The sun had disappeared below the horizon, and she shivered. It was time to return to the great hall.

THE VISCOUNT'S DAUGHTER

* * *

The next day, Ermengarde and Missee, relieved to be alone, sat side by side on the settle in the bower they shared with the women of the Château Comtal. The others didn't usually gather here. Heated only by a small brazier and with only two high narrow windows, the chamber was cold and dark. Missee picked out a melody on her lyre while Ermengarde read Boethius' *Consolation of Philosophy*. Damian had recommended it, but she couldn't keep her mind on the words. She had a frightening dream the night before, and it still haunted her. In her dream, she had again fallen into a fire like she had when she was child, but in the dream, no strong arms rescued her. Instead of the minor burns she received as child, the fire had consumed her. She awoke in a sweat, wondering what it portended. A loud knock sounded on the door, interrupting her thoughts.

"Enter," Ermengarde called, putting down her book, but not rising from her chair by the brazier. A page, a small boy not more than eight or nine, awkwardly came into the room.

"Lady Ermengarde," he said in a high thin voice. "My Lord, the Count of Toulouse, requests your presence in the great hall."

The moment for her decision had come. All the thinking and agonizing over it would soon be at an end. "Tell his lordship that I will attend him directly."

The page bowed and then left to convey his message.

"What will you tell Toulouse?" Missee asked anxiously as soon as he was gone.

Ermengarde didn't respond, just twisted her lips in a grimace, her own powerlessness almost overwhelming her. They had not discussed her decision. Even at Missee's young age, she seemed to realize Ermengarde had no other choice.

Missee went to the table by the bed. "Let me brush your hair. I'll make it shine as it never has before, and I'll braid ribbons into two small braids beside your face."

Ermengarde was proud of her luxurious black hair, and clearly, Missee had been planning how her hair should look on this special day. "Yes, please do. But you mustn't take long. The count is a wolf waiting for a lamb."

Missee giggled. "That nose of his does look a bit like the snout of a wolf." She brushed Ermengarde's hair, and her scalp soon tingled from vigorous strokes.

"There." Missee pulled the brush through her hair one last time. She parted Ermengarde's hair in the middle, plaited the two side braids with ribbons, and handed her the polished bronze hand mirror. "See how lovely you look."

Taking the mirror from Missee, Ermengarde held it and inspected her appearance. She did look well, except for the sadness in her eyes. She sighed and gave the mirror back to Missee.

"You must put on your best gown. I'll get it for you." Missee went to the chest where they kept their clothes. She took out the green-and-blue silk gown, woven with silver thread.

From her enameled box from Limoges, Ermengarde retrieved the rich silver ring Toulouse had sent her at the time he proposed. She had tried to return it, but he wouldn't accept it. She had not yet worn the ring with its intricate spirals. Since she didn't want to marry him, it had seemed like a bribe and somehow unclean.

Ermengarde slipped into the soft silk gown that clung to her chainse and drew attention to her slim figure. It was flared in the latest fashion, with its wide sleeves lined with green. It was elegant. She was elegant, once she put it on and fastened the embroidered girdle across her hips. The finery gave her the confidence she would need in the upcoming encounter with Toulouse.

"You look like a queen, a countess," Missee said. "Here, put on a bit of rose water." She anointed Ermengarde's wrists.

Ermengarde had often worn this fragrant scent when she met Damian for lessons. He was so otherworldly; he'd probably never noticed it.

"I guess I'm ready, like a suckling pig on the table. All I lack is the apple in my mouth."

Missee wrinkled her forehead trying to look disapproving. "Ermengarde, you shouldn't say such things."

"I can't help it." Ermengarde leaned again the wall, taking a deep breath, steeling herself for what lay ahead. She had to be strong and not let her misgivings and fears show.

Missee put her hand around her sister's waist. "I'll come with you."

Together they made their way to the great hall, full at midday with knights and their retainers. All eyes, except those of Minerve who seemed purposely to be ignoring her arrival, turned toward Ermengarde, and silence settled over the crowd. Missee left her side to join Jordana and the other noblewomen sitting in front of the fireplace.

Ermengarde threw back her shoulders, tilted her head as if in challenge, and walked gracefully the length of the hall to where Toulouse sat in an ornately carved oak chair on the dais. He wore a dark blue-striped surcoat that flattered his thick form. He rose, took her hand in his blunt, calloused one, and led her to the seat beside him. Damian's hands with the long slim fingers and well-cared-for nails came to mind. The comparison almost unnerved her, but she managed to keep her composure.

"My lady, wearing my ring becomes you," Toulouse said, looking her up and down appraisingly.

Ermengarde's heart descended into her slippers. "Thank you, my lord." Her own voice surprised her. She had almost whispered.

Toulouse cleared his throat and stroked his beard. "Have you reconsidered my proposal?" He spoke loud enough for everyone in the great hall to hear, as if daring her to refuse him in front of all those assembled.

"I have indeed, my lord," she said, trying to speak up and keep her voice even.

40

THE VISCOUNT'S DAUGHTER

Toulouse shifted impatiently in his chair, as if he wanted to get this necessary but burdensome task over with as quickly as possible. "And your decision is?"

She was unable to keep a quiver from her voice. "I accept your offer of marriage."

The people in the great hall responded with a spontaneous chorus wishing the couple well. Toulouse held up his hand for silence. "Thank you." His voice was full of self-satisfaction.

When the tumult died down, he turned to Ermengarde. "Come with me. There's something I want to show you."

He led her out of the door near the dais along a narrow corridor to the new defensive tower he was building. It was still under construction, but it was to be the highest in the city, if not in the whole county. He indicated the stairs that wound up the tower.

For just a heartbeat, Ermengarde saw herself falling from the tower to her death. The thought passed as quickly as it had appeared. "My lord, please, let's save it for another time. The tower isn't yet finished."

"You'll be safe with me. I'll be right behind you."

Gritting her teeth, Ermengarde began to ascend. Up and up they climbed. There must have been 200 or more steps. The stairs became narrower and narrower. There was nothing to hang onto, and she began to feel dizzy. She paused to momentarily steady herself against the rough stones of the wall.

Toulouse stopped also. He was breathing heavily and sweat glistened in his beard. Ermengarde continued climbing. The

41

stairs ended and, squinting in the bright sunlight, she stepped onto a windy mason's platform of rough boards. The platform was sturdy enough but there was no railing, nothing between her and the ground hundreds of feet below. Toulouse clambered onto the platform after her. His weight caused the boards to creak.

The wind tugged at Ermengarde's gown and loosened her hair from its braids. She gazed at the recently harvested fields that stretched in all directions, looking very much like a chessboard. In the far distance was the narrow blue line of the sea.

Toulouse came to her side. "Look." He pointed in the direction of Narbonne. Then with a motion of his hand, he indicated the territories that lay below. "What you are seeing will one day be the Kingdom of Toulouse. I'll rule everything from the Pyrenees to the Alps."

Ermengarde wrung her hands. *He hadn't said: "We" will rule.* The devil tempted Christ by offering him dominion over all the kingdoms of world. Like the devil, Toulouse wanted absolute power and he might do anything to get it. If he just gave her a little push, then he could marry compliant Missee when she came of age. The fact she had thought of such a thing made the world spin. Someday, she might grow to be like Toulouse. She not only wanted to control her own life, she wanted to rule her patrimony in her own right. Ermengarde reached out to Toulouse to steady herself. With her hand on his arm, she regained her balance.

Toulouse's face was hard, unreadable. Had he entertained a similar thought? She turned abruptly and started the long descent on unsteady legs. Toulouse and his ambitions frightened her as much as the thought of becoming like him.

Chapter 3

ONCE TOULOUSE AND ERMENGARDE HAD exchanged their *verba de futuro*, their binding commitment to marry, they could have been married as soon as the banns were read. But she begged her future husband for time to get ready. He had grudgingly given her two weeks to see to the necessary preparations. It was not as long as she'd wished. The two weeks passed swiftly, too swiftly. The time was taken up with visits to shops to select fabrics, to a shoemaker to arrange shoes to be made to match the fabrics, and finally, to seamstresses who sewed and fitted her wedding clothes and a new outfit for Missee.

The morning of her marriage, Ermengarde's empty stomach growled as a servant laid out her hastily made wedding gown. She had to admit that in spite of everything, it had come out well. She had searched the shops of Toulouse until she'd found the most elegant material. She put on the sky-blue, silk gown—rich enough to be the Virgin's robe—with its wide border of pearls at the hem and neckline. At the waist, she cinched her mother's delicate gold girdle inlaid with pearls. Over the gown, she placed her contrasting purple mantle, the color of the night sky just before it went black. The mantle was trimmed with sable. She stroked the soft fur, the same fur her mother had worn on her wedding day. Ermengarde retrieved her silk shoes, dyed blue to match the dress and also embroidered with pearls. She would look the part of Lady Ermengarde, Viscountess of Narbonne and soon to be Countess of Toulouse. If she was to be the queen on the chessboard, she must play the part. She would show everyone she was equal to her fate. She would not betray her true feelings in front of the citizens of Toulouse or the guests invited to the wedding and to the wedding feast.

Two hours later, she was ready, physically, if not mentally, to go to the Basilica of Saint Sernin. There, according to the custom, in front of the Porte des Comtes she would be wed. Minerve, with his beard and hair neatly trimmed and dressed in a dark red tunic, patterned with the castle with three white towers—the symbol of his viscounty—came to escort Missee and her to the ceremony.

"Doesn't she look beautiful?" Missee chirruped.

Minerve studied her for a moment. "She's a picture that a smile would make complete."

Ermengarde couldn't force a smile. Her heart was too heavy. "Marriage is serious business," she said, meeting his gaze with such intensity that he looked away.

"Toulouse has asked that you wear this today," he said, holding out a girdle of old gold adorned with the twelve-pointed cross of Toulouse. Each arm of the cross was embellished with large rubies.

Ermengarde touched the slender gold girdle that circled her waist. She had deliberately commissioned her wedding dress with it in mind. "Isn't the bride to choose what she wears on her wedding day?"

"Toulouse insists."

Ermengarde shook her head. Toulouse's deceased wife had once worn this same girdle. The belt seemed to carry with it the taint of her corpse. "I won't wear it."

Minerve looked worried. Apparently, he wasn't used to women with minds of their own. "I fear you'll displease your future husband."

Ermengarde suddenly understood her uneasiness with Minerve. She recalled his comment that she was young and a woman. He was misogynist—one of those men who feared and mistrusted women—and this had overshadowed his loyalty to her father. "We'd best be on our way," she said. "Send a servant to return the girdle to Toulouse."

"Toulouse has already left the castle."

"I don't care what you do with it. I shan't wear it."

Minerve seemed befuddled for a moment. "I'll meet you in the bailey," he said, leaving hurriedly.

Ermengarde took a deep breath as Missee and she made their way down the twisting stone steps to the bailey. It was unusually quiet. Toulouse's retainers must have been given leave to attend the wedding. They waited for a few moments before a scowling Minerve reappeared without the girdle.

They passed through the castle gate into the gray day, walking toward the basilica. Ermengarde hadn't seen Damian since she'd sought him out there, two weeks before, but she guessed she'd see him today. All the clergy connected to the basilica would be in attendance at the count's marriage. Dark, rain-filled clouds hung above the usually sunny city, a fitting backdrop for her own somber thoughts.

The citizens of Toulouse had turned out in numbers to see their count married. They lined the main road to the basilica and cheered as Ermengarde passed. Brides were expected to be beautiful, and she had clearly not disappointed them. She looked neither left nor right, but held her head high, her hair floating behind her as she walked, falling in dark waves over her mantle. She knew that her clothes, bearing, and appearance were regal. Yet her stomach churned with misgivings. The murmur of the crowd grew into a roar, and people shoved and pushed to get a glimpse of her as she neared the basilica. Their enthusiasm made her fears seem unfounded, ridiculous. She was surely the envy of many women who wanted the power and position that came with being the Countess of Toulouse. Was she wrong to feel she was trapped like a rabbit caught in a snare?

Her bridegroom, looking very much the part of a powerful lord, waited for her outside in front of the decorated doorway. He wore a splendid, deep red tunic, embellished with a gold, twelve-pointed cross. Raymond his eight-year-old heir stood nearby. Jordana, dressed in a new green gown with silver threads woven through it and a matching mantle trimmed with silver fox fur, headed the contingent of palace ladies. Jordana caught Ermengarde's eye and gave her a forced smile.

A few steps behind Toulouse, off to one side, the Templar lurked. Even though Ermengarde had greeted him in the hall on his arrival weeks ago, he'd refused to speak to her then or any day since. Jordana had told her that Templars never spoke with women, and this Ranulf would be assisting her father indefinitely. The Templar's pale eyes were the blue-green of ancient Roman glass and as cold as crystals of ice. Ermengarde had taken an immediate dislike to him.

A score of Toulouse's important vassals, all dressed in their best, gathered behind the groom. A cold shiver went down her spine. Apart from Missee and Minerve—and she wasn't sure of him—she had no friends here.

Moments after Ermengarde's arrival the doors of the basilica opened. The Archbishop of Narbonne, Arnold of Levezou, one of her relatives, came forth magnificently dressed in a white silk robe and miter, richly embroidered with gold and silver. He carried a bishop's staff, a gold crosier studded with gems. Her mouth fell open in surprise at the sight of the stern-looking old man with his beaky nose and hawk-like eyes. His appearance at the wedding was proof that he and Toulouse were in collusion. Together, they'd continue to exploit her city. A bitter surge of resentment shot through her, giving her a bad taste in her mouth. Even the powerful church acquiesced to

Toulouse. It was as if she were the unprotected queen on the chessboard about to be eliminated by the bishop.

With his tall pointed hat and bishop's crosier, the archbishop loomed above them like a threatening bird of prey. The Bishop of Toulouse and twelve of the basilica's priests accompanied him, Damian among them. Ermengarde no longer considered him a friend. But she noted his face looked strained, as if there had been a difference between what he told her and what he actually thought.

Gently, yet firmly taking Ermengarde's elbow, Minerve escorted her to Toulouse's side. She didn't look at him. There would be plenty of time for that. She looked over the head of the archbishop to the carved sculptures of Lazarus over the door.

The crowd grew quiet as Archbishop Arnold began the outdoor ceremony. His mumbled Latin was difficult for Ermengarde to hear, and try as she did, she couldn't force herself to concentrate on the meaning of the words. Almost before she knew it, the time came for her to give her consent. Her mouth was as dry as November grass. She tried to speak loudly and clearly, yet she only murmured the fatal words. It was only then that she turned to Toulouse, who slipped a heavy, ruby ring on her slim finger, the weight of the ring anchoring her to him. He had a self-satisfied look on his face, as if he had just slain a wild boar. Nausea almost overcame her, and her head reeled. She struggled to keep her face neutral, to keep up appearances.

The wedding ceremony had taken only minutes. What she had done, the vow she'd just taken, almost took her legs out from under her. They walked inside the basilica, lighted on this dark day by the huge candelabra over the splendid main altar.

In front of the altar, Ermengarde knelt beside her husband, grateful for the prie-dieu that protected her dress and knees from the cold stone of the floor, grateful that she no longer had to stand on her unsteady legs.

The church rapidly filled, and she heard rustling behind her. The spectators grew quiet. The mass began, the familiar Latin echoing in the vast open nave. Damian, his head bowed in prayer, stood with the other priests in the choir. He was no more than two horses' length away, but the distance separating them now was as far as the moon. She would never study with him again.

Ermengarde tried to pay attention to the service, but the archbishop's betrayal further unsettled her stomach. At the Eucharist, a cloud of incense filled the nave, replacing the stench of unwashed bodies with the sweet smell of frankincense. She focused on keeping her back straight and her face composed. Her eyes rested on a small, exquisite statue of the martyred Saint Agnes, holding a lamb, in an alcove near the main altar. The female saints invariably had sad eyes and met terrible fates. She'd been taught that such women were models of sanctity to emulate. Clearly, the church used the saints' lives to keep women subservient.

The mass was interminable, but it finally ended. Ermengarde rose stiffly from the kneeler. Toulouse took her hand and placed it firmly on his arm as they walked down the long aisle. His gesture was proprietary, and she found it disconcerting. She turned quickly for one last glance of Damian, disappearing off to the left with the other priests. He didn't look in her direction.

* * *

With Ermengarde at his side, Toulouse passed out of the basilica into the gray day, amid cheers from the assembled crowd. He noted with approval the bonfires that blazed throughout the city, filling the air with fragrant wood smoke. Inebriated revelers were already dancing in the streets. Hawkers circulated through the crowd selling honey cakes, meat pies, and wine. A raucous parade of musicians, led by a drummer, arrived to escort the wedding party to the Château Comtal.

Ermengarde's hand slipped from where Toulouse had placed it in the church. He grabbed her arm, holding it so tightly he was sure he was bruising it. He did not look at her, and said nothing.

"You are hurting me," she whispered, trying to ease her arm from his grip.

"It is time you learned who is in control." He grunted and tightened his hold.

For the first time, he noticed she wasn't wearing the traditional bride's belt of Toulouse. He ground his teeth. It didn't bode well that she had refused to honor his wish and his

51

heritage. She would soon learn her place. He'd personally make sure of that.

The crowd roared as they passed, and Toulouse's anger lessened with the realization that a long sought goal was at last attained. He now had a clear title to Narbonne. His long rivalry with Ermengarde's dead father, Aymeri, was over. No longer could the rulers of Narbonne use their close connections to the Count of Barcelona to undermine his efforts to unify the south. It was Aymeri, more than anyone else, who had kept the other nobles from acquiescing to his plans. But no more. This day Toulouse would celebrate.

* * *

The journey from Rocamadour to Toulouse was uneventful, and Anduze was making his way to the Basilica of Saint Sernin to arrange masses for his deceased wife when he met a boisterous crowd headed toward the great church. Curious to see what was happening, he joined them.

"What's going on?" Anduze asked a shopkeeper in a leather apron who was hurrying along with the others.

"Count's being married today," the man replied. "They'll soon be walking back to the Château Comtal from Saint Sernin where the wedding took place."

Anduze slowed his pace, but caught in the crowd, he moved forward with it. At the market square, he found a place where he could watch the wedding party as it passed. As much as he didn't want to see Toulouse, or be seen by him, in his pilgrim garb, he was indistinguishable from the workmen, goodwives, shopkeepers, and other townspeople. He could safely satisfy his curiosity.

Anduze didn't have long to wait before the wedding party appeared. First came a group of rowdy musicians. Two knights on caparisoned white horses, their ceremonial blankets displaying the twelve-pointed cross of Toulouse, led the official party. A gaggle of churchmen surrounded the archbishop. Following them were the bride and groom and a long procession made up of family, the ladies of Toulouse's court, and well-dressed nobles. Two other horsemen brought up the rear.

As they drew near, Anduze stepped back into the shadows, but he need not have bothered. Toulouse looked straight ahead. He was heavier than he'd been all those years ago, and the features of his arrogant face had coarsened. Anduze clenched and unclenched his fists and turned his attention to the bride. She carried herself with great dignity. He noticed her long, graceful neck, her high cheekbones, and deep-set, dark eyes. She had a long, thin nose on which there was a slight bump. Curiously, Anduze found this nose attractive. It kept a pretty woman from being beautiful and made the bride's face memorable. Toulouse bent close to say something to her. Her back stiffened, and she responded with flashing eyes.

Anduze turned to a gray-haired woman, with a baby in her arms, standing next to him. "Who is she?" he asked, with a nod of his head toward the bride.

"I see you are a pilgrim and not from here," the woman said. "Otherwise you'd know the count has married Ermengarde, Viscountess of Narbonne."

Anduze turned back to the bridal party. "She's lovely."

The old woman harrumphed. "Men always want what they can't have."

Anduze sighed, wishing things were that simple. The bride and groom passed the place where he stood and, moments later, he detached himself from the crowd. Although the day was cool, his palms were sweaty. Seeing Toulouse with the lovely young woman brought back memories he'd long suppressed. Anduze retreated into a dark side street to a small tavern with two tables outside. He needed wine. Perhaps if he drank enough he could forget.

* * *

At the Château Comtal, the wedding celebration, the feasting and dancing that would continue throughout the rest of the day and for the next three days, was already underway. Many people had gathered in the doorway to greet the bride and groom. Ermengarde's head pounded, and she wanted to flee like a hen from a fox. Instead she made a determined effort to hold her head high and appear poised and noble. She greeted the wedding guests with a smile. Toulouse continued to grasp her arm, and his possessiveness worried her. She tried not to think what tonight, her wedding night, would hold.

THE VISCOUNT'S DAUGHTER

The cavernous great hall with its huge, centuries-old oak beams blackened by the smoke of many fires, had been transformed since last evening. New banners and pennons bearing the family arms augmented those already in place. Fresh rushes covered the stone floor. A big, wooden bowl of red apples and vases of autumn poppies and broom sat on the raised dais. Garlands of apples had been strung from one huge beam to another. A blazing fire roared in the huge fireplace at the end of the hall. For once, the room looked warm and welcoming. The transformed great hall gave Ermengarde a glimmer of hope. Something positive might come of her marriage.

A white linen tablecloth covered the head table and two large, carved oak chairs stood at its center. Toulouse led Ermengarde to the one on his left and seated himself beside her. Raymond and Jordana, her new stepchildren, were already seated at the head table. The Templar, ever at Toulouse's elbow, sat next to Raymond. Jordana, seeing Ermengarde glance in her direction, sniffed, and looked away. Missee, her jaw firmly clenched, was seated beside Jordana. From the time Missee was a small child, whenever her jaw clenched, she was trying to hide her feelings. She looked small and alone, and Ermengarde inwardly wept for her. An empty place at the head table next to Ermengarde was reserved for the archbishop. He was the last person she wanted to sit beside. She didn't know if she'd be able to conceal her anger at his betrayal.

The wedding guests found places at long tables parallel to the dais. Those of the highest status, wearing their best velvets and silks, chattered noisily as they settled into their appropriate places nearest the dais. Minerve was in this group, and he wasn't looking in her direction. Behind them, Toulouse's hearth knights, wearing matching surcoats, found seats.

Further back in the hall, lesser nobles, court officials, and wealthy merchants were noisily taking their places. At the very back of the hall, the invited townspeople gathered. Ermengarde didn't see her new husband's mistress, but knew she probably was watching the banquet from somewhere, as she had been watching Ermengarde for months.

Archbishop Arnold arrived with several churchmen. Ermengarde scanned their faces, letting out a breath of relief. Damian wasn't with them. His comeliness and intellect attracted her in a way her new husband never would. Archbishop Arnold sat next to her without even a perfunctory greeting. He immediately began to chat with the Bishop of Toulouse on his left. She didn't know whether to be relieved or offended.

Servants appeared and filled their wine goblets and the cups of the many guests. When the cups were full, Minerve stood, holding up a hand for silence. "A toast to the Count and Countess of Toulouse."

Everyone in the hall rose and raised their cups. Ermengarde acknowledged the toast with a slight inclination of her head as she had seen ladies in the great hall do when toasted. The wedding guests cheered.

She lifted the heavy, jeweled goblet to her lips and took a sip. The liquid failed to sooth her dry lips and throat. Toulouse raised his goblet and drained it with a satisfied grunt, before signaling the servant to refill it. He undoubtedly was celebrating his success in finally having full claim to her inheritance.

The archbishop gave a blessing and everyone made the sign of the cross. Then with a loud scraping of benches, everyone sat and resumed talking. Servants began to carry in platters of food, including a huge boar with an apple in its mouth. They placed a roasted peacock, festooned with its own tail feathers, in front of Ermengarde. Platters of pheasants, swan, duck, and hart appeared at regular intervals.

Toulouse took something from every platter and bowl, washing down the various meats, fish dishes, breads and sweets with copious amounts of wine. In her years in the Château Comtal, Ermengarde hadn't paid attention to the count's table manners, but now she was disgusted. His mustache was greasy, and crumbs of bread stuck in his beard. It was this, more than anything else that brought home to her the physical reality of being married to Toulouse. He revolted her, and she would be expected to touch him, caress him even kiss him. All day her stomach had been queasy, now it cramped. She usually loved elderflower cheesecake, but she pushed it away. She couldn't eat it, or any of the other elaborate pastries the cooks had concocted. As she watched her husband wolf them down, bile rose in her throat, and she almost lost what little she'd eaten. Fortunately, Toulouse did not speak to her, and she had nothing to say to him.

The wine took effect and the crowd grew boisterous. Four of the count's knights, seated together, began singing a bawdy song, drowning out the troubadour and his lyre. A knight grabbed one of the serving wenches as she passed and seated her on his lap. Loud laughter came from another table.

Musicians joined the troubadour, and the wedding guests cheered. The musicians took out their instruments and began to play festive music. The drone of the bagpipes mingled with the lilting sounds of the cithara, flute, vièle, and the pulse of the tambourine. The crowd clapped and stomped their feet to the music. *Everyone, except me, is enjoying the banquet.*

The last gray daylight coming through the high fenestral windows faded, and servants lit candles in the huge oak chandelier in the center of the great hall and in the sconces along the walls. As if this was a sign for a change, eager hands pushed the tables and benches to the walls and cleared the floor. Toulouse took her hand and led her to the center of the hall to begin the dancing. Ermengarde joined the circle of young women forming in the center of the hall. All eyes were upon them and the noisy hall grew quieter. Toulouse joined an adjacent circle of young men. The lilting music signaled the beginning of the dance. Forcing a smile, Ermengarde joined hands with the others and twirled and bowed, as if she were enjoying herself. As they circled, she caught sight of Toulouse. For a man of his girth and stature, he danced well, but tonight, he was a bit unsteady from the wine.

Others joined in the whirling dance, and the floor was soon full. Silver and gold and bright colors flashed by her and she spotted Missee's rose-colored gown trimmed with miniver. Her cheeks were flushed, and she smiled as she passed. Ermengarde tried to return her smile, but it died before reaching her lips.

The dancing continued. The hall grew hot, and the dancers began to perspire in their heavy clothes. Sweat mingled with smells of the leftovers from the banquet and the smoke from the fireplace. The smokiness, the shadows cast by the flickering candlelight, and steamy heat made Ermengarde feel like she was in hell. She was taking part in a dance macabre, and the devil was her new husband.

Toulouse finally signaled for the musicians to stop playing. He came to Ermengarde's side and leaned close to her. His breath smelled rancid, as if he had eaten rotten meat. "It's time we are to bed," he said. His eyes were fever bright, the eyes of someone deep in his cups.

Toulouse led her to the archbishop. "Your eminence, 'tis time for you to bless the marriage bed."

The archbishop led the way to Toulouse's private chamber. The bride and groom fell in behind him and a large crowd trailed after them. Ermengarde had been in the count's solar a number of times, but never in the room where he slept. They entered a drafty chamber containing a large bed with curtains of faded, red brocade, the color of dried blood. In spite of the warm fire that blazed in the fireplace, a chill passed over her.

Archbishop Arnold intoned the words of a blessing, finishing with a sign of the cross. They all said the obligatory amen, and then he left the room along with Toulouse and all the men. The women of the castle remained, as was the custom. They were to undress her. Usually, this task fell to the mother of the bride and close relatives, but since she was an orphan, a number of women had taken the honor upon themselves, among them Jordana. Something inside Ermengarde knotted. Jordana and the others would see the unsightly scars on her arms from her fall in the fire when she had been a toddler. Ermengarde had kept the ugly scars hidden since coming to Toulouse, and she had no intention of revealing them now. "I wish for everyone to leave," she said with all the command she could muster. "I'm quite capable of undressing myself and would prefer it so."

The women looked chagrined and started to chatter their objections. But Ermengarde made a sweeping motion with her arm in the direction of the door. "*Certes*, it is the prerogative of the countess to make herself ready for her wedding night with the count."

With murmurs of complaint, the women left. She couldn't resist giving Jordana a triumphant look. But Ermengarde's victory was a Pyrrhic one, because as soon as the women left, Toulouse entered the bedchamber. A shiver of dread ran down her spine as he closed the heavy, carved oak door on the men who lingered in the antechamber. A drunken reveler began to serenade them with a bawdy song. The lewdness of the lyrics, more appropriate to the brothel than the bridal bed, heightened her unease. She'd had no time to undress, no time to gather her resources to withstand whatever lay ahead. She moved to the far side of the room, away from her husband.

THE VISCOUNT'S DAUGHTER

The commotion outside of their door died down. Toulouse weaved drunkenly. He tossed his velvet tunic into a heap on the floor, then removed his shoes, red silk stockings, and embroidered shirt. In only his braies, his underwear, he appeared heavier than before. Ermengarde stared at his bulky body, dreading what she knew must come and not knowing what to do.

He strode to her and pulled her to him. "'Mistress, 'tis time to pay the marriage debt." His voice was slurred, and his eyes bright with lust. He groped for her breast and kissed her roughly on the lips.

Ermengarde gagged from his wine-soured breath. How dare he manhandle her like a common tavern wench! Her rising panic gave her strength to struggle out of his grasp. He stumbled after her, grabbing her around the waist in a bear hug. He kissed her again, this time forcing his thick tongue between her lips and into her mouth.

Ermengarde freed her fists and shoved him away. He momentarily let go of her, and she struggled from his grasp.

Toulouse's eyes became narrow slits. "How dare you defy me!" He advanced in her direction. Fury made him look like one of the horned gargoyles on the basilica.

There was nowhere to go. Ermengarde glanced around frantically for something, a weapon, anything she could use to defend herself from her drunken husband. She spotted the poker. A careless servant had left it half in and half out of the fire. She raced to it and picked it up, but her hands were shaking so much, it clattered to the floor. Toulouse was right behind her, breathing heavily. Choking down her fear and revulsion, she stooped and picked it up.

Toulouse snarled and grabbed the poker, wrenching her outstretched arm as he did so. Something snapped, and she fell forward doubled over in pain. The poker clanged to the floor. He picked her up, threw her on the bed, and ripped off her handsome wedding gown. "I'll teach you to raise a poker at me!" He unsteadily picked up the poker from where it had fallen.

"Please don't hurt me," Ermengarde sobbed. She closed her eyes and gritted her teeth, trying to will herself anywhere but here.

Chapter 4

FROM ONE OF THE NARROW windows of Sandeyren Castle at Tornac, Bernard of Anduze surveyed his ancestral lands. They stretched far beyond the Gardon River to the Cevennes Mountains, now colorful in their late autumn foliage. His visit to Toulouse had been unsettling, and he'd returned to find his son and heir had disappeared.

Anduze rejoined Nicholas who sat at a trestle table in the center of the great hall. "Nicholas, Storm's been gone a sennight, a whole week. How could he spend seven nights away from home without telling anyone he was leaving? Where in the name of all the saints in heaven has he gone?"

His trusted retainer and friend shook his head. "I'd say he'd gone after some woman if he wasn't so sweet on Matilde, the miller's daughter. And I saw her yesterday in town."

Anduze sat across from Nicholas and placed a hand thoughtfully on his chin. "He has resisted my attempts at arranging a suitable marriage for him, and I suspect it's because of his devotion to that little minx. What my son doesn't know is the fair Matilde first attempted to entice me with her wiles."

Nicholas guffawed. "And you resisted, of course."

"At the time, she was little more than a child, and there are limits to my philandering, believe it or not."

Nicholas' face softened. "'Tis something I well know."

"I should have never left my son's rearing to his mother. Now that she's gone…" Anduze made the sign of the cross "…he has no one to make excuses for him."

"It's not your fault," Nicholas said. "Marriages sealed with rings oft end with drawn knives. From the day of his birth, Lady Petronilla excluded you, undermined you. It's a case in point that though he was named after you, she never called him by his given name, calling him instead 'her small storm cloud.' And he's been Storm ever since. Lady Petronilla aptly named him. I'll say that for her."

Anduze smiled at the memory. "With his baby scowls and black looks, he did indeed call to mind a storm cloud. Perhaps if I'd cared for his mother, she wouldn't have turned him against me."

"Having no other weapons, women use whatever, whomever they can to establish their control, exercise power. And it isn't as if you abandoned or mistreated her. In fact, you treated her kindly. You have your faults, but you are kind."

In spite of the somber tone of the conversation, Anduze raise an eyebrow and chuckled. "I have faults?"

Nicholas ignored his question. "It's understandable after so many miscarriages and the death of your daughter that she'd hover over her only son. When she was ill and loath to have Storm leave for another castle to begin his training for knighthood, you did the right thing by providing excellent training in arms here for him."

Anduze leaned back in his chair. "And, God's bones, a lot of thanks I got for it. I tried to make sure my son was the match for any man on the battlefield and a fit ruler for his patrimony. And he is proficient in arms, if not yet ready to rule. I have done what I could, but I was never able to win his affection."

"I wouldn't be so sure of that. You have a way with everyone, a genial manner that makes you friends wherever you go. Gilles and the other lads around the castle worship you. Perhaps he's jealous."

"Jealous? Of Gilles? You more than anyone, should know I had no intention of training him in arms. I only considered it because Storm needed someone roughly his own size and age to exchange blows with. Granted, Gilles tries hard to please me where my son balks at my every suggestion."

"Have you thought Storm may be more like you than you realize?"

"How so?"

A twinkle came into his Nicholas' eyes. "The herring barrel always smells of herring."

It took Anduze a moment to get the gist of the proverb. As often as they were together, so great was the old man's store of peasant wisdom, there were still proverbs Anduze hadn't heard before.

"Perhaps you've forgotten," Nicholas continued. "You were once headstrong like Storm, chaffing under the heavy hand of your father."

Anduze leaned back, clasping his hands behind his head. "So I have a heavy hand? I think I've been more than lenient with Storm."

"What you think and what he thinks may be entirely different things."

Anduze shook his head. "Nicholas, how did you get so wise?"

The old man's face lined face crinkled into a grin. "Sixty years of living should teach you something."

"What will we do now? I have to oversee the collection of the harvest dues and hold court. After that, we are to meet Abbot Stephen for our annual hunt."

"We should go look for the boy."

"Might he not come back of his own accord?"

"Yes, he might, but I think it's essential we track him down. I don't think he'll go to join another conroi. It would be hard for him to attach himself to another fighting group. He's too used to fighting with Gilles and your knights. Like you, he's loyal."

"I hadn't thought he might seek employment in arms. What if he approached the Count of Toulouse? He's always in need of knights. Storm has no idea of my history with that man. Fighting for Toulouse would be much worse than running off with Matilde. Do you have any idea where he might have gone?"

"I don't know where he's gone. But it's time for the fair in Nîmes, and if I was young and looking for excitement, I would head there."

"I suppose you're right." Anduze shook his head. He didn't like the prospect of going after Storm, but he so trusted Nicholas, he was prepared to follow his suggestion. "I'll make preparations. I want you and Gilles to come with me. We'll leave tomorrow at first light."

* * *

Morning found Ermengarde huddled in her bloodstained chainse in a corner of the bed, cradling her twisted, broken arm and crying from pain and despair. Her private parts were on fire, and the sheet was damp with blood. Her bridegroom had fallen into a drunken sleep after violating her and now, thankfully, he was gone, probably to spend the rest of the night with Mahalt.

Ermengarde had waited for daylight and the time when everyone was at morning mass to seek help. She had to pull herself together, get dressed, and seek a bonesetter for her arm. She struggled to sit up, wincing with pain. She examined herself. She no longer bled, but dried blood smeared her legs. She had fainted, and she wasn't sure exactly what happened the night before. Yet, from the burning inside her, Toulouse clearly had damaged more than her arm. A terrible thought came to her. If the damage was extensive, and it felt like it was, she might never be able to have children.

A servant had brought her chest to the count's bedchamber before the wedding, and she needed to make her way to it and dress. No servants would disturb a bride the day after her wedding night. She was on her own. It was just as well since the room was in disarray. Her wedding gown lay in a tangled heap on the floor. The bloodstained poker rested at an odd angle on the hearth of the now extinguished fire. One of the bed curtains had come loose from its hanging, the sheets were in a wad, and pillows were strewn about.

She gingerly slipped her legs off the side of the bed. The movement brought a wave of dizziness. She closed her eyes to steady herself. As the feeling passed, she placed her feet uncertainly on the cold stone floor and stood. The room reeled about her, and she grabbed the bedpost to stay upright.

With her good hand on the wall to steady her, she slowly shuffled to the cruet on the window ledge. Each step tore at something inside her. She poured water into a cup and drank. It calmed her a little. She wanted to wash herself, to have a bath. She trembled, fearing she might never be truly clean again. First, she must deal with her broken arm.

From the window ledge, she wobbled to her chest and took out an old, everyday gown. She put her broken arm into the sleeve and pulled it over her head, gasping from how much it hurt. The room swirled, and she was afraid she might faint again. Slumping onto the lid of her chest, she sat until the weakness passed. It was impossible for her to put on her shoes and stockings with one hand, so she shoved her bare feet into her wedding shoes.

Her hair was a tangled mess, with the decorative ribbons that Missee had woven into the braids, hanging at odd angles. She undid the braids with one arm, removing the ribbons, found a comb, and neatened her hair. Taking a deep breath, she gingerly struggled to the door of the bedchamber. She had to think up something to tell people. Toulouse probably didn't know he'd broken her arm. He was so drunk he wouldn't remember anything of their wedding night. She hastily prepared a story and opened the heavy door.

Threading her way down the narrow, winding stairway to the first floor, she spotted a servant, carrying an ewer of water. "Come over here," she called in a loud voice that surprised both of them.

The woman came to where Ermengarde leaned against the wall. "I've fallen. I'm quite certain I've broken my arm. Fetch my sister, a bonesetter, and an herb woman. Now. I'll be in the women's bower. Bring them there."

The woman seemed taken aback. "Yes, my lady." She put down the ewer and hurried off.

Wincing with each step, Ermengarde tottered along the corridor to the stairway leading to the women's bower. At the top of the stairs, she entered the empty chamber and went directly to the bed in the alcove she'd shared with Missee. She eased herself onto it with an intake of breath. With her uninjured arm, she closed the bed curtain. She closed her eyes, hoping if she lay still, the pain would lessen.

The next thing she knew the door to the women's bower opened, and Missee rushed to her side. Her face was pale and her eyes frightened.

"Ermengarde, what has happened?"

Seeing her beloved sister, Ermengarde's resolve failed, and she began to sob. "Missee, I'll explain later," she managed to say between sobs.

Missee took Ermengarde in her thin arms, and Ermengarde cried and cried. When there were no more tears, she forced herself to think. "Missee, Toulouse and the other wedding guests will wonder why I didn't appear at mass. You must go and tell them I am ill. And that in my weakness, I fell and broke my arm."

Missee gave her an uncertain look. "Of course. But, oh, Ermengarde I'm not a very good liar."

Ermengarde squeezed her sister's hand. "Missee, you can do this for me."

Missee still seemed hesitant. "What if they don't believe me?"

"I don't care whether they believe you or not. That's not important."

A knock on the door brought their discussion to an end. A servant showed in the bonesetter, an old man with a shaggy white beard and a dark-skinned woman Ermengarde recognized as the herb woman, who lived on one of the narrow streets near the Château Comtal.

"Go," she said to Missee.

Missee took a deep breath, and then pursed her lips, as if summoning courage. She turned and left.

* * *

Toulouse, his head still pounding from last night's excesses, found Jordana sewing in front of the fire with the other women. He whispered in her ear, "I need to speak with you privately."

Jordana put down her sewing. She followed her father out of the great hall and outside into the bailey. The day was cool, and gray clouds hung ominously on the horizon. Jordana sat on a bench near the stables, out of the hearing of the many retainers in the bailey busily going about their morning work. "What is it, Father?" she asked. "I'm guessing it concerns your new wife since she wasn't at mass this morning."

Toulouse put one foot on an overturned bucket and ran his fingers through his hair. Nearby, the blacksmith worked at his anvil, and the sound of his hammer echoed the throbbing in Toulouse's head. "The wedding night didn't go well. The wench continues to defy me. I had a lot to drink and well, you can imagine my response when she didn't cooperate."

"I'm afraid I can," Jordana said curtly. "What do you want me to do?"

"Find out why she hasn't appeared and what lies she is telling everyone about last night. I've made her countess, and I've been generous to her. But apparently, that isn't enough."

Jordana gave her father a smug look. "I could have predicted you'd have trouble with Ermengarde. But you never asked my opinion. She's obviously smitten with her tutor, the handsome young priest, with his soft hands and good manners."

A look of surprise passed over Toulouse's face. He swept his hand to one side. "A girlish fantasy, no more. I've seen the fellow. He's more monk than man. Go see her, and let me know what is going on."

"As you wish, Father. I'll do it right away." She gave him a self-satisfied look.

After Jordana left, Toulouse climbed the stairs to the curtain wall, grinding his teeth. *So the wrench fancies her tutor. Her rejection of me wasn't only because I was drunk. She prefers that prissy priest. The wedding night went so wrong because she'd already given herself to him. What an affront to my house and me! I'll teach her. She'll bend to my will. She'll be my wife in more than name.*

* * *

Later that day, Ermengarde lay in the bed with the bed curtains closed. The pain in her arm and burning in her groin dulled her mind. Her arm had been set, and Missee had helped her bathe. The herb woman had given her fennel for her female complaints, a chervil salve for her burns, and comfrey tea for the pain. But so far, these ministrations had given her little relief. She listened to rain, splashing off the windowsill. Missee, her face pale and drawn, sat next to her.

THE VISCOUNT'S DAUGHTER

When someone opened the door, Ermengarde's muscles tensed. Perhaps it was her husband, although few men in the castle came willingly into the women's bower. "I do not want to see anyone," she whispered, turning her face to the wall.

Missee sprang to meet whoever was approaching. "Hello, Jordana. My sister is sleeping, and we shouldn't disturb her."

"My father is concerned. All the wedding guests are asking what has happened to the bride."

Missee was ready with the story Ermengarde had concocted. "My sister became sick during the night," she said, sounding older than her twelve years. "Dizzy and weak this morning, she tripped on the bedclothes and broke her arm. It is very painful, and she's still quite ill."

There was a pause, and Ermengarde imagined Jordana craning her long neck to look around Missee to where she lay still behind the bed curtains with her eyes closed.

"This is most inconvenient," Jordana said tersely. "My father is furious. He must host a day of banqueting without his bride by his side."

"Yes, that is inconvenient. But she is seeing no one." Missee's firmness surprised and pleased Ermengarde.

Jordana muttered something under her breath. Moments later, Ermengarde heard the sound of Jordana's retreating footsteps as she left the chamber.

Shutting the door, Missee came to her side. "I'm not sure she believed me. Did Toulouse do that to you?" She pointed to Ermengarde's bandaged arm.

She nodded. "He also hurt something inside me."

Missee's eyes filled with tears. "Oh, I'm so sorry. What will you do?"

"There's naught I can do. I never should have married Toulouse. He's a beast." She choked up but continued. "I wish I could run away. *We* could run away. But where could we run that Toulouse wouldn't find us and bring us back?"

"Ermengarde, for the nonce you're in no shape to walk, let alone run anywhere. I doubt you could ride a horse."

Missee was right. Ermengarde ached all over and, with her arm tightly bound and in a sling, she was sure she wouldn't get far. Her pain was intense, but even worse was the feeling of utter despair that threatened to crush her like grapes in a winepress.

"What will you do?" Missee repeated.

Ermengarde managed a bitter laugh. "If Toulouse and I are playing a game of chess, for the moment, he is checkmated. My broken arm, for all the pain, 'tis a visible sign to everyone that at least for a while, I'll need help with dressing, bathing, and toileting. I'll need to stay in the women's bower while the arm heals, and I cannot share Toulouse's bed."

"I'll take good care of you." Missee spoke with determination. "The same way you've always cared for me."

Missee's obvious concern and dedication lifted Ermengarde's spirits a little. Her marriage, the world, had gone terribly wrong. She didn't know what she could do, but she resolved to do something. The first thing was to regain her strength. Then she must somehow escape her marriage. She wouldn't stay married to Toulouse.

THE VISCOUNT'S DAUGHTER

* * *

Anduze headed down the rocky road of the escarpment with Gilles, Nicholas' grandson, leading the way. Nicholas rode by Anduze's side. The morning fog was thick, but it would burn off by midmorning, long before they reached Nîmes. It would be a fine day, but the thought didn't cheer Anduze. He dreaded hunting down Storm as if he were a runaway serf. He half hoped his son had more imagination than just running off to the fair. On the other hand, the sooner they found him the better.

Gilles seemed excited, as if they were going on a heroic adventure instead of to Nîmes. Anduze had ignored Gilles until Storm needed a sturdy training partner. Without land and a position in society, Gilles could never become a knight, even though he'd been trained as one. The best he could hope for was to be a man-at-arms. Anduze's affection for Nicholas had been the determining factor. The more skills Gilles had, the better his life would be. Anduze hoped he hadn't inadvertently raised the boy's expectations.

By early afternoon, they drew near Nîmes. Anduze pulled up his horse and called to Gilles who during the journey had gotten a furlong ahead of them. He galloped back to join them.

"We'll go into town before we visit the fair, have something to eat, and find lodgings," Anduze said.

Gilles' face fell. Anduze reconsidered. "Unless, Gilles, you would prefer to begin looking for Storm. You could grab something to eat from one of the vendors. Meet us at the Black Boar near the Maison Carrèe, the Roman temple, at nightfall."

"Yes, sir, I'll do that." Without hesitation, Gilles kneed his horse in the direction of the fair.

"Ah youth," Nicholas said. "'Tis better to give it free rein sometimes." He leaned forward on the cantle of the saddle. "I've been thinking about your problems with Storm. They say a wise man never gives advice, but I have a suggestion. If and when we find him, could you say you seek him so he can collect the harvest dues and hold the manorial court while you go hunting?"

Anduze frowned. "But the boy can't be trusted to manage the rents and even for me, holding the court is a challenge."

"How do you know Storm can't manage until you allow the lad to try? You can't eat the almond without breaking the shell. Such a plan would also save Storm the shame of having his father drag him home."

Nicholas had apparently thought this through. "You are very clever, Nicholas. I like your plan. It will no doubt be adequate punishment for Storm to stay home and work while we go on our annual hunt with Abbot Stephen."

* * *

The next morning, Anduze, Nicholas, and Gilles stood outside the Black Boar. The ancient inn, with its tiled roof and bright yellow sign painted with a black boar, had long been a landmark in Nîmes. Anduze had chosen it because it was centrally located and a good place to begin their search for Storm. "I've decided to divide the city into three sectors," he said. "Gilles you're to search the area near the archbishop's palace, Nicholas, the inns near the amphitheater, and I'll cover the rest. We'll meet back here when we're done."

Gilles' brow furrowed. His excitement of the night before apparently had given way to more practical concerns. "What will we do when we find Storm?"

"Bring him here to the taproom."

Gilles shifted from one foot to the other. "What if he refuses?"

Anduze reached into his purse for some coins. "Hold out your hands."

Nicholas and Gilles each held out a hand, and Anduze deposited a few coins in each. "I know my son well enough to be assured he will have spent most of his money, and he'll not refuse the offer of food and drink."

Gilles shook his head as he put the coins away and then departed. Nicholas gave Anduze an appreciative grin. "Well done, Anduze. I was wondering how Gilles would deal with a difficult situation if one arose. But a few coins in the hands of the youngster will smooth his way."

"Gilles' position isn't an easy one. He tries hard to please me and still be on good terms with Storm." Anduze rubbed his eyes, still irritated from sleeping in front of the smoky fireplace in the tavern. "We best be on our way. 'Twill not be an easy or a pleasant morning."

He headed to the narrow streets and dark alleys in the roughest section of the city. Mostly likely his son would be attracted to the stews and seedy taverns. He rested one hand comfortably on the pommel of his sword. Unlike Nicholas and Gilles, who were unarmed except for their daggers, Anduze was prepared to deal with any troubles he might encounter. He went down a dark lane that smelled of urine and manure. A goodwife opened a shutter on a window above him. She was about to empty a chamber pot into the street. Seeing Anduze, she hesitated, and he saluted her with a wave of his hand and a smile. Although it was still early morning, a few unsavory-looking men stood around a cockfighting pit, wagering on a cockfight. A glance told Anduze that Storm wasn't among them. Anduze's first stop was a well-known bawdy house. He pounded on the door and waited.

Finally, a blousy young woman, dressed only in a chainse with one shoulder exposed opened the door. "What can I do for you, handsome?" She thrust out a hip suggestively.

Anduze looked the woman up and down, and his eyes crinkled at the corners. "As delectable as I find what's on offer, unfortunately today, I am looking for my son. He's taller than I am and dumber."

The woman laughed. "What makes you think he might be here?"

He raised an eyebrow. "He is my son."

The woman laughed again. "I do recall someone looking a bit like you visiting here a couple of days ago, but I haven't seen him since."

"Thank you. He's probably run out of money, or I'm sure he'd be back to visit."

The woman had been standing in the doorway. She stepped back to close the door. As she did so, her chainse slipped down further revealing her breast. She gave Anduze a coquettish smile. "Come to see me sometime."

He inclined his head in a bow and smiled. "It will be my pleasure."

Across from the bawdy house was a tavern, so old and decrepit, its timbers had settled at odd angles. A glance told Anduze it had no stable so Storm could haven't made it his base. Nonetheless, Anduze went inside to question the barkeep. Having no luck there, he went from place to place. His diplomatic skills were wearing thin when he approached the last tavern on the street. It was a sprawling, rundown establishment with seven stars painted on its crude sign.

The barkeep, unshaven and wearing a dirty apron, came from the back to serve Anduze.

"I'm looking for a young man," he said.

The barkeep gave him a surly look. "What's it to me?"

Anduze took coins from his purse and placed them on the bar. "These are yours if you give me information about my son. He looks a lot like me although he's taller."

The man reached out a grubby hand, missing an index finger, to take the coins.

"Not so fast." Anduze covered the coins with his hand. "I'll hear what you have to say first."

The barkeep seemed uncertain, possibly wondering how he might extract more money from him. Anduze sensed the man was up to no good, and he scooped up the coins.

"Wait," the man said. "There's a drunk of that description sleeping it off near the stable."

Anduze dropped the coins. "Show me the way."

The barkeep led him out a side door to a rutted, open space before a rundown stable. Storm lay where he had passed out in his own vomit, now swarming with ants. Disgusted, Anduze flipped the man another coin. "Bring me a basin of water and a cloth."

The barkeep disappeared. Anduze's disgust gave way to compassion. It was bad enough to be lying in your own vomit without having your father find you in such a state. Nonetheless, when the man returned, Anduze dumped the whole basin of cold water on Storm's head. His son struggled to sit up, wiping at his face with his sleeve.

Anduze led a befuddled and chagrined Storm to the city's bathhouse, ordered a bath and, once his son had undressed, took the dirty clothes to the Black Boar to be washed. There, he found his saddlebag containing the change of clothes he had packed for the trip. They wouldn't fit Storm very well, but at least they were clean.

Leaving a message with the innkeeper for Nicholas and Gilles, Anduze returned to the bathhouse. He still wasn't sure what to do about Storm, but having no clear plan in mind decided to adopt the course of action Nicholas had suggested.

A sullen Storm was still in the tub when Anduze arrived back at the bathhouse. "Here put these on." He tossed the clothes on the bench beside the tub. "There's a cook shop across the street. Meet me there when you're dressed. I can imagine you're ready to put something in your sour stomach."

Anduze settled on a bench in front of the cook shop, and before the girl had come to take his order, Storm joined him. He cleared his throat. "Did you have to come and find me like I was a small boy who'd run away?"

"I assure you, I like the task no better than you do."

"Then why did you do it?"

"Because you are my son and heir and have responsibilities, though you've shown little interest in fulfilling them."

The serving girl came to their table, and they ordered cider, leek soup, white bread, and goat cheese. "It's appropriate you should mention responsibilities and my unwillingness to fulfill them. Matilde is pregnant, and she wants me to marry her."

Anduze rubbed his head that was beginning to ache. This was a cause for additional concern. "Do you want to marry her?"

"No," Storm said emphatically. "She's become a shrew, always teasing me, telling me of all her other admirers."

Anduze breathed a sigh of relief. "I'm glad you are no longer smitten with her since you couldn't marry her."

"I know you have an heiress in mind for me, Father. But what can I do?"

"You can take responsibility for your bastards the same why I've provided for mine. You'll give the fair Matilde a dowry, large enough to induce someone else to marry her. From what you've said, the child may not be yours in any case. Nonetheless, the dowry is only the beginning. You'll have to see to it that Matilde and her child never are in want."

Storm gave Anduze a black look. "How will we manage all this?"

"As you know most of our wealth is not in coin. So you'll have to turn some of our assets into silver." Anduze leaned forward, resting his elbows on the table and thoughtfully stroking his chin. "This year you'll see to the collection of our manorial dues and then arrange to sell whatever is given in kind."

"But...I've never done that! I wouldn't know where to begin."

"I'll tell you what you need to know before I leave for our annual hunt with Abbot Stephen."

Storm seemed taken aback. "You mean I'm not to go on the hunt?"

"You'll be busy, collecting manorial dues and holding manorial courts throughout our lands. For a long time now, I've wanted to explore a bit of wild country between Toulouse and Narbonne, belonging to the Abbey of Fontfroide, as a possible area for future hunts with Abbot Stephen. I haven't been able to do it because each fall I've been burdened with the harvest dues and our manorial courts. This is my chance."

Storm shifted uneasily on the bench. "When is all of this going to happen?"

"As soon as I get you settled at Sandeyran."

Chapter 5

CHURCH BELLS RANG THROUGHOUT THE city. Toulouse sat in his solar with Jordana. He didn't like the bells. They reminded him of the passage of time. It had been ten days since his wedding, and Ermengarde still remained in the women's bower. He cleared his throat. "I was deep in my cups, celebrating my acquisition of Narbonne on our wedding night, and I fear I went too far."

Jordana gave him an incredulous look. "You mean to say she didn't fall and break her arm?" Her tone suggested that she hadn't for one moment believed the story.

Toulouse shook his head. "I don't understand it. I've never had problems with women before."

Jordana's brow wrinkled. "I've made no secret of the fact that I don't like Ermengarde, Father. I've always thought her willful. She has an unwarranted estimation of her own worth."

"She has her father's stubbornness. But it doesn't look good for us to live apart."

"Ermengarde is feeling better, although she's not completely recovered. She's walking about the women's bower, and her appetite has returned."

"Find her and tell her to wait on me here, immediately." Toulouse tried and failed to keep the exasperation from his voice. "I must bring an end to our estrangement."

Jordana headed to the door to do her father's bidding. "I wish you luck." Her voice was thick with sarcasm.

When she closed the door, Toulouse took a gold necklace from a pouch on the table. He'd intended it to be a wedding gift for his bride, but failed to present it to her the night of the wedding. The necklace, wrought by the best goldsmith in Toulouse, glinted in the sunlight. It was a handsome piece and would look well on his wife's long neck. Perhaps if he gave it to her today, he could make amends, since there would be many years when they would live together as man and wife. Yet he couldn't dismiss the idea Jordana had put in his head earlier. He made a fist. To think Ermengarde had played him false with the priest, and he'd been cuckolded before his marriage. His drove his fist into the palm of his other hand with so much force that both hands stung. He shook them to relieve the stinging sensation and then put the necklace back into the pouch to await her arrival.

* * *

Ermengarde was beginning to feel stronger. She was able walk around a little now although she hadn't yet ventured from the women's bower. She was alone in the chamber and was surprised shortly after terce around the ninth hour when Jordana came in.

"My father summons you to his private solar. He's impatient to have you at his side." She was unable to keep the acrimony from her voice. "It's hardly suitable for you to hide yourself in the women's bower."

"I'll attend him at once," Ermengarde said, dreading the meeting. In the time she had been indisposed, she hadn't seen her husband, but he must have heard she was again on her feet. No doubt Jordana was spying on her and informing Toulouse of her every move.

Ermengarde walked tentatively toward the solar, her legs aching. Tension made her head pound. She paused at the door. Toulouse sat at the small table, empty except for a green velvet pouch. He was picking his teeth with a sharp sliver of wood. She composed her features, fearing her disgust would show on her face. He glanced up, saw her in the doorway, and spat out the piece of wood.

"How does my countess fare?" He looked her up and down. "Come in. Have a seat." He indicated a chair by his side.

Ermengarde was determined not to cower before him. She sat on the hard, straight-backed chair, raised her chin, and looked at him directly. "I am gradually mending, my lord.

Toulouse's presence and their proximity to the bedchamber put Ermengarde on edge. She waited for him to speak.

He put a possessive hand on her knee. "It's unseemly for a new wife to be separated from her husband."

The heat of his palm brought back the terrible memories of her wedding night. His touch was like a spark that ignited the dry leaves of her fear and loathing. Her temper flared and she glared at him. "It is unseemly for a bride to have the bridegroom break her arm on their wedding night and treat her so roughly she has yet to recover. Fortunately, I had the presence of mind to make up an excuse for your beastly behavior."

Toulouse's cold eyes became narrow slits. "That's enough! You needn't have bothered with excuses. No one questions my behavior. NO ONE. Let me assure you, wife, you will NEVER defy me again in word or in deed." He leapt to his feet and loomed over her. "It's unseemly for the woman I've honored with marriage to have already given herself to a priest."

Ermengarde's chest tightened. She had to deny this outrageous accusation. "You can believe what you like, or what Jordana mayhap put into your head, but I came to you a maiden."

Toulouse grunted. "We'll never know now, will we? If I were to ask your priest, he'd deny it."

"He is not MY priest." She glared at him.

Toulouse's face reddened. "Do you deny your involvement with him?"

She shook her head, before spitting out the words. "He was ONLY my tutor."

"It was through my benevolence that I allowed you to continue your studies. And this is how you repaid me." Toulouse grimaced, making him look like one of the gargoyles on a cathedral. "I want you at my side."

Ermengarde needed time. Time to make a plan. She might be only his pawn, but she'd learned enough of chess strategy to know even a pawn could act decisively. "My lord..." her voice wavered, and she demurely lowered her eyes in a calculated effort to appear submissive. "My arm will not be fully healed."

Toulouse took a deep breath, as if trying to control himself. "I'll give you a fortnight, and then I expect you to return to my bed. At that time, I will make arrangements for any servants you need to assist you in dressing and the things you can't do for yourself. In the meantime, you are to begin acting the part of countess. You'll accompany me to mass each morning, sit at my side at meals, and join the other ladies of the castle in the great hall. You will defer to my wishes in all things."

Realizing the futility of further argument, she bowed her head to Toulouse. "As you will, my lord."

Toulouse sat. His anger seemed to be expended. "You may go. I will see you at dinner."

"Yes, my lord." She stood, and the room began to pitch and spin, as if she were aboard ship. She steadied herself for a moment, looking at her feet, instead of at her husband. Fourteen days. Her mind flew. It was not enough time to devise and carry out the plan just beginning to take shape in her mind.

"A fortnight," he said again. It was not a request, but a command.

She glanced up at him. He inclined his head slightly with a begrudging acknowledgement of deference. As she left the room, she heard a thud as something hit the wall. She didn't turn to see what it was.

Ermengarde fled to the chapel and leaned against a cold, stone pillar. It took her a moment to calm herself. In the days since her wedding, she had begun to formulate a plan to escape Toulouse. Now that he had given her an ultimatum, she had to move ahead before she had thoroughly thought through how to proceed. The first step was to confront Minerve. He was her only possible ally, and perhaps if the incentive was lucrative enough, he might be convinced to help her.

The day after Ermengarde's meeting with Toulouse, she sent a page to find Minerve. He'd been staying in the Château Comtal since the wedding. She asked for him to wait on her in the small vestry near the chapel where she and Damian had had their lessons. Centrally located near the chapel and the great hall, with the door open, it was far from being a private space.

Returning to the vestry for the first time since her marriage, Ermengarde spotted the blue-and-yellow enameled box of chess pieces on a shelf. She experienced a twinge of longing for Damian, her lessons, and their chess games. Gray light from the dark, rainy day filtered in through the window slit. She sat on the familiar settle where so often she had studied with Damian, feeling as empty and desolate as the dreary room.

Through a long night, she'd rehearsed what she would say to Minerve. She was no longer a child and didn't wish to be treated like one. She must act decisively. Her talk with him would be a test. If she could convince him to aid her, perhaps there was hope she could outmaneuver Toulouse.

With her uninjured hand, she nervously smoothed the folds of her wool everyday gown. A knock finally came and, with a settling breath, she prepared to risk all in the next few moments, not only for herself, but also for her sister. Missee would never suffer her fate. "Come."

Minerve put his head into the room, a quizzical look on his face. "You wanted to see me?" He was dressed today in an expensive-looking, apparently new, purple surcoat, trimmed with yellow.

"Minerve, do come in, shut the door, and be seated. I have much to talk over with you."

He found a seat on the bench across from the settle. "I was sorry to learn of your broken arm," he said politely. "But do you really think it is wise to shut the door? Won't it endanger your reputation?"

An ugly laugh rose in Ermengarde's throat, but didn't reach her lips. "At this point, I'm unconcerned what others think. When I had lessons here with Father Damian, the door was always open. And still tongues wagged. I must speak with you alone. It is either here, or again on the ramparts, and the rain has not let up." The little hairs on the back of her neck prickled. If she was going to take a stand, this was her opening.

Minerve looked taken aback. "I'm not sure I understand."

Ermengarde studied the familiar lined face of her father's friend for a long moment before speaking. He appeared uneasy, as if he suspected she was about to ask him something. Taking a deep breath so she could speak without her voice shaking, she plunged ahead with the words she had practiced over and over to herself. "Minerve, you were my father's loyal ally. You know I had reservations about my marriage to Toulouse. Your part in the marriage negotiations was substantial. I trusted you because of your friendship with my father." She paused coming to the crux of what she wanted to say. She swallowed hard. "I want to give you the chance to serve me, too."

Minerve leaned forward on the bench. Clearly, she had his attention. He must have realized she was not the child he had advised only weeks ago. "My lady, I am at your command."

His immediate response was a good sign, but was he to be trusted? She looked into his one good eye, trying to measure his sincerity. "I am prepared to reward you handsomely for your loyalty to my family, if..."

Minerve's expression was wary, but interested. "What would you like me to do?"

Heartened by his response, she continued. "I'd like you to be my ambassador, so to speak."

"Ambassador?"

"Before I tell you more, I must have your pledge of secrecy. You must pledge it on your life and sacred honor."

Minerve rose and paced from his chair to the window and back, as if he was trying to decide what to do. "Do you know what you are asking?"

"You must choose between your loyalty to my family and to Toulouse."

"Ermengarde, believe me, I had no idea you'd come to this." He paused apparently searching and not finding words to describe the state he found her in.

She raised a hand to silence further discussion, her heart in her throat. She had to take the chance Minerve would be loyal to her. "I trusted you. I still trust you."

A look of sad realization passed over his face. He took his heavy sword from its scabbard and awkwardly knelt before her. He kissed the sword and handed it to her. "I swear on my sacred honor to keep whatever you tell me secret. I will forfeit my life, if I divulge a word of what you say to anyone."

She gave him back the heavy sword. "Rise, Minerve, and please be seated."

Now that she had sworn him to secrecy, Ermengarde got to the difficult part of the discussion. "I need not burden you with the sordid details." She hesitated, feeling her face grow red with embarrassment. Yet she had to tell him of Toulouse's shameful behavior toward her, even though it was generally accepted that women didn't discuss the details of what transpired in the bedchamber. She took a deep breath. She mustn't look back, she must move forward. "It is enough you know that Toulouse broke my arm on our wedding night and cruelly assaulted me. I will not stay married to that man."

Shock registered on Minerve's face. "I didn't realize…"

She waited for him to digest what she had told him. "Minerve, I will not stay married to that beast."

His shocked look gave way to one of puzzlement. "But what can you do? An annulment?"

Ermengarde was very glad she had planned what she was going to say. "I have thought of an annulment, but that is further down the road. As long as I am here, under Toulouse's roof, under his power, it will never happen. I have to get away from here, from him."

His face hardened. "What do you want me to do?"

Relief swept over Ermengarde like a breath of cool air on a sultry day. She had his support. "I want you to go to Narbonne and see if any of my father's vassals will help me if I go there. And after that I'd like you to approach father's old allies. Perhaps some of them will rally to my side. I will make it worth your while and reward anyone who comes to my aid."

He clasped his hand behind his back and began to pace again. "My lady, what you are suggesting could lead to war."

Was he having second thoughts? Ermengarde gave him a surprised look. "It may come to that, but only if Toulouse starts it."

Minerve was silent for a moment, as if he were considering many variables. "You would have allies. Just last year Toulouse alienated William of Montpellier by encouraging the citizens of Montpellier to rebel against him. And not everyone in

THE VISCOUNT'S DAUGHTER

Narbonne is pleased that Toulouse has made common cause with Archbishop Arnold. Raymond of Béziers has allied himself with Toulouse, but it's possible he and his Trencavel brothers fear Toulouse's growing power."

"And my father was half-brother to the Count of Barcelona. That makes Raymond Berenguer IV of Barcelona my half-cousin."

"Surely Barcelona would want an independent and neutral Narbonne." Minerve's voice rose in excitement. "The more powerful Toulouse has become the more of a threat he is to every noble in the region, including me. Be assured, I have sought his friendship only when no viable alternatives were available."

"The Templar is new in court. I've heard his order has released him to serve Toulouse. What do you suppose that portends?"

"It's understandable that Toulouse, having been born in Outremer, would have strong connections to this crusading order. The Templars are growing in power and importance everywhere, and they are answerable only to the pope. At some point, they might counterbalance the power of the church in the lands of the southern Franks. Toulouse is probably up to something with them, but I don't know what."

Ermengarde took from her finger her emerald ring, a rare cabochon that her father had long ago given to her mother. "Take this as token, a talisman."

Minerve shook his head as if he was beginning to reconsider the wisdom of her proposal. "Are you sure you want to do this? This could put you and your sister in danger, and you could lose everything. It is hard for me not to think of you as a child.

Tears rose in Ermengarde's eyes. "I ceased being a child on my wedding night."

Minerve walked back and forth in front of the settle. "You must realize that taking up your cause will forever alienate me from Toulouse. I need time to think over your proposal."

Ermengarde struggled to control her rising fear that he would not help her. "I want your answer now. I don't have the luxury of time. Toulouse has given me notice. In a fortnight, I must…" she almost most choked on the next words, "…return to his bed. I'd rather die." She held out the ring to him again.

He let out a deep breath. Giving her a compassionate, fatherly look, he took the ring from her outstretched hand. "My lady, I'll leave for Narbonne this very day. I'll test the waters. But two weeks is not much time for such an undertaking."

"How long will it take you to get there?"

"I will make it tomorrow tonight if I ride hard." He looked down and continued. "I'll do what I can. And I'm sorry, very sorry. What will you do in the meantime?"

"It's best you don't know my plans," she said. She hadn't thought beyond getting his aid. The next step would be to get away from Toulouse, and she hadn't figured out yet how she'd accomplish that.

THE VISCOUNT'S DAUGHTER

After Minerve left, Ermengarde was drained and elated at the same time. Her eyes were wet with suppressed tears. She daubed at them with a cloth, her hand shaking. It had a taken tremendous effort for her to rein in her emotions enough to admit to someone, other than Missee, what she had endured and then to press forward with a plan. Yet she, with no experience of such things, had done it. And now she had an ally, even if it was someone she knew so little about. Now she had hope. It was as if after a long difficult winter, she spotted the first green shoots beneath the snow.

When her elation passed, she began to have doubts. She wasn't sure why she didn't trust Minerve. Perhaps it was his inability to look her in the eyes. In spite of her brave assertion that she was no longer a child, she knew little of men and their motives and had no experience of politics or war. And her actions could lead to war. Yet she had set a plan in motion. She must act on the plan. She had no viable alternative.

Chapter 6

ERMENGARDE AND MISSEE RETREATED TO the women's bower supposedly to rest. But for Ermengarde it was just as excuse to get away from the others. She had been dutifully attending morning mass with Toulouse, sitting at his side during meals, and spending her days in the company of the women of the castle. Her outward calm belied how much she despised her husband and how much his nearness unsettled her. She even found her time with the women of the castle strained since they no longer openly gossiped in her company. That made her think she was the main source of their gossip.

She went to the window. "Look Missee, just there, beyond the far gatehouse, the Via Aquitania. I wonder if those ancient Romans could have imagined that their road could lead me to Narbonne and my freedom. How I long for us to be on it, leaving behind Toulouse and our life here forever."

Missee's jaw clenched. "What are we going to do?"

Ermengarde didn't know how to answer. She didn't know if Missee meant today, or about her impossible situation. She had thought of nothing but escape since Minerve had left for Narbonne and now, he had been gone for more than a week, and she hadn't heard from him. Each day brought her nearer to the end of the fortnight Toulouse had allowed her, and she still didn't know what she was going to do. She'd been up half the night, pacing the corridor outside the women's bower, but she still hadn't been able to decide on a course of action. She'd seen frightened rabbits freeze in place, hoping that no one would see them. Now fear froze her in the same way, and she had been unable to move forward with the only option open to her. She answered Missee as if she had meant today. "It's a nice day. I want to see if I can ride. Will you come with me?"

Missee frowned. "Do you really think you are ready?"

Ermengarde sighed. "I have to find out."

"I'll come along."

"Good, I need to talk with you alone, and I'm hesitant to do so in the Château Comtal where Toulouse's eyes and ears are everywhere." Ermengarde looked at her sister's serious little face and smiled. Hopefully outside, she could take Missee into her confidence. If she could find a way to escape, her sister had to come with her. During their wardship, she had been both mother and sister to Missee. Whatever course of action Ermengarde took, she could not leave her here with Toulouse.

They made their way to the stables with its familiar smells of dusty hay, oiled leather, and sour-sweet manure. They entered the dark interior where a single window cast a shaft of bright light, leaving all else shadowed and dim. A stable boy with a shock of reddish hair and a mouth full of protruding teeth came forward to greet them. He bowed deferentially to Ermengarde. "My lady."

"Ready our horses," she said. "We'll wait without."

Before long, the stable boy brought out the large bay gelding named Titan, that Ermengarde customarily rode, and Missee's little mare, Hebe. Hebe neighed a greeting and nuzzled her hand for a treat. She put her arms about the mare's neck. Missee wasn't fond of riding, but she visited Hebe every day and had made the mare into a pet.

Lack of exercise had made Titan rambunctious. He pranced and snorted, and the prospect of getting on him filled Ermengarde with dread. Her injuries weren't completely healed, and it might not be wise for her to ride. Yet she was an accomplished rider, and riding Titan would be crucial to any hope she had of escape. She had heard of women riding aside, but she'd never seen anyone do it. She was grateful for her tunic with its slits up the side, making it practical to ride astride.

The stable boy steadied Titan, and Ermengarde used the mounting stool to swing into the saddle. Hot fingers of pain spread through her loins. She had stopped bleeding two days after her wedding night. However, as the days had gone by and the ache in her legs and groin continued, she couldn't set aside the fear she'd never be able to have children. With a sharp intake of breath, she shut her eyes for a moment. Titan reared, skittered sideways, and almost threw her from her precarious seat. It was difficult to control him with only one hand. She loosed her injured arm from the sling and pulled up decisively on the reins. Her arm throbbed, but Titan calmed.

The stable boy helped clenched-jawed Missee into her saddle. "Are you sure you're ready to ride?" she asked.

The bay's strong haunches were poised for action, and Ermengarde urged him forward in answer. Missee followed her out of the bailey. The stable boy mounted an old hack to follow them at a discrete distance. They headed out of the Château Comtal by the gate that led into the rolling countryside. Ermengarde relaxed her hold on the reins and returned her injured arm to the sling. The bay lurched forward. Every movement seemed to reopen the tear she imagined Toulouse had rent in her womb. She held Titan in check with difficulty, trying to keep beside Missee and Hebe.

Ermengarde bit her lip as the bay jounced along the uneven rutted road. Blood trickled down her chin, and she wet her fingers and then wiped it away. The November day was chilly, but the bright sun was warm on her shoulders. They rode for several minutes in silence alongside the brown stubble of the recently harvested fields. The scattered stone farmhouses, with their tiled roofs, barns, and outbuildings became fewer and fewer as they lengthened their distance from the city.

They were well out in the countryside, when Ermengarde turned off the road onto a muddy track filled with potholes.

They slowed their pace. The stable boy kept a respectful distance behind them. Now was their chance to talk privately.

"Missee, I've determined two things," Ermengarde began. "I will not stay married to Toulouse, and you will never be forced into a marriage."

The color drained from Missee's face. "But what can you do? You've taken a holy vow before the archbishop in the basilica."

Ermengarde told her she had pinned her hopes on Minerve. "Whether he is able to find me support in Narbonne or elsewhere, I must somehow manage to escape from the Château Comtal, the city, and the territories controlled by Toulouse." She paused for a second, wondering how much she should say to Missee. But her pent-up emotions overflowed. "As for the archbishop, I hope he burns in hell for his collusion with Toulouse. And if the church condemns me for breaking my vow, so be it."

Missee's eyes grew large. "You mustn't say that."

"I've never seriously questioned the church until now. But if the archbishop represents God on earth, I don't like God, or his church, very much."

"Oh Ermengarde," Missee said. "It frightens me to hear you say such things about the church, but I can understand how you must feel. Is there nothing else you can do besides escape?"

"I have wracked my brain for an alternative plan. Each day brings me closer to returning to my duties as Toulouse's wife, and…" She hesitated, knowing she needed to tell her sister more than she had before. "And he's a beast." Ermengarde told her sister what she remembered from her wedding night. She shifted uneasily in the saddle, trying to ease her discomfort. "I don't know that I'll ever again be able to have relations with any man…" she shook her head, "…let alone with my vile husband."

Missee may have suspected Toulouse had seriously injured her, but this was the first time Ermengarde had revealed the extent of his brutality. Tears welled in Missee eyes. "What if you try to escape and Toulouse catches you?"

"What worse can he do to me than he has already done?" As soon as Ermengarde said the words, she knew they weren't true. He could claim she was crazy and lock her away in a dungeon, where he could do whatever he wanted to her physically and emotionally. And if he married Missee, he might drive her mad in reality. Ermengarde rubbed her forehead, trying to dismiss her fears. She had wanted to have choices and clearly now, like a deer cornered by hunters, her only choice was to run away.

"What if the knights of Narbonne and Father's old allies won't rally to your support?"

"That's a chance I'll have to take."

As they talked, the stable boy, behind them, came closer. Ermengarde didn't know if he was within hearing distance, but she leaned closer to Missee. As she did so, the pain in her groin became intense, worse than any pain she'd had during her flux. She wanted to scream. Instead, she whispered with unconcealed urgency. "You will come with me, won't you?"

The tears that had been threatening rolled down Missee's cheeks. "Yes, of course, whatever happens I want to be with you."

"My two weeks are up the day after tomorrow. So there's no time to concoct an elaborate escape plan."

"What do you have in mind? I heard you up last night, pacing. Certainly, Minerve hasn't had time to make any arrangements."

Ermengarde pressed her lips together into a thin slash. "We'll have to take our chances. If tomorrow is fair, we'll do as we did today. Go out for a ride. However, we'll just not come back. It isn't much of a plan, but it's all I could come up with."

Missee wiped her eyes on the sleeve of her gown. "But how can we travel without an escort? It's not safe."

Ermengarde swallowed her rising fear. "We'll be all right on the main road, but if we have to leave the road, we'll have to take our chances."

"Women never travel without an escort."

"I know, but I'm out of time and out of alternatives."

"What about our clothes, your embroidery, my lyre, our mothers' chests?"

"We'll have to leave them. I know you hate to part with your mother's things, and it's the same for me. I promise you that as soon as I can manage it, I'll buy you a new lyre. We'll secure our jewelry and any coins we have on our person."

Missee turned to glimpse the stable boy. "What will we do with him?"

"I'll take care of him." Ermengarde spoke resolutely, but at the thought of having to deal with the stable boy, her throat tightened, and she found it hard to breathe. She had no idea how she'd handle whatever escort they had.

"What if he rides back to the castle and alerts the castle guards and Toulouse?"

Ermengarde took a deep breath. "We'll have a head start."

"Can we make it to Narbonne? And if we do, will we be welcomed there?"

Ermengarde struggled to keep her voice steady. "We'll make our way to the Abbey of Lagrasse where our uncle, Berenger, is abbot."

"But he doesn't know us. He's never come to visit us."

"He's a monk, but he's still our father's brother, even if he rarely leaves the shelter of Lagrasse."

"Ermengarde, I'm scared."

"Missee, haven't I always taken care of you?" Ermengarde spoke lightly, trying to dispel her sister's anxiety.

"Do you know the way to Lagrasse?"

Ermengarde smiled at Missee, but she only had a vague idea of the location of the monastery. It lay south of the Via Aquitania and was alongside a river, but she wasn't clear how to get to it. She could consult the map she had studied months ago with Damian, but requesting it would make Toulouse suspicious. She tightly clutched the reins with her one good hand, trying to mask her apprehensions. She must do something, but could she really get them away from Toulouse?

It rained the next day. Not just a gentle drizzle but a deluge. The streets flooded, turning those without cobblestones into seas of mud. Water pounded on the shutters so furiously Ermengarde couldn't even open one enough to look out. She sat in a chair in the women's bower and stared off into nothingness. The shattering of her hope of escape left her weak, overcome with despair. The persistent, heavy rain had prevented them from going for the ride that could free her from Toulouse. Her fortnight was up on the morrow. She closed her eyes, trying to formulate a prayer that heaven would intercede. But words failed her.

"Holy Virgin, intercede for me," she finally managed to pray. Again and again, she repeated the words, hoping, but not really believing, that the Queen of Heaven would answer her pleas.

That night she and Missee tossed and turned in the bed they shared. "What will happen if it rains again tomorrow, and we can't ride?" Missee asked.

Panic engulfed Ermengarde. Perhaps her escape plans were the foolish imagining of a young girl, a girl who hadn't taken something as elemental as the weather into consideration when making her plans. She stifled the sob that rose in her throat. "I don't know."

After their uneasy night, the first gray light of dawn finally came through the narrow windows. Struggling out of bed in the early morning cold, Ermengarde hurried to look outside. To her relief, the first rays of sun appeared over the distant horizon.

She gently shook Missee. "The rain has stopped," she whispered as her sister's blue eyes fluttered open. "I must attend mass with Toulouse. Then we'll break our fast as is our custom and, afterwards, we'll be off for an early morning ride."

The girls and young women who shared the bower with them got up slowly, dressing for morning mass. Missee's nervous fingers tied Ermengarde's embroidered purse, containing her mother's jewels and a few coins, around her waist. Then Missee helped her on with a heavy woolen riding gown, woolen stockings, and her sturdiest leather boots.

"Missee, do you have everything?" Ermengarde asked in a whisper when they were ready to leave the chamber.

Missee glanced about the chamber and sighed. Her eyes filled with tears, but she didn't say anything or allow the tears to fall.

Ermengarde took her sister's hand and gave it a squeeze, hoping her own misgivings at what they were about to do didn't show.

Missee went to the hooks where their mantles hung. She put them both over her arm. With a last look at the chamber where they'd spent so much time together, she followed Ermengarde downstairs.

In the chapel, Missee joined the women, and Ermengarde stood at her husband's side as Father Hugh from the basilica said the morning mass. The kindly old priest with his wisps of white hair had taught Ermengarde to read and write. Later, he had found Damian to tutor her. The unheated space was gloomy, damp, and smelled of beeswax candles and incense.

Toulouse watched the service through half-closed eyes and paid no attention to Ermengarde. In her desperation, she prayed fervently for their deliverance.

The mass ended, and they entered the great hall where a fire burned in the huge fireplace. The two long tables nearest the fire were filled with knights, men-at-arms, squires, and other early risers. A big hound lay in front of the hearth, running in his sleep. Toulouse stopped to talk to one of his men.

"Let's warm ourselves before we eat," Ermengarde said to Missee. The morning's bone-numbing chill overcame Ermengarde's usual reluctance to get close to an open fire.

Carefully stepping over the hound, they both stood with their backs to the fire until the warmth penetrated their heavy gowns. The radiating heat eased Ermengarde's persistent pain. She surveyed the tables, wondering where it would be best for them to sit.

Toulouse came in their direction, his expression unreadable. Ermengarde had only moments to hide her revulsion. She bowed her head in wifely submission, peeking up at him through her thick lashes.

"Wife, 'tis time you returned to your husband. This morning, I'll send servants for your belongings."

"Yes, my lord. As you wish."

"I hear you are strong enough to ride."

"Yes, my lord, my arm is mending." Ermengarde wasn't sure where the impulse came from, but she turned her head to one side and managed a maidenly smile. "I must be able to ride," she paused, "before I resume my wifely duties."

Toulouse clearly caught the suggestion in her words, and this left him without a reply. Before he could think of something to say, one of his knights, a swarthy, furtive-looking, young man named Wulfrid, approached. He held a helmet in one hand and ran a hand through his greasy hair. "My lord, I'm just back from Narbonne. I beg a word with you." He glanced from Ermengarde to Toulouse. "Alone."

"Until later, my lady," Toulouse said, bowing before turning to walk to the far corner of the hall with Wulfrid.

* * *

Toulouse stared at his vassal. "And what is so urgent that can't wait until after I've broken my fast?"

"I've just returned from Narbonne," Wulfrid began. "And whilst I was there, who should turn up but your late guest, Minerve."

Toulouse laughed. "He, no doubt, couldn't wait to spend the purse I gave him on new finery."

Wulfrid frowned. "He was meeting with a number of the city's knights."

"I can imagine he couldn't wait to brag about his part in the marriage. We have nothing to fear from that man. He's an ass-licker, all bluster and no balls."

Wulfrid's frown deepened into a scowl. "He seemed pretty serious. I thought you should know."

Toulouse laughed, confident in his judgment of Minerve. "That kind always puts on a show of seriousness. But I don't think we have a thing to worry about." With a wave of his arm, he dismissed Wulfrid and returned to the front of the great hall to break his fast. He was more confident of his understanding of men than of women. He would try again to come to an accommodation with Ermengarde.

* * *

Alarmed, Ermengarde whispered to Missee. "Is it possible that knight has learned something of Minerve's mission?"

Missee blanched. "It's possible. But I'm sure Toulouse has lots of other things on his mind. Let's try to eat something."

Again carefully stepping over the dog that groaned in his sleep, they found a place to sit at the end of a table near the castellan, one of Toulouse's oldest servants who oversaw the smooth running of the Château Comtal. They helped themselves to bread from a basket on the table, cut pieces of cheddar from a round yellow cheese, and filled cups with pear cider from a jug on the table.

Ermengarde forced down a hunk of bread and a slice of cheese. She fingered the heavy ring Toulouse had given her when they were wed. She'd like to take it off and leave it in a prominent place. But that would be foolhardy. It would reveal her intentions before they managed to get away from the city. Finally giving up trying to eat more, she turned to her sister. "It's time."

"I'm ready." Missee smiled her sweet, trusting smile.

THE VISCOUNT'S DAUGHTER

If Ermengarde had any doubts about what she was doing, they were allayed. Missee mustn't fall into the hands of Toulouse. Ermengarde managed to smile back at her sister. "My prayers have been answered. It's a gorgeous day for a morning ride."

Missee helped her on with her soft blue mantle, and they left the great hall. It took considerable effort for Ermengarde not to look around to see if anyone was taking notice of their departure.

The bailey of the castle was coming to life. Steam rose from a huge laundry kettle boiling over a fire and, as they passed, a laundress was putting linens into it. A farrier was stoking his hearth, preparing to shoe a horse tied nearby. A maidservant chased after a squawking chicken, obviously bound for the stewpot. The ordinariness of the chores gave Ermengarde an unexpected twinge of regret. They were leaving the world they knew for the unknown. She hadn't been happy in Toulouse before her marriage, but her existence was safe, predictable, and privileged. It was here also that she'd learned much from Damian of the world beyond the castle and the city. Now she feared she'd learned too little.

They made their way into the stables. As Ermengarde's eyes adjusted to the gloom, the first thing she saw was Toulouse. Her hand flew to her mouth. She pretended she needed to cough. Did he guess her plan? She struggled to hide the fear that chilled her like yesterday's cold rain.

If Toulouse was suspicious, he didn't let on. In all probability his knight had asked to speak with him on another matter. "Good morrow, again, lady wife," he said, coming to her side. "I see you are headed out for a ride. Perhaps you won't mind if I accompany you?"

Chapter 7

ANDUZE HAD BEEN BACK AT Sandeyren a sennight, and this morning the sumpters were packed and waiting in the courtyard. It was a fine morning to begin his trip to explore the Abbey of Fontfroide's more far-flung holdings. In his chamber, he collected the last of his gear, put the hunting bow in its leather sheath, and secured his sword at his side. Mentally reviewing what he had packed, he headed toward the bailey.

Storm waited for him in the hallway. His dark eyebrows were knit together in a frown. "Wouldn't it be better if the first time I undertook the viscountal duties, you were here to guide me?" he blurted out.

"We've been over this again and again, Storm. You're staying here. If I accompany you, you'll defer to me, depend on me. It's past time for you to settle down and assume your responsibilities as the next lord of Anduze."

"But you're not yet in your dotage."

"No, and while I can still enjoy myself I'm going to let you do the burdensome tasks I have shouldered these last fifteen years since your grandfather died. Every year, I had to wait until all those chores were done before I could leave."

"But you're taking Gilles with you."

So that was what was behind this. Storm resented the fact that Gilles was going on the hunt, and he was not. "Gilles is not the next viscount. You are, and it's time you began to act like my heir to the viscounty."

"You just don't want to deal with all the accounts and squabbles between the peasants."

Storm was right about that. The young man was as feckless as he had been at his age. Anduze grimaced at the memory. Yet unwilling or not, there were responsibilities that went with rank. Perhaps without his father always looking over his shoulder, Storm could manage the collection of the rents and settle the peasant disputes, always brought to the lord's courts after the harvest. Before Anduze could think of an appropriate reply, Storm turned abruptly, hastened down the stairs, and disappeared.

Nicholas and Gilles were waiting in the bailey. Anduze attached his bow to the saddle and mounted. "I don't think Storm will be wishing us a safe journey," he said. *God's teeth, Storm is just like I was at age nineteen.*

The grass was still wet and the road muddy when they left Sandeyren. Before they reached the village below the castle, Anduze was having doubts. He pulled his horse up beside

Nicholas. "I'm not sure I've done the right thing," he said, pursing his lips.

"Storm will be fine. He who loves well, punishes well."

"What if he doesn't do what I've assigned him?"

"Oh, he'll do it. You didn't tell Gilles and the others about his humiliation in Nîmes, and I suspect he's grateful for that. And yet, that is something you could do if you a mind to."

"What if he does what's required, but does a half-hearted job of it?"

"As for not doing a good job, I've discovered people don't often make mistakes where money due them is concerned."

Anduze clapped Nicholas on the shoulder. "What would I do without you?"

* * *

Ermengarde's hopes for escape plummeted. She thought fast, trying to keep her voice casual as she spoke. "My plan today is to introduce Ermessende to some of the refinements of the skilled rider." She took a breath and continued. "She has dearly loved the little mare you gave her. She visits her everyday and brings her carrots and apples. But you may have noticed, she prefers sewing by the fire and playing games to outdoors activities. I have failed to teach her to be a good horsewoman. If you accompany us, your expertise would be a great help to her."

Toulouse grunted. Ermengarde wasn't sure if that meant he was or wasn't coming with them. The red-haired stable boy brought his stallion. "Get their horses!" Toulouse bellowed.

The stable boy scurried to do his lord's bidding. Ermengarde stood uneasily beside Missee and Toulouse as the stable boy readied Titan and Hebe. Before the silence between Toulouse and Ermengarde grew uncomfortable, the boy appeared with their saddled horses. Titan nickered in greeting. Toulouse handed her up, and she winced as she found her seat astride the bay. He didn't appear to notice her discomfort. He turned to assist Missee. A look of surprise flashed over her face at the unusual attention of the count.

Ermengarde's shoulders tightened with tension as they went out the castle gate and into the countryside. The early morning sun glittered on drops of yesterday's rain, still clinging to the grass along the road. The racing of her heart sharpened her senses. The sparkling raindrops, the rain-freshened fields, and the bright, beautiful morning seemed to mock what would probably be her failed escape attempt. She remembered the day of Missee's mother's funeral mass. That terrible day, of yet another loss, had been a bright, beautiful day too.

Needing to keep up the pretense that the purpose of the outing was a riding lesson for her sister, Ermengarde spurred Titan into a field where grain had recently been harvested. "Missee, this will be a good place for us to practice," she said. "I'll demonstrate what I'd like you to try."

Doing her best to ride proficiently, Ermengarde cantered and steered her palfrey into a figure eight. Pain shot through

114

her groin with each step of her horse. She galloped back to where Missee sat on her mare. "Now you try it." Ermengarde forced a smile.

Missee had little experience in the formal aspects of riding. She dug her heels into Hebe's side and tried to bring her into a canter. The mare whinnied and bolted, either misunderstanding her intention or in a burst of willfulness. Missee, clearly out of control, screamed.

Toulouse galloped after her. With her one good arm, Ermengarde held on to the reins and spurred the bay, drawing in deep breaths in an effort to manage the daggers of pain that shot through her. Missee's mare tired and stopped running before they caught up with her.

Missee's cheeks were red with embarrassment. Ignoring her obvious distress, Ermengarde put on her best big-sister voice. "Missee, you must be in control at all times, and the horse must know you are in control. Watch me again." She cantered through another figure eight.

Missee tried again to copy Ermengarde. This time, she applied too little pressure to Hebe's flank, and the mare began to walk slowly forward.

Ermengarde glanced at Toulouse. He appeared impatient with their little lesson. "Do you have any suggestions, my lord?"

Toulouse's face clouded. "I've never taught a lady to ride, but Lady Ermessende, the control of the horse is a matter of feeling. You have to feel with the horse, feel when to spur her on or when not to."

"I've been trying to learn that." Missee choked back tears.

Ermengarde turned to Toulouse and spoke calmly, even though her uneasiness made it difficult to control her voice. "All she needs is practice. I suspect the very fact a great lord is watching has made it even more difficult for her."

"Then practice she must." Toulouse was curt. Clearly, he was irritated. "I'll return to the castle and send out the stable boy." Toulouse was obviously eager to make his exit.

Ermengarde wondered what prompted him to accompany them. It certainly wasn't suspicion or he never would be leaving them alone. He spurred his horse and headed back toward the city and the Château Comtal, the battlements of which could be dimly seen in the distance. Her spirits soared. Now was their chance, mayhap their only chance to escape.

Toulouse was barely out of sight when she dropped the pretense of Missee's lessons. "We must away before the stable boy rides out to find us."

Missee, looking pale and apprehensive, nodded.

Ermengarde gingerly rearranged her seat on the saddle, and they urged their horses to gallop in the direction of Narbonne. It was imperative they put as much distance between themselves and Toulouse as possible. Her mind racing as fast as her heart, Ermengarde tried to calculate how long they would have before the stable boy found they'd disappeared. She guessed it would be no more than a quarter of the sand in an hourglass. Otherwise, Toulouse wouldn't have left them without an escort. It wasn't much time, and they had to make the most of it.

Their horses soon began to tire and they had to slow their pace. Ermengarde glanced anxiously behind them to see if anyone was following.

Missee came to Ermengarde's side, her face pinched with worry. "How far is the monastery at Lagrasse, and how long do you think it will take us to get there?"

Ermengarde wasn't sure, and her own uncertainty unnerved her, but for Missee's sake she mustn't show her fear. She only had a general sense of the monastery's location. "It's not all that far, but it's very isolated. We'll have to leave the main road to get there. Perhaps a knight on horseback could make it in a day's ride. It might take us longer."

Shock registered on Missee's face. "I didn't realize it was so far. Do you think anyone will come after us?"

"Yes, it's just a matter of time. The stable boy probably will look thoroughly for us before returning to inform Toulouse we are missing. And Toulouse may be riding elsewhere. Then he will have to assemble four or five knights to accompany him. All that will give us a bit of time." Ermengarde repeated to herself the prayer that had lately become her favorite. *St. Just and St. Pastor, patron saints of Narbonne, protect us.*

Missee's looked worried. "Will it be enough time?"

Ermengarde needed to reassure her sister, but they didn't have much of a lead. "I hope so."

"Oh Ermengarde, I'm scared. If we get away from Toulouse, we'll still be in danger. I've heard awful things about women travelling alone. What will become of us?"

Ermengarde wanted to tell her she was afraid too, more afraid than she'd ever been, but instead she said, "I'll take care of you, like I always have."

* * *

Toulouse was in the great hall, listening to a petitioner. The man was complaining one of his vassal's horses had gotten into his field and damaged his harvest. The red-haired stable boy approached the dais. Something was wrong. Toulouse held up his hand. "A moment," he told the petitioner.

The stable boy approached Toulouse. "They've disappeared," he said, his voice shaking.

"Disappeared! You fool! How could you lose them?" He struck the stable boy with a fist, and he crumpled.

Toulouse turned to the petitioner. "This will have to wait."

Wulfrid was lounging near the fire talking with the Templar. "Wulfrid," Toulouse ordered. "Find five knights ready to ride at once. Meet Ranulf and me at the stables."

Hearing his name, Ranulf came to Toulouse's side. He gave Toulouse an inquiring look.

"My willful wife and her sister have absconded. We're going after them. I can't imagine they'll get far." Toulouse spat out the words as if they were poison.

"Where will they head? Narbonne?"

Toulouse brought his anger under enough control to think. "Narbonne or Lagrasse. Their uncle is abbot of the monastery at Lagrasse."

"Don't be concerned, my lord. We'll catch them."

It flashed through Toulouse's mind that he should probably put on his mail, but the very thought of donning his battle armor to capture his wife stoked his anger. "Enough talk. We're wasting time. We leave immediately."

* * *

Ermengarde and Missee rode in silence. The sun climbed ever higher in the sky. Ermengarde kept turning in her saddle, hoping she wouldn't see the glint of sun off mail, helmets, and shields in the distance. When she could no longer see the battlements of the Château Comtal in the distance, she took off the heavy ring Toulouse had given her at their wedding. She wanted to throw it into the bushes, but it was valuable and might come in handy. She stuck it in her purse, and the very act made her feel freer, more in charge. Her next impulse was to remove her gauzy veil, identifying her as a married woman. But a well-dressed married woman traveling unaccompanied with a young girl would arouse less suspicion than two girls traveling alone. In her heightened emotional state, the brown fields stretching out against the brilliant blue of the sky looked heartbreakingly beautiful to her. It was as if her precarious freedom allowed her to see the world in all its wonder for the first time.

They met a peddler in a jaunty feathered hat with a bulging sack of goods. Seemingly intent on getting to the city, he passed with a mere glance in their direction. Ermengarde stiffened as a man on a horse approached. Yet he had no weapons other than a dagger at his waist. From his fine mount and deep purple velvet mantle, he looked like an official of some sort, perhaps even one of the town counselors of Toulouse. She let out her breath. This man wasn't a threat. Nonetheless, on this busy thoroughfare they were as vulnerable as a fly on the cook's worktable. They would have to leave the road at the first opportunity. Yet venturing into the woods was extremely dangerous. Wild boars and the wolves of Ermengarde's dreams lurked there, along with outcasts from society who lived by attacking and robbing others.

They passed fields with haystacks, prosperous farms with many outbuildings, and small peasant holdings with thatched roofs. Late-blooming, pink flowers with white stamens bordered the road. From time to time, Ermengarde got a strong whiff of anise. At other times, the heavy odor of manure was the only smell. They came to a small village near a stream crossed by an arched Roman bridge.

Ermengarde held up her hand as a signal for them to halt. She hated to stop, even for a moment, but they had been riding their horses hard, and this was a good chance to water them. She slipped off Titan and let him drink. Missee came to her side.

"Are you all right?" she asked. "I've noticed you keep wincing."

"I'm hurting a little," Ermengarde lied, "but it will be worth it if we get away from Toulouse."

"I think you're awfully brave."

"I'm not sure desperation is the same as bravery."

The horses finished drinking. "'Tis best that we keep going," Ermengarde said, glancing nervously in the direction of the city behind them.

Using a tree stump to help her mount, she managed to get back on the bay with only her one hand for support. Missee used the same stump to mount her little mare, and they continued on their way.

As they traveled farther from the city of Toulouse, they rode through unfamiliar countryside. Peasants stopped working in the fields to stare at the unusual sight of a noblewoman and girl traveling without an escort. They passed rich vineyards, with plump grapes ready to be harvested and almond groves. In one place, a pig squealed as young boy struggled to capture it. They overtook a farm cart filled with turnips. The peasant, leading the donkey, took off his hat in deference. They traveled past several side roads. Ermengarde studied each of them, wondering which one might be the road to Lagrasse. None of them looked promising. The cool sun was directly overhead when they stopped again.

"They must be close behind us," Ermengarde said, trying to keep her rising apprehension from her voice. A rocky outcropping crowned the hill beside where they stopped. "I'm going to the top of that knoll to see if anyone is behind us." She pointed to the hill." Stay with the horses. I'll be right back."

"Let me go," Missee protested. "I'm tired of riding. I want to stretch my legs."

She had assumed the big-sister tone of voice that Ermengarde often used.

"All right," Ermengarde said, unable to keep from smiling. She rubbed her aching arm, glad just to sit and watch Missee run off.

In moments, her sister reached the top of the hill and shaded her eyes against the glare of the sun. Suddenly, she crashed down the hillside to arrive breathlessly at Ermengarde's side.

"I see smudges: horsemen, traveling fast. Ermengarde, it's them. They're coming."

* * *

The thudding of his destrier's hooves on the rough paving stones reverberated through Toulouse's tense body. "Hell and damnation!" he muttered. It was unseemly for the Count of Toulouse to be running after a woman, any woman, even his wedded wife. He had often laughed at men who were cuckolded, and this was worse. If he couldn't capture her and return her to Toulouse, he'd be the butt of jokes from the Middle Sea to the Atlantic. *Christ's blood, what have I done to deserve this?* He had more important things to do than discipline women. Once as a young lad, he'd been hunting and gotten lost. He wandered into a swampy area where swarms of mosquitoes almost drove him crazy. At the time, he'd been annoyed with himself for being so careless as to get lost and angry that something as small as mosquitoes could drive him crazy. His dealings with Ermengarde now recalled that experience.

Ranulf rode by his side, his face composed. He was seemingly unaffected by the seriousness of the situation. Toulouse respected the Templar's intelligence and prowess, but the man struck him as bloodless, and now the man's detachment riled him.

They came to a crossroad, and Toulouse pulled up his winded horse. "Ranulf, I want you to take one man and head to Lagrasse. My men all know the way." He indicated the narrow road that snaked through the hills. "If they decide to head there, you'll be there to greet them."

"My lord, I'll be ready." Ranulf signaled to one of knights, spoke with him briefly, and they headed down the road.

For the first time, it occurred to Toulouse that he should have taken seriously Wulfrid's warning about Minerve. Perhaps the bastard was plotting something. Toulouse regretted that he hadn't had time to assemble a bigger force. *Hell and damnation. What problems that woman is causing.*

* * *

Missee didn't need to say more. They hurriedly mounted and urged their tired horses onward. They rode as if the devil were on their heels, and Ermengarde couldn't help but feel that he was. Her heart raced, and her chest constricted as if a giant hand had grasped it. She dared not think what Toulouse would do to her if they were caught.

After a while, Ermengarde's exhausted palfrey slowed, his sides heaving, and began to walk. He refused to respond to her efforts to get him to go faster. She turned to Missee who rode just a few paces behind her. She looked tired and frightened. "How are you managing?"

"Not much better than my mount. We're both spent."

Missee's little white mare did indeed look spent. They would have no chance of outrunning knights on sturdy destriers. What should they do? Ermengarde hastily looked around and made a decision. "We're leaving this road. That'll make it harder for them to follow us. We'll head south toward Lagrasse."

She steered Titan toward a twisted, rock-strewn, muddy trail that led off to the right. They couldn't help leaving hoof prints, but she hoped the men, riding fast, wouldn't notice them.

"But isn't it dangerous to go into the woods?" Missee protested. "Are you sure we're doing the right thing?"

"We're doing the only thing we can do," Ermengarde said, trying to sound certain, strong, and unafraid. Yet the shadowy woods made her ill at ease. The terrain ahead was inhospitable, and she grasped the reins tighter with her gloved hand that in spite of the afternoon chill had grown sweaty.

"Where will this take us?" Missee asked tremulously.

Ermengarde took a deep breath to calm herself before speaking. "Away from Toulouse and his men."

THE VISCOUNT'S DAUGHTER

They rode through a deep puddle and around a large boulder. Evergreens shaded the trail. They hadn't gone far before Ermengarde smelled fresh-cut timber. The trail climbed up and up, until it became little more than a path, filled with gullies and strewn with rocks and fallen leaves.

"We'd better walk the horses." She dismounted awkwardly. The tensions and fears of the last hours had all but ossified her muscles. She turned her head from side to side and stretched her legs, trying to relax.

Missee got down too. "I'm not sure we should have come this way." She expressed the very thought that had been Ermengarde's mind.

Ermengarde looked around with growing concern. "I'm not sure either. The sun will set in the west toward Toulouse, and if we keep going in a southerly direction, mayhap we'll find the road to Lagrasse."

She began gingerly walking. As she picked her way over the uneven ground, her riding boots sank into mud. With each step, mud splashed onto her mantle and gown. *Was coming this way a terrible, perhaps a fatal mistake?*

They walked and walked, and the sun began to slide downward. Ermengarde stopped for a moment. She strained her ears, trying to determine if they were being followed. She heard no telltale commotion behind them.

Missee pulled a fluffy fragment of something from one of the gorse bushes. "What's this?"

She handed Ermengarde the fragment. She fingered the soft fibers for a moment, before it dawned on her. "'Tis wool.

125

Look there are bits of it caught on the brambles and gorse. A flock of sheep has passed through here," she said, trying her best to sound cheerful. "And that may mean a farm or a shepherd's hut is somewhere near."

The path grew narrower and narrower until it almost disappeared. Ermengarde's shoulders tensed. *Had we come so far only to get lost?* There was nothing to do, but to keep going. They picked their way forward as the thin November light faded, and the path became nearly impossible to follow.

Ermengarde turned to Missee. In the last rays of the fading light, she looked paler than usual and Ermengarde could tell by the way her sister walked that she was exhausted. Ermengarde smiled. "We'll rest for a bit. 'Twill be difficult for them to find us in this wilderness."

"Mayhap no one will *ever* find us," Missee replied gloomily. She sat on an ancient stone fence they had been following for some time.

Ermengarde sat beside her. "Would that be so bad? We'd be together at least."

Missee shook her head. "The woods frighten me. The trees that have lost their leaves look like skeletons."

A twig snapped somewhere nearby, and they both jumped. They looked in the direction of the sound, but didn't see anything.

Struggling to keep her anxieties at bay, Ermengarde asked, "Do you think I could become an Amazon?"

Missee laughed a tired laugh. "I've always thought Amazons were mythical creatures. But I suppose you could do anything you set your mind to. You've always been a fighter."

"I hope you are right," Ermengarde said, heartened by her sister's confidence. "But you're quite a little wood sprite yourself. We've come a long way without rest or nourishment and you've not complained. You're stronger than you think."

"I didn't mind leaving Toulouse, but it was hard for me to leave my few things. I know that sounds silly."

"It's not silly at all. I loved your mother, too. She was the only mother I ever knew. Leaving the lovely little triptych filled with scenes from the life of Mary in front of which she prayed was hard for me to do." Ermengarde made the effort to cast off her gloomy thoughts. "We'd best be on our way again."

"How can we keep on in the dark when there isn't even a clear path to follow?" Missee whispered, as if speaking out loud would betray their location.

"When it's completely dark, we'll be able to see any lights in the area. This path must lead somewhere."

They used the stone fence to mount again and gave the horses their head, trusting that they would lead them along what little there was of the path. Ermengarde worried what would happen to them but, at the same time, she was grateful she was not with Toulouse at the Château Comtal. The blackness around her was frightening, but it was nothing compared to that dark, horrible reality.

It was almost totally dark when she spotted a dim light through trees off to their left. "Missee, look! We'll head for it."

Ermengarde dismounted, sliding from her horse and hitting the ground with a sharp uptake of breath. Leading the bay, she headed towards the light with Missee behind her.

"What if it is Toulouse and his men?" Missee asked in a low voice, hardly more than a whisper.

"If they found where we left the road, they're probably behind us. Most likely, we'll come to a small farm or shepherd's hut where we can ask for shelter for the night."

The woods were thick and brambles caught at Ermengarde's mantle as they made their way slowly toward the light. She expected the woods to give way to a clearing and a farm. Then as they neared the light, she saw the flickering of a campfire through the trees. *Who, other than thieves or outlaws, would be deep in the woods this time of year?*

A man's gravelly voice called out. "Who goes there?"

Ermengarde wasn't sure how to answer. But she had to say something. She had to tell them that they meant no harm. "We're lost and saw your fire. We need help."

"Throw down your arms!" the voice came again.

"We are unarmed." As soon as she said it, Ermengarde wondered if she should have admitted it.

"Show yourselves."

Ermengarde took her sister's cold hand and gave it a brief squeeze. Inhaling deeply, she walked slowly toward the fire with Missee at her heels.

They came into a small clearing. Two men sat at the fire while another man stood just behind them. In the flickering firelight, he held a bow with an arrow in it. The arrow was pointed directly at Ermengarde's chest.

Chapter 8

TOULOUSE PULLED UP HIS TIRED horse, grasping the reins tightly. He hated to abandon the chase, but it was pointless to go on in the dark. The moon had not yet risen, and the stars gave little light. If only he had spotted the place earlier where they'd left the road. By now, he'd have captured Ermengarde, and they'd be on their way back to the Château Comtal. He addressed his men. "The night's as black as sin. We'll not find them tonight."

Blood pulsed in his temples, and he fumed as he urged his horse in the direction of the Via Aquitania. He let his horse lead the way. They slowly made their way along until trees no longer brushed them, as the narrow path widened. A short time later, the horse's hooves clopped on the paving stones of the Roman road.

Toulouse remembered passing an inn several miles back where they could spend the night. He told himself things would look better in the morning. They'd be rested and well fed. The horses would be fresh. The two young women couldn't go far in the dark. By tomorrow, after a night in the woods, they'd be more likely to return willingly to Toulouse. He contemplated sending for more men. No, he wouldn't do that. It was humiliating enough to have not caught Ermengarde right away, without summoning an army to capture her.

* * *

Ermengarde froze, not knowing what to do. All her instincts told her to turn and run, but they would never get away. "Don't shoot," she said, summoning all the command in her voice that she could. Still, to her it sounded weak.

"Come closer!" the man bellowed.

They moved closer. Ermengarde's legs trembled with every step. It had been a difficult day, and it wasn't over. She didn't take her eyes off the man with the bow.

As they came into the flickering firelight, the man lowered the weapon. He was somewhere in his middle years, tall and muscular. Several days' growth of beard gave him a roguish appearance. He was dressed like a woodsman in a leather jerkin, breeches, and a felt hat. His aspect was not that of a peasant, yet he was no one she'd seen frequenting the Château Comtal.

Ermengarde glanced from him to the two men by the fire. One had a white beard with the deep lines of age chiseled in his face, making it as craggy as the side of a cliff, and the other was a stocky young man of no more than twenty years. Both of them were attired in hunting clothes. A large hare was roasting on a makeshift spit over the smoking fire. A horse neighed somewhere nearby. These men were undoubtedly highwaymen. Images of the violence of her wedding night flashed to mind. *Have I saved myself from my disastrous marriage only to place Missee and myself in even graver danger?*

Ermengarde took a deep breath. Whoever they were, she had to deal with them. At least if they were outlaws, they were not likely to want to bring themselves to the notice of Toulouse and his men. Summoning reserves of strength she didn't know she had, she threw back her shoulders and stood tall. "We're tired and hungry. And we seek your aid."

The man with the bow laughed a deep, not unpleasant, laugh. "What makes you think we just won't rob you, have our way with you, and leave you for dead? Two women alone are but flowers, waiting to be plucked."

Her blood ran cold, but there was something in the way the man spoke that was more teasing than threatening. "I suppose that is an option," she said as calmly as she could manage. "But I assume you are too smart to do anything foolhardy."

The man with the bow, obviously their leader, seemed to consider. "Hobble their horses," he said with only a slight nod of his head that made her think he was used to giving orders and having them obeyed.

The young man was as tall as the leader, with wide shoulders and a thick neck. Something about him seemed vaguely familiar. He approached and held out a hand. She gave him the reins, wondering if she'd ever see Titan again. Missee handed over the reins to her mare.

Moving closer to the fire, Ermengarde stretched out her hands to warm them as if it was the most natural thing in the world for her to do. Missee followed her lead. The rich smell of the sizzling meat made Ermengarde's stomach growl.

"Make yourself at home," the leader said, inclining his head in a mocking bow. He came to join them. His hair was as dark as the eyes that looked at her with an air of amusement and curiosity. His hunting attire was neat and without stains. His obvious good humor was combined with a relaxed confidence, a self-possession that she found both intriguing and worrying.

Damian's cool reasonableness flashed into Ermengarde's mind. In spite of her overwrought state, she must keep her wits about her and decide upon a strategy to deal with this situation. She didn't know what she should tell this man, or if she should reveal her true identity. In the duress of the last hours, she hadn't thought up a yarn to spin in case someone stopped them, or when they might ask for refuge for the night. In her chess games, she had learned that offense is often the best defense. She decided to take that tact.

"Whom do I have the honor of addressing?" she asked, as if she had every right to know the man's identity and business.

The leader cocked his head slightly as if wondering what all this was about. "I'm called Anduze."

Ermengarde had heard of Anduze, a viscounty north of Nîmes. The viscount there was said to be a distant relative of hers. But this man wasn't very forthcoming. Was he a man of substance, an errant member of that noble family, or a highwayman who came from that area? "Fortune smiles on you this day, Anduze," she said evenly. "We'll discuss it after we've rested and eaten. The hare looks like 'tis ready to eat."

Ermengarde eased her aching body to the ground, knowing otherwise she might collapse. The ground was damp and cold, but she was beyond worrying about such a minor thing. Missee sat beside her.

"You have a lot of nerve," Anduze said in a mocking tone.

"Yes, I do. Or I wouldn't be here."

Anduze gave her a questioning look. "And who might you be?"

She hesitated, fearing to reveal her true identity. Yet she had come this far, and she had no alternative but to take the chance this man could be reasoned with. "I am Ermengarde, Viscountess of Narbonne, and this is my sister Ermessende, Missee."

Anduze laughed. "I like a woman with spirit, and you are one whose ransom would be worth her weight in Moorish gold."

Ermengarde forced out a laugh. Two could play this game. "Perhaps I was wrong to guess that you were too smart to do anything foolhardy."

The young man who had taken their horses returned and stood awkwardly by the side of the leader. Ermengarde had the fleeting impression he was uncomfortable in his hulking body, as if he had grown too big, too fast.

"The ladies are hungry," Anduze said. He approached the spit, took out his eating knife, and hacked at one of the haunches of the rabbit until it was almost off. Then he skewered it. "My lady," he said, with mock reverence as he held it out to her.

Ermengarde removed her eating knife from its sheath and leaned toward him to take the meat. He smelled of wood smoke, and the look he gave her was arresting. She took the meat from him. "You are most gracious, Anduze," she said with courtly civility.

Anduze smiled. "A woman of fine manners, spirit, and a sense of humor, a rare find indeed."

"Keep in mind, sir, I found you and not the other way around."

He laughed. "And luckily for you, you found us just in time to eat." He skewered another haunch with his knife and gave it to Missee, before serving himself. The two other men cut their own shares and seated themselves next to Anduze. They must have made a curious sight. Ermengarde and Missee were on one side of the fire, and the three woodsmen on the other. A slight breeze stirred, and the smoke from the fire made Missee cough. No wonder the men were sitting next to Anduze.

Ermengarde blew on the steaming meat to cool it, made a hasty sign of the cross, and gratefully sank her teeth into the tender flesh, seasoned by wood smoke. "Very tasty. My compliments to the cook."

The man with the craggy face and the white beard spoke. "Nicholas is my name, my lady. I'm glad our humble fare meets with your ladyship's approval. The youngster is called Gilles." Nicholas' accent revealed his humble origins, but there was something about him Ermengarde found appealing. Winkles of good humor lined his aged face, and he spoke gently as if he were calming a spooked horse.

The lad, Gilles, was of an age to be Anduze's squire if this man was a knight. But in the darkness and dressed in hunting clothes, she couldn't judge the men's relationship to each other. Whoever this Anduze was, she had to deal with him. She considered what incentives she could offer him to gain his help. She thought back to her dealings with Minerve. Maybe this man could be influenced by money or land.

"I am pleased to make your acquaintance," Ermengarde said, not to be outdone in politeness.

"And I am too," Missee said, mimicking her good manners.

The tension of the last moments eased a little. Anduze produced a stoppered costrel, opened it, and passed it to Ermengarde. She sniffed the contents and, assured of the hearty smell of new wine, took a deep drink. She coughed, but managed to swallow it. Welcome warmth spread through her. Wiping her lips, she passed the costrel to Missee. Neither of them had ever drunk rough wine like this before. Missee's eyes got big, and she also choked on the wine. Ermengarde took another drink, before passing it back to Anduze, who drank and then passed it to the others.

The hare soon disappeared. "Now that we have eaten," Anduze said, wiping his knife on fallen leaves before putting it away, "'tis time for you to tell me why I shouldn't ransom you."

"What ransom would you demand for me?" Ermengarde asked, raising an eyebrow.

Anduze thoughtfully rubbed his face with one hand. "I already said, and I wasn't jesting, I would ask your weight in gold."

He clearly thought she was worth a lot. She had to come up with something to offer this Anduze that would make him her man. "Gold I have none." Ermengarde spoke very deliberately. "But I am willing to offer you wealth, land, and privileges in return for your service."

In the firelight, it was hard to read his expression. "How much land and what kind of tenure?"

"A knight's fief," she paused, and the unimpressed look on his face compelled her to continue, "in the beginning."

She heard a rustling in the bushes somewhere nearby. Anduze and the others heard it, too, and they all fell silent. A whooo, whooo brought a smile to Anduze's lips. "Only an owl. And I'm curious. How can you offer me land?"

"I am on my way to claim my inheritance, the Viscounty of Narbonne."

"What of your husband? I was in Toulouse the day you were wed and saw the bridal party. I didn't recognize you in the darkness."

"My husband can go to the devil!" Ermengarde shocked herself with her vehemence and choice of words. It wasn't that she hadn't thought it. It was just that she hadn't said it before.

"And I wager you'll not want to have any dealing with him. I'm offering you protection and—"

"You're offering me protection?" Anduze chortled. "You have confused the chickens and the fox."

Ermengarde refused to rise to his smart remark. "Decide if you will deal with me or with Toulouse and the law." She knew she was taking a chance with this complete stranger. "Tell me Anduze are you an outlaw?" She shifted her position on the hard ground and looked intently at him.

"I have no problems with the law." Anduze shook his head. "But helping you might give me problems with Toulouse, problems I don't need. Why are you running away from him?" He indicated her arm with a nod of his head. "Did he harm you?"

Ermengarde didn't reply, and Missee spoke up. "He's… he's a beast. He broke her arm and…."

Anduze's face grew somber, hard. "Is he the one I should thank for the pleasure of your company in the middle of nowhere?"

Ermengarde recovered her voice. "We left the Via Aquitania when we sighted his men behind us. We will seek sanctuary with our uncle, the abbot of the monastery of Lagrasse." The moment she spoke she wondered if she was telling this stranger too much.

Anduze disappeared into the shadows to return a few moments later with a log. He threw it on the fire, and a cascade of sparks leapt into the darkness. Then he turned to his followers. "What say you, Nicholas? Shall we aid these ladies in distress?"

The old man took off his cap and scratched his head. "As you will, my lord. The days follow each other and don't look alike. We can hardly desert two young ladies alone in the woods."

The words "my lord" took Ermengarde aback. The nobles she knew were forever strutting about, letting no one forget their rank and position. And she had never known a noble to defer to a man who, like Nicholas, had every appearance of being a commoner. "Are you the Viscount of Anduze, whom I've been bargaining with like a fishwife at the market?"

"At your service, my lady," Anduze said, with a bow. "And Nicholas is right. We can hardly desert ladies in distress. We'll leave first thing in the morning."

The thought of spending the night in this deserted place in the company of this unforthcoming man and his huntsmen made Ermengarde recoil. She took a deep breath, straightening her spine. "We need to go, now."

"We'll leave at first light."

Horrid thoughts of what might be befall them this night made it difficult for Ermengarde to think clearly and speak calmly. She glanced at Missee who looked terrified. "But…we're being followed," Ermengarde said feebly.

"My lady, if you're seeking my help, you'll have to trust my judgment." Anduze spoke respectfully, but firmly. "Your husband can't follow you in the dark, and if you push on now, you'll ruin your horses. We'll stay here until dawn." He took a faggot from the fire, lighted a small lantern, and gave it to the young man." Gilles, fetch the ladies their horse blankets."

Did they really need to wait until morning? The thought of spending the night in the company of these unknown men was daunting. She'd rather die than be ravaged again and the possibility of innocent Missee being raped made her apprehensive, yet Ermengarde had no alternatives. Without a lantern, they couldn't go on in the dark. Something told her these men would do them no harm, but she wasn't sure she could trust her instincts. She hoped she hadn't unwittingly put them into an untenable position. She let out her breath. She had no choice but to stifle her fears and do as Anduze suggested. Whatever the outcome, they couldn't go on tonight alone. Someday she'd control her own fate and not be set upon by circumstances.

Gilles returned with their blankets. With a determined effort, Ermengarde kept her voice even and confident. "Come, Missee, we'll spread our blankets over there." She indicated a flat area a little distance from the others.

"I'm cold. Couldn't we get a little closer to the fire?" Missee asked.

Ermengarde shook head. "You know how frightened I am of fire. There's a bit of breeze and a spark from it might set our blankets afire." Before moving away from the others, she inclined her head in Anduze's direction. "My lord, Gilles, Nicholas, may God be with you 'till the morn."

Anduze acknowledged her nod with one of his one. "And with you."

Gathering a few leaves for a mattress, Ermengarde and Missee arranged their blankets close together, lay down, and used their mantles for covers. "Missee, do you think you'll be warm enough?" Ermengarde whispered.

Missee yawned. "I'm so exhausted and so glad we're not going on tonight, I think I'll be able to sleep." She turned on her side, pulling herself into a fetal position.

Ermengarde squirmed, trying to find a place where the pulsing ache in her loins eased. Taking her eating knife from its sheath, she resolved to stay awake and defend them, if they were attacked. Huddling close to Missee for warmth, Ermengarde listened to the murmur of voices as the others made themselves ready for the night.

Before long, Missee's breathing quieted and snores came from the other side of the dwindling fire. In spite of her anxiety and best efforts to stay awake, Ermengarde drifted into an exhausted, uneasy sleep, only to wake moments later, whimpering. She had dreamed Toulouse was coming at her with a fiery poker. She stared into the blackness, relieved that the woodmen had made no move in their direction, but disquieted by her dream.

* * *

Anduze lay for a long time watching the embers of the fire. He heard Lady Ermengarde whimpering in her sleep. God's teeth, what was he was getting himself into? This hunting trip was to be an escape from the troubled last weeks with Storm. He was just beginning to unwind from his pilgrimage, the upsetting visit to Toulouse, and his confrontation with Storm when rain had driven them to a squalid inn for two nights and a day of wenching and drinking. Muzzle-headed, they'd made a slow start this morning and only this afternoon was he beginning to feel like himself again. Now he was faced with two runaways.

Anduze turned uneasily on the hard ground, dislodging a stone that had been sticking into his back. The young woman and her little sister were trouble. Trouble he didn't need or want. Yet he couldn't leave them to fend for themselves in the woods with Toulouse—that rotten bastard—hot on their trail. Anduze thought back to the one and only time he'd met Toulouse, and his stomach churned. Yet, thwarting the most powerful man in the land of the southern Franks had a decided appeal.

He sat up and reached for the costrel of wine. He took a drink and then lay back down. Lady Ermengarde. He didn't fully understand why he was drawn to her. Perhaps it was her self-possession. Perhaps it was as the old woman in Toulouse had said. It was in his nature, and that of all men, to want what they couldn't have. The viscountess had been foolhardy to flee into the woods without an escort. She was young and vulnerable, and her proud defiance was enough to inspire lust in any man. The thought of her being raped aroused him, yet the same time engendered a feeling of protectiveness. She must be truly desperate, and who knew better than he, what evil Toulouse was capable of. But such thoughts were getting him nowhere.

He had to focus on the problem at hand. He rubbed his eyes, as if doing so would clear his head. In making the decision to help the runaways, he had clearly deferred to Nicholas. Long ago, he'd promised Nicholas he'd not seek revenge. The old man knew better than anyone what might be at stake, and yet had agreed they should help the women. Nicholas had whispered to him, before going to sleep, that their paths hadn't intersected with Ermengarde's by accident. Perhaps this was his opportunity to finally confront Toulouse. However, it made more sense that this meeting was a coincidence, and they only had to deliver the two noblewomen someplace where they'd be safe. Then with any luck, the coming hunting trip wouldn't be ruined after all.

* * *

"My lady," a voice came through Ermengarde's sleep. "It's time we were on our way."

She opened her eyes. Nicholas was bending over her, a look of urgency on his lined face. The pale suggestion of morning was just beginning to lighten the sky. She gingerly stretched her legs and wiggled her cold toes, before using her good arm to sit up. Her eating knife lay on the ground beside her. She put it away relieved she hadn't had to defend Missee and herself.

Turning to Missee, Ermengarde gently shook her. "*Ma petite soeur*, we must be up and on our way."

Missee rubbed her eyes sleepily, and they both got up, shaking twigs and leaves from their mantles. Missee's hair was mussed, and Ermengarde patted her own, neatening a few unruly wisps.

Gilles brought their horses. "Anduze is scouting to see if your *friends* are nearby. We're to meet him ahead."

Ermengarde's fears of the night before resurfaced and her muscles tightened. Could she trust Anduze? It was possible he was the lord of Anduze and an outlaw at the same time. At his very moment, he could be seeking Toulouse to arrange her ransom.

Her unease must have registered on her face because Nicholas said, "Not to worry, my lady. Anduze knows what he is doing."

Nicholas helped Missee and Ermengarde into their saddles and then mounted his own horse. "Follow me," he said.

Ermengarde nudged the bay and followed Nicholas through thick ground fog along a barely discernible trail. Missee and Gilles rode single file behind them.

They traveled this way in the cold, still morning until finally Ermengarde could see slivers of sun through the bare tree branches. They rode on and on. Finally, they came to a dolmen, two huge stones with a cross piece, often thought to be an ancient tomb. On the other side of the trail was a stone cross, probably to ward off the evil spirits of the dolmen.

Nicholas pulled up his horse and then dismounted. "We're to wait here for Anduze."

Ermengarde and Missee dismounted also, tethering their horses where they could graze on the sparse grass along the trail. Nicholas took a round loaf of bread from his saddlebag and tore it into four pieces. "You better eat something," he said, passing out the bread reverently, as if it were the Holy Eucharist. "It'll be a long day."

Ermengarde took a bite of the chewy, brown bread, unlike the soft, white bread regularly eaten at the Château Comtal. She'd heard about twice-baked bread, used on military campaigns and long journeys, but she'd never tasted it. "It's very good," she said.

Nicholas smiled. "I made it myself before we left Sandeyren Castle. It's by forging that one becomes a blacksmith." Something in Nicholas' kindly manner reminded Ermengarde of her confessor, Father Hugh. If as people aged, their faces revealed their true characters, the deep lines of Nicholas' face seemed to have been etched by a lifetime of goodness and of caring for others.

"I take it bread making is just one of your talents?" she asked with a hint of levity.

Nicholas laughed not only with his mouth, but also with his eyes. "I'm not sure what you take us for, my lady. Outlaws I imagine."

She raised an eyebrow. "I never knew outlaws were also bakers."

"And I would wager they're not. I don't generally do the baking at Sandeyren Castle, but before we left, I made this special hunter's bread that travels well."

"Nicholas, do you know if there is water nearby?" Missee interrupted. "I'm very much in need of a drink."

"I was beginning to think you didn't have a tongue." The deep lines in Nicholas' face gentled. "There's a stream a little further on where we can drink and water our horses, but until then perhaps I can offer you a drink." He took a gourd from his pack and held it out to her.

"Oh, yes, thank you." Missee drank and passed the water to Ermengarde. "I am not usually this quiet. These are unusual circumstances."

Nicholas chuckled. "Very unusual."

As Ermengarde took a deep drink of the refreshing water, she heard horse's hooves and the clinking of a bridle. She stiffened, choking on the water. Had Toulouse found them?

* * *

Toulouse and his knights picked up Ermengarde's trail that led along a stone fence. His head throbbed from the wine he had drunk the night before, and he squinted in the early morning sunlight. He'd ordered the best wine in the inn, but it had still been raw and of poor quality. This morning, he regretted drinking so much of it.

They followed the hoof prints of the two horses for some way and came to a place where the women had dismounted. At that point the trail disappeared.

"Dismount," Toulouse ordered. "Search the area." He stayed on his horse, and the others began searching the woods.

It wasn't long before Wulfrid called out, "They went into the woods here."

Toulouse rode to his side and examined the disturbed earth. "This way," he called to his men. He followed the indistinct hoof prints into the woods. Branches, wet with morning dew, brushed his clothing. He shook the wet drops from his mantle. *By the Holy Rood, Ermengarde will pay for this.* He came to a clearing and an abandoned campfire. "Damn it all to hell." He shook his head. "They met up with somebody." He studied the leafy ground.

"It's hard to tell, but I think there were three additional horsemen." Wulfrid indicated the many hoof marks.

Toulouse didn't think it was possible the women had met Minerve by prearrangement. Wulfrid had reported seeing him in Narbonne just yesterday morning. Besides, Toulouse couldn't imagine Minerve having the balls to take such a decisive step. So if they had encountered men, perhaps they were now captives and would have to be ransomed. In any case, this development was a complication he didn't need. "Let's find which way they went. They didn't return to the path. That we know."

He and his men searched the woods adjacent to the campfire until he spotted telltale horse droppings. "This way. It's not long after daybreak. They can't have gone far."

* * *

Anduze rode into the clearing on a handsome, dappled-gray stallion. He was alone. Ermengarde smiled in relief. He hadn't betrayed them. When he dismounted, she noted the finely worked silver trappings on his horse and the Damask sword at his side. He was not as young as she had thought, seeing him only in firelight. In spite of his trim, athletic figure, there were tiny lines around his eyes and a few gray hairs in his shoulder-length hair. A jagged scar along his right eye marred an otherwise handsome face.

"Your *friends* spent the night not far from here at an inn," he said. "They're not far behind us."

"How many of them are there?" Nicholas asked.

"Four men and Toulouse."

Ermengarde's stomach lurched. "How will we ever get away?"

"Don't worry, my lady," Anduze said with a glint in his gray eyes, "I have a plan."

She looked at him curiously. "Would you mind sharing it with me?"

He studied her for a moment. His intent look made her uneasy. He might be as wary of her and the trouble that followed her, as she was of him. "I don't know if it's safe for you to head to Lagrasse with Toulouse hard on your trail. 'Tis the obvious place for you to go. He may already have other men stationed there, waiting for you. Instead, it makes more sense for us to head for the monastery of Fontfroide where we'll seek sanctuary."

Thoughts tumbled through Ermengarde's brain. One day during their lessons, Damian had mentioned that her grandfather had founded the Abbey of Fontfroide and it was within an easy day's walk of Narbonne. Going there was a possibility. She hadn't heard from Minerve, and it was probably too soon for him to have gathered supporters for her in Narbonne. Toulouse knew her uncle was abbot of Lagrasse, and it was likely that he'd guess they were headed there. She laughed a bitter laugh. "I'm not sure Toulouse will honor sanctuary. I am, after all, his wife."

"Your situation is precarious indeed. Having you run away is a huge affront to Toulouse's pride. I can imagine he's furious. But we'll worry about him later," Anduze said. "He and his men aren't far behind us. We'd best be on our way."

They mounted, and Ermengarde wondered again whether or not she should trust Anduze. She had to admit he was an attractive man, and it was obvious he was used to commanding others. He had an appealing equanimity of manner, and it was clear from various things he said that he thought deeply. She'd never seen him at the Château Comtal, but she'd been relegated first to the children's quarters, and then, to the company of women.

They rode on. Ermengarde strained her ears, listening anxiously for the sounds of horsemen behind them. Not hearing anyone coming, she relaxed a little. Then it occurred to her that in this dense forest, Anduze could be leading them into a trap. Her husband could be in front of them, waiting poised like a snake ready to strike. She tensed again, aggravating the persistent pain in her loins.

Water splashing over rocks broke the stillness of the forest. They came to a stream filled to overflowing from the recent rain. Dismounting, Ermengarde took a deep breath to come to terms with her physical and mental discomfort. The smells of mud and wet grass filled her nostrils. Nicholas filled his water gourd, offering it first to her and then to Missee. The shock of the freezing water gave Ermengarde goose bumps, but Nicholas' gentle attention was comforting. After everyone drank, they watered the horses before going on.

Leaving the stream, they followed a sinuous trail for a long time. The early morning sunshine gave way to dark clouds, heavy with rain. Late autumn gorse was in bloom on the hillsides, its golden flowers a sharp contrast to the gray sky. Ermengarde began to feel as gloomy as the day. Small needles of rain stung her face from time to time, but thankfully, most of the threatening rain held off.

More time passed, and they didn't ride into a trap. With the realization that so far she had escaped from her husband, Ermengarde's mood lightened a little. She was still unsure of Anduze. She studied his broad shoulders on the horse in front of her. He rode with confidence and a keen awareness of their surroundings.

The trail widened into a narrow, muddy road, filled with puddles. They weren't on the road very long when Ermengarde heard the clop, clop of horses' hooves, coming from the opposite direction. She and Missee had met no travelers on horseback since leaving the Via Aquitania. Was she being delivered to Toulouse like a lamb to the slaughter? Two horsemen, knights from the quality of their horses and the long swords at their side, came around a bend and rode steadily toward them. A glance told her they weren't Toulouse or his men. Nonetheless, she pulled up the hood of her mantle, hiding her face in case they, too, were searching for her. She held her breath as they approached. They rode past, and she breathed again. Anduze had not betrayed them. Not yet.

Well past midday, Anduze called a halt. "Our progress is slow. I'm going to double back. Rest while you can." He turned his horse and disappeared from sight.

Ermengarde hoped with all her heart that her trust in this stranger was not misplaced. She dismounted. After two hard days of riding, she walked back and forth on the grassy verge to ease the stiffness in her limbs. Missee sat nearby on a rocky ledge, watching her progress. If her sister shared her fears, she didn't let on. Nonetheless, Missee's face was pale and drawn.

Nicholas approached with a chunk of cheese. Taking out his knife, he cut a slab and then held it out to Ermengarde."

"Thank you. You seem to have thought of everything. What else do you have in your saddlebags?

"A bit of ham in case our hunting doesn't go well. Anduze never seems to think about provisioning until he's hungry. So I always make sure we've got plenty of food."

"We are appreciative of your foresight. How much farther is it to Fontfroide?"

Nicholas glanced at the sky as if calculating the time and distance. "We should be there soon."

He didn't sound very sure. But she needed to keep her spirits up for Missee's sake. "Good," she said, trying to sound confident and enthusiastic.

Nicholas cut another slab of cheese and brought it to Missee. Ermengarde sat beside her sister on the ledge, and they ate in silence.

They'd just finished eating when Anduze rode toward them. She noticed how well he sat his horse, as if he had spent much time in the saddle.

"I've spotted them." His gray eyes were worried. "No more than a Roman mile behind us. We must be on our way."

Chapter 9

*A*NDUZE SIGNALED GILLES WITH ONLY a nod, and the young man brought their horses. With a boyish grin, he helped Ermengarde mount the bay and Missee her mare. He was obviously enjoying their adventure a lot more than Ermengarde was. Moments later, they were on their way again.

Scrub oaks with their leathery leaves grew on the wild, deserted hills. Here and there gorse half-heartedly sent forth scraggly, yellow blooms. The riders left the road again and followed a rough track so rarely used that in one place a fallen oak blocked their way. They dismounted, and Ermengarde found her legs were as unsteady as those of a newborn colt. *I am Ermengarde, Viscountess of Narbonne. I must be strong.* She led Titan around the root ball and then glanced back at Missee, grim-faced and pale behind her, leading the flagging Hebe by the bridle. Once around the obstacle, they remounted and struggled onward.

Ermengarde envisioned Toulouse, on his huge destrier, closing the distance that separated them, and her breath came faster and faster. She couldn't help turning to look behind them. They crested a hill. Far below, the gray-pink stone buildings of the Abbey of Fontfroide, surrounded by protective hills, came into view. The monks had little land under cultivation, and hills almost encircled the monastery. If the founders of the monastery had desired to escape into the wilderness, they had done so.

Their horses picked their way down the steep trail, their hooves dislodging rocks that skipped and clattered down the mountainside. Ermengarde's heart plunged with each tumbling stone. It was taking them forever to navigate the descent.

They were almost to the bottom when they heard a cascade of rocks, dislodged above them. She craned her neck. Missee was close behind her with Nicholas and Gilles bringing up the rear. Above them on the steep hillside four men, led by Toulouse—unmistakable on his powerful black stallion—were gaining on them. Her shoulder hunched at the sight of him. She turned away and urged on the tired bay.

* * *

Toulouse spurred his horse. Ermengarde and those with her were just ahead of him, making their way down the steep embankment. Unfortunately, the Abbey of Fontfroide wasn't one of the monasteries that enjoyed his largesse. He couldn't count on any special treatment there. He took the measure of the men with her. They weren't heavily armed and were dressed as woodsmen. One was white haired and one was young. The only one who looked like he might present a problem appeared to be their leader. He rode a fine horse and sat easy in the saddle, as if he were a knight or a noble.

Toulouse's horse stumbled, dislodging a sizeable stone. He must intercept them before Ermengarde reached the abbey. If she reached the safety of the monastery and word of her presence spread, her defiance might unite the whole south. He had dismissed Wulfrid's account of Minerve's doings in Narbonne, but now he ground his teeth. His elaborate plans to control the lands of the southern Franks were in jeopardy.

He lurched in his saddle as he plunged down the slope, displacing stones and earth. Ermengarde would pay for this, and he'd flay alive the men who were helping her.

* * *

Ermengarde and her party reached the bottom of the slope and the wagon road that passed through fields surrounding the monastery. The grain had been harvested months before, leaving only brown stubble in the fields.

"Come on!" Anduze yelled as he spurred his tired mount forward.

They again pressed their horses onward. Ermengarde's breath became constricted, trapped. She couldn't believe she might be captured now, before the very gate of the abbey. They skirted a vineyard and raced through an orchard, heading for the drawbridge that led across the vallum, the dry moat, to the main monastery gate.

The pounding of their horses' hooves and the pounding in her chest were one. She turned again in her saddle, almost losing her balance. Toulouse and his knights had reached the valley and were closing on them. Hot tears spilled from her eyes. She had been hasty in thinking she might escape from Toulouse.

Just as they reached the moat, their horses lathered and laboring, the drawbridge swung up with a creaking groan. The wary monks were taking no chances with the approach of two groups of unknown riders. In the time it would take to reopen it, Toulouse would be upon them. Ermengarde wiped decisively at her eyes to dry her tears. She couldn't let him see her crying. She was through crying. It was bad enough she had failed in her escape attempt, but she wouldn't give him the satisfaction of seeing her cry.

Toulouse and his men were gaining on them fast. Anduze veered his horse away from the drawbridge. Ermengarde and the others followed him. They skirted a long wall to where the side of a hill abutted the back of the monastery. Then she saw it. A small door, half-hidden by a twisting vine, the postern gate to the monastery. She gasped in surprise.

In one swift movement, Anduze leapt from his horse, put his shoulder to the door, and forced it open. He stumbled through the door, holding it open for them. The bay was frothing at the mouth as Ermengarde dug her heels once more into his sides and galloped through the door, followed by Missee and rest of their little party.

Ermengarde glanced back. Toulouse was so close she could see the sneer on his hard face. Anduze closed the door with a loud bang and threw a heavy bar across it.

Her eyes wide, she looked around at the place that had delivered them from the very jaws of her nemesis. The abbey, built in her grandfather's time, was in need of repair. It was clearly a poor place, and they were apparently in the monastery's kitchen garden. Two monks in black robes working in the garden stopped and stared incredulously at them.

Ermengarde heard the neighing of horses and the clatter of horses' hooves as their pursuers circled outside the door. A moment later, someone pounded on it. "Open this door! I demand my wife be returned to me!" Ermengarde, holding her breath, glanced at Anduze and then at the monks. No one moved to disbar the door.

Outside the door, Toulouse bellowed. "I demand to see the abbot! Immediately!"

Hearing the hatred in Toulouse's voice, Ermengarde drew back on the reins of her exhausted bay as if getting farther from the door would protect her from him. Would she ever get away from that man?

Titan refused to move, and she slid down from his back, with an uptake of breath at the sharp pain in her loins. Missee's little mare frothed at the mouth and quivered. Ermengarde's legs buckled, but she managed to grab the mare's reins so Missee could dismount. Her face was drawn with concern. As soon as she dismounted, Missee put her arms around Hebe's heaving neck. "Poor, poor little Hebe," she murmured.

Toulouse stopped shouting, and the pounding on the door ceased. The horsemen galloped off, probably to seek admission to the monastery by the front gate.

One of the monks, a stocky fellow of middle years, with a work apron covering his habit, put down his spade and walked toward them. He seemed to have recovered from his astonishment at their arrival and smiled widely. "Welcome Anduze. May the peace of the Lord be with you."

"And with you, Brother Hubert," Anduze replied evenly, as if they'd just been out for a pleasant afternoon ride. "We are seeking sanctuary. Please inform Abbot Stephen."

"I'll do so at once." Brother Hubert called to the other monk. "Brother Gervais, please see to the horses. They've been sorely pressed."

Brother Hubert left to find the abbot and Brother Gervais, a much younger monk with a protruding Adam's apple, shyly approached. He didn't look at Ermengarde, but bowed and held out his hand. She gave him the reins of the bay. Missee stood back and gave him the reins to Hebe.

She turned to Anduze. "Will Hebe be all right?"

"Yes, she's in good hands. Brother Gervais has a way with animals." Anduze's voice was calm, reassuring.

Collecting the other horses, the monk led them away.

"Ermengarde, you're shaking and pale. Are you all right?" Anduze asked.

Ermengarde let out her breath. "I'm much better than I was a few minutes ago. Thanks to you."

Anduze came to her side. He bowed slightly. "At your service, my lady." He gave her wry look. "There's nothing like a heated pursuit to get the blood stirring."

Again, she wondered at this stalwart man, this stranger who was her savior. Anduze was an exceptional man, whoever he was, for braving Toulouse's wrath for her and Missee.

As her composure returned, she became curious. "How did you know about the door?"

Anduze smiled. "I visit here from time to time. My brother, Peter, Abbot of Saint Gilles, introduced me to Abbot Stephen, who shares my love of the hunt. Though many frown on monks hunting, he often joins us for that purpose."

Ermengarde's mind flew. They'd been fortunate indeed to come across Anduze and his men. Yet with Toulouse demanding to see the abbot, they were still in grave danger. Before she could focus on what to do next, Anduze took charge.

"Nicholas, take the ladies to the guest house. And Gilles, help the monks with the horses. I'll deal with Abbot Stephen. Toulouse will seek an audience with the abbot, and it's best that I speak with him before that happens."

Ermengarde and Missee followed Nicholas along an uneven brick path, passing the cloister, chapel, and the monks' dormitory. The guesthouse nestled up against one of the outer walls of the abbey. Built of the same soft-colored stone as the walls, the two-story building was small, and Ermengarde noticed no chimney. A leafless almond tree, heavy with nuts, and a few late autumn flowers relieved the austerity of the setting. Nicholas led them up a steep stairway to an unadorned, lime-washed room containing a bench, two chairs, and a trestle table. The bleak sun coming in the open window offered little warmth.

Suddenly, Ermengarde was more exhausted than she had ever been in her life. Her whole body ached from the rugged ride. She sat gratefully in one of the chairs and tried to compose herself. Missee sank down beside her.

"What will happen now?" she asked, regarding Ermengarde with troubled eyes.

"*Ma petite soeur*, I think it unlikely Abbot Stephen will refuse us sanctuary." Ermengarde spoke reassuringly and hoped what she said was true. But she was full of doubts. If they did obtain sanctuary, how long could they stay here? She was sure of one thing. No matter how long they stayed here, whenever they left, Toulouse or his lackeys would be waiting for them outside the monastery gates.

She barely had time to catch her breath when Anduze entered the guest parlor with a monk. He was as tall as Anduze, but more slightly built, with a high forehead, and the fringe of hair surrounding his tonsure was completely gray. Their visitor was clearly Abbot Stephan, and they stood to greet him.

"Abbot Stephen," Anduze began formally, "I'd like to introduce Lady Ermengarde, Viscountess of Narbonne and her sister, Lady Ermessende."

Abbot Stephen inclined his head, and then met Ermengarde's gaze. His blue eyes were kind. "I'm pleased to meet you, my lady. I knew your father. He was a good man."

She acknowledged his bow with a slight nod of her head. In her years at Toulouse no one had ever spoken of her father, and the abbot's mention of him unsettled her for a brief moment. She remembered being a small girl and riding here to this very monastery with her father before he left to fight the Moors. He'd given her a spotted pony, and when he asked her to accompany him, she'd been pleased. Her father was physically powerful and much admired for his prowess, and she'd ridden proudly by his side, savoring the appreciative glances of people along the way. He had presented the abbot, whom she assumed was Abbot Stephen's predecessor, with a purse of coins, and then they returned to Narbonne the same day. Yes, her father was a good man. She recovered herself, returning to her predicament. "I am seeking sanctuary."

Abbot Stephen didn't seem surprised, and she suspected that Anduze had already explained her situation. "Please be seated," the abbot said. He sat on a bench across from them. "You must be tired from your journey." He clasped his hands in such a way that they were completely hidden by the voluminous sleeves of his robe. "Sanctuary is not given lightly, my lady."

"Justice is on my side, Abbot Stephan," Ermengarde said. "I seek sanctuary from my husband, Count Alfonse Jordan of Toulouse."

Abbot Stephen gave her an inquiring look. "And is Count Alfonse Jordan of Toulouse such a bad husband?"

Ermengarde was disconcerted by the abbot's question, coming as it did after his kind words about her father. "Judge for yourself." She indicated her arm in the sling, her voice wavering. "He broke my arm and injured me on our wedding night."

Abbot Stephen seemed taken aback by her bluntness. She hadn't meant to tell anyone the specifics of Toulouse's violence, but too much was at stake for her to equivocate. He removed his hands from his sleeves and sat back on the bench. "We are greatly indebted to your grandfather, who founded this monastery. Forty days is the limit on sanctuary, but 'tis unseemly for women to stay long in an abbey with only men for company. I'll grant you sanctuary for a sennight."

"Thank you, Abbot Stephen." Ermengarde tried to remain calm. Seven days wasn't very long.

"Perhaps in time," Abbot Stephen said, assuming the tone of a counselor and confessor, "you can make peace with your husband."

Ermengarde sucked in her breath. "Never," she said, her voice filled with venom.

A look of pain passed over the abbot's face, as if fully understanding her situation for the first time. "This room and the cells adjoining it are our guest quarters for members of the nobility, and they're at your disposal. I'm afraid you will find them rather barren. The monastery has suffered from the lack of vocations, and our endowment is small. Pilgrims and others guests stay in the hall below."

"I'm sure the cells will be fine," Ermengarde said. "I hope Toulouse's presence without won't cause duress to the monastery."

Abbot Stephen seemed to consider. "I wager the Count of Toulouse will not dare to interfere with the operations of the monastery or the sanctuary it offers."

Ermengarde turned to Anduze. "Perhaps now, you can return to your hunt."

Anduze snorted. "What? And miss the continuation of the compelling drama in which I have been able to play a small part? Besides, my lady, I seem to recall you offered a substantial reward for my help."

Ermengarde felt her face redden. "I have not forgotten our bargain."

"We will discuss it when you have taken refreshment and rested," Anduze said.

Abbot Stephen rose, indicating their talk was over. "I've asked the cook to bring you bread and soup. He should be along directly. Anduze and his men will join the pilgrims below in the great hall. If you follow me, I'll show you your cells." He led them to small monastic cells side by side. "We ask that you confine your activities to the guest parlor, your cells, and the chapel."

Ermengarde gave him a gracious smile. "Of course. And thank you."

* * *

Toulouse and his men milled about before the front gate of the monastery. Again, he yelled, "I demand to see the abbot!"

No one answered his yells. He pounded on the door. An arrow, shot from a narrow slit, landed in the dust near his feet. Wrapped around the shaft was a piece of parchment. Toulouse bent, picked it up, and untied the bit of fabric holding the parchment to the arrow. He unfurled the message. He squinted at the words. Although he had learned to read, it was not his habit. Word by word he puzzled it out: "You may enter, if you send away your soldiers."

Toulouse sighed and handed Wulfrid the reins of his horse. "Wulfrid, take the others over there to that hillock where you can see both the drawbridge and the postern gate. Make sure no one leaves."

His men retreated to the nearby hill. With a groan and a grating sound the great drawbridge opened. Toulouse took a deep breath before walking into the courtyard of the monastery.

An old monk tottered forward to greet him. "Follow me, Abbot Stephen will see you in the chapterhouse."

Toulouse followed the monk through the cloister where birds chirped and flitted to and fro. Upon entering the octagonal chapterhouse, Toulouse's eyes took a moment to adjust to the dim interior. The abbot rose from his seat and advanced in his direction. Toulouse immediately sensed he was in the presence of an astute man. He wished he'd not sent the Templar to Lagrasse. Ranulf would know how best to deal with this monk.

"Your lordship," the monk said with a slight bob of his head. "I'm Abbot Stephen. I don't believe we've met."

"Alfonse Jordan, Count of Toulouse," he said in a commanding voice. "And I demand to speak with my wife."

Abbot Stephen seemed unimpressed with the fact he was dealing with the most powerful noble in the area. "She has sought sanctuary here and doesn't wish to speak with you."

Toulouse couldn't contain his anger and frustration. "How dare you come between a woman and her husband!"

Abbot Stephen opened his arms in a helpless gesture. "It's not my wish to have women in the monastery. And yet Fontfroide is a sacred space and, as such, offers refuge to those who seek it. Please be seated. I'll tell you what I've decided."

A stone bench ran along the wall of the chapterhouse. Toulouse sat on the cold stone. He cracked his knuckles, deep in thought. He had heard of cases where monasteries gave sanctuary to people for years.

Abbot Stephen sat beside him. Toulouse opened his mouth to threaten him.

The abbot put a finger to his lips. "Hear me out. I've offered the women sanctuary, but only for a sennight."

Toulouse grunted. The abbot was clever. He was honoring sanctuary and being careful not to unduly offend him. One way or another, the situation would be resolved in a week. Yet he wanted it to be resolved immediately. He struggled to control his impatience and to appear more conciliatory than he felt. "Will you please ask her to speak with me? Will you reason with her? This situation, her situation, has gotten out of hand. It's my hope that we can't settle our differences amicably."

"I will do as you wish. Lady Ermengarde is distraught. Perhaps in a day or so, she will be more amenable to a meeting."

Toulouse could contain his anger no longer. "God's teeth, I have made her Countess of Toulouse, and she spurns the honor and me."

Abbot Stephen seemed uncomfortable, hesitant. "I will speak with her. But in the meantime, I will expect you will honor the accommodation I've made. I'll walk you to the drawbridge."

Toulouse pursed his lips and nodded his head. He didn't like the situation, but couldn't risk alienating the church by attacking the monastery. Someday with the help of the Templars, he'd not have to worry about the power of the church.

Toulouse walked with Abbot Stephen toward the extended drawbridge. "I regret I cannot offer you or your men the hospitality of our poor house. Our monastery is a stopping place for pilgrims on their way to the shrine of Saint James at Compostela, and I don't intend that in this desolate spot they should be without a roof and a meal."

Toulouse scowled. "So my men will stay without while you host pilgrims?"

"They come in peace. There is surely a difference."

Toulouse let out a long breath. "My men will stay without, honoring the week of sanctuary you have granted. They will wait for the Countess of Toulouse, my wife, to emerge."

"I have your word on this," Abbot Stephen ventured.

"You have it," Toulouse said.

They had reached the drawbridge, and Toulouse, although unhappy with the arrangement, was already thinking of his next move. He'd wait to see if the abbot could convince Ermengarde to speak with him, and if she wouldn't, he would go into Narbonne and see for himself what, if any, damage Minerve had done to his support there. He'd leave Wulfrid in charge of his men here and send to Toulouse for more knights. He wouldn't let Ermengarde's rebellion get out of control.

Chapter 10

G RAY MORNING LIGHT CAME THROUGH the cracks around the shutters of the window in Ermengarde's cell. She rubbed her eyes, wondering how long she'd slept. She'd lain awake for a long time, worried about the future. But she finally fell into an exhausted sleep, and now, from her grogginess, she guessed it had been for many hours. With a sense of urgency, she stepped from her narrow cot onto the cold stone of the floor. An arrow of pain brought her fully awake. Gritting her teeth, she walked to the window and threw open the shutters. Dark clouds, filled with rain, obscured the horizon. Closing the shutters again, she broke the ice in the ewer beside the washbasin. She winced as she splashed the frigid water on her face.

Before she had the chance to dress, there was a knock at her door. She put on her mantle over her chainse and opened the door a crack. It was only Missee, fully dressed.

"I've come to help you dress. I didn't want to wake you. I waited until I heard you stir." Missee came into the cell and took Ermengarde's gown from its hook. Her sister gave her an anxious look. "I dreamed last night Toulouse was just outside, waiting in the parlor. In my dream, he looked more like a vulture than a man. Do you suppose he's here in the abbey?"

Ermengarde gazed sleepily at Missee. "I don't think so, but there is no way of knowing. I'm not sure Abbot Stephen knows how to handle a situation like ours."

Missee's jaw clenched. "I'm afraid. What's going to happen to us?"

With so many things on her mind, Ermengarde hadn't been sensitive to how her sister must feel. "I really don't know. Perhaps I shouldn't have brought you along. But I couldn't leave you there with…with him."

Missee's face relaxed. "Oh, I'm so glad you didn't. I couldn't stand being left behind. I might never know what happened to you. And if something did happen to you, Toulouse might make me marry him."

Ermengarde's eyes widened. "I didn't know you suspected that mayhap you would have to marry him."

Missee held out her gown, slipped it on over her head, and tied the side ties. "I may be your little sister, but I'm not deaf and dumb. Lady Jordana even suggested that someday I might marry her father."

"Lady Jordana." Ermengarde rolled her eyes.

A brief smile stole across her sister's face. "Sit and I'll help you on with your stockings and boots."

Missee finished helping her dress, and Ermengarde put her good arm around her sister's shoulder. Even though Missee was clearly worried, the events of the last two days had aged both of them. "*Ma petite soeur*, you mustn't worry. We've gotten this far. Everything will work out."

There was another knock on the door. Ermengarde's heart began to race. Had Missee's dream been prophetic? Perhaps Toulouse was in the parlor. She took a deep breath and opened the door. A young oblate, his face broken out with pimples, stood uneasily in the doorway with a tray. On it were two steaming cups of cider, a loaf of bread, and what appeared to be a pot of honey. "My lady, Abbot Stephen asks to meet with you in the parlor after you have broken your fast."

For a moment, Ermengarde couldn't respond. Missee came forward to take the tray. "Please tell Abbot Stephen we'll be there after we have eaten," she said, sounding very grown up.

The oblate's face grew red, and he addressed Ermengarde. "My lady, the abbot would like to see you alone."

Ermengarde fought a wave of dizziness. This was ominous. "Please tell Abbot Stephen I will attend him after our meal."

The oblate hurried off in the direction of the guest parlor. She shut the door and then leaned weakly against it. She hoped Abbot Stephen hadn't allowed Toulouse into the monastery, but perhaps the abbot had been unwilling to alienate such a powerful noble. If only she'd asked the oblate. She sunk onto the cell's only bench.

Missee put the tray on the small table and then handed her a cup. Ermengarde sipped the warm, sweet cider. Her sister tore off a hunk of the bread, spread honey on it with a spoon, and offered it to her. Ermengarde's stomach knotted. "Maybe later," she said.

Missee finished eating, and Ermengarde could delay no longer. She left the cell for the guest parlor, her heart in her throat. She entered the room where Abbot Stephen sat alone, reading his breviary. Relieved, she managed a thin smile.

He looked up at her approach and put down the breviary. "Lady Ermengarde, good day to you. I hope you slept well."

"Good day to you, Abbot Stephen. Thank you, I did sleep well." Her voice may have evidenced more cheer than was called for. But not seeing Toulouse lifted her spirits.

"Lady Ermengarde, please be seated." He indicated a chair beside his. "Your husband has asked to speak with you."

She sat in the chair and spit out the words. "I don't want to speak with him today, or ever again."

Abbot Stephen didn't seem to know how to respond. "I have little experience of problems between husband and wife," he said slowly. "But if Toulouse treated you as badly as you say, perhaps he wishes to make amends."

"Before I married Toulouse, it was explained to me that he was a politician. If he wants to speak with me, it is only because my defiance is spoiling his plans."

"You did agree to marry him."

"I never agreed to be bullied and maimed." Ermengarde tempered her emotional response with a more conciliatory tone. "I can imagine your situation is a difficult one, Abbot Stephen, but not as difficult as mine."

He cleared his throat. "Your husband has asked me to reason with you, to remind you that your marriage was sanctified by the church, that you took a sacred oath."

Ermengarde tried to read his plain, sober face. Was he fulfilling his Christian duty as an abbot, or did he really believe she should return to her husband?

He continued. "You surely must know that your continued defiance of your husband could have dire results. Anduze tells me you seek to claim your inheritance. If you do find supporters in Narbonne or elsewhere, it could end in war. Have you considered your father's vassals and allies might not be willing to rally to the cause of a woman, a young woman at that?"

The relief and high spirits Ermengarde experienced moments ago vanished, and her temper flared. "Have you considered that many of the Narbonnese and the leaders of the southern Franks may dislike Toulouse as much as I do? And my age and sex may inspire, rather than deter, them."

Abbot Stephen got to his feet. "Lady Ermengarde, this discussion is getting us nowhere. I'll convey your wishes to your husband."

Ermengarde murmured her thanks and returned to her cell where Missee was waiting.

"Was Toulouse with the abbot?" her sister asked anxiously.

"Thankfully, no." Ermengarde related what had transpired and concluded, "I need to come up with a plan."

"Why don't you ask Anduze for help? I like him. He has a sense of humor, and you don't."

Ermengarde felt her face relax into a smile. It was good to hear Missee express an opinion. "I like him, too. We are indebted to him and his men, but we can hardly expect him to further involve himself in our troubles."

"He's still here," Missee said.

"I'll ask to talk with him, but first I need to come up with a plan."

"When you do speak with him, I have a favor to ask"

Ermengarde gave her sister a questioning look.

"I'm worried about Hebe." She faltered. "I know I can't go to see her, but perhaps you could ask Anduze to have Nicholas look in on her."

Ermengarde gave Missee a sisterly pat. "*Certes*, I'll ask Anduze. I don't think Nicholas would mind. But before I speak with Anduze, I'm going to rest for a few minutes and think."

Missee returned to her room, and Ermengarde stretched out on the hard cot. She stared at the simple crucifix hanging above the bed. She wanted to pray, but couldn't find words. Father Hugh had patiently seen to her religious education and, until now, she had faithfully observed all the teachings of the church. Why was it then that in the last crisis-filled weeks, prayer had eluded her? A pang of guilt unsettled her. If her faith was being tested, she was failing.

The deep silence of the abbey gradually seeped into her, and the churning within slowed. She began to understand why someone would enter a monastery. She probably wasn't the only one who found it impossible to pray amid the tumult and trials of a disordered world. She held on to this thought, closed her eyes, and prayed for deliverance. Finally, it came to her. A plan. She would ask Anduze to locate Minerve. Perhaps together, they'd be able to find enough men to free her from the monastery.

With this plan in mind, Ermengarde left her cell. The oblate was sitting on the stairs, and she sent him to find Anduze.

She was waiting in the guest parlor when Anduze came in. He was clean-shaven, making the deep scar on his face more noticeable.

"Good morrow, Anduze. I haven't thanked you for getting us here." She indicated for him to sit in the only other chair.

"I seem to recall you were going to thank me with a knight's fief," he said, with hint of merriment in his eyes.

His comment, accompanied as it was with an appreciative gaze, momentarily disarmed Ermengarde. "Of course, when I come into my inheritance."

Anduze raised an eyebrow. "And just when will that be?"

His directness caught her off guard. She wasn't sure how to answer. His eyes sparkled, and he laughed.

"I see you find my words amusing."

His face grew somber. "Not at all, my lady. It is your defiance that amuses me. Your situation is grave. Toulouse left after you refused to see him. I assume he's headed for Narbonne to shore up his support there and be more than ready for us, if we make our way there. Gilles reports that he has left men to guard the monastery. There's no way out without confronting them. "

"I fully realize our situation is dire. I have something to ask you. I have purchased your services once and I'd like to do so again."

Anduze's face grew serious. "How do you know they are for sale?"

"Since you say you are the Viscount of Anduze, perhaps you're not interested in the knight's fief I promised you."

"I'm interested in the fief, but not for myself." He leaned forward. "I'm not sure my services are for sale. But I would be curious to know what you have in mind."

Ermengarde told him about Minerve laying the groundwork for her to claim her viscounty. "If I give you my jewels, perhaps you can meet up with him and bribe knights in Narbonne to come to Fontfroide and rescue us." She removed her pouch from her girdle and spread the jewels out on the small table beside her—rings with precious stones, a gold Roman necklace and an assortment of pearls. He didn't appear impressed.

Anduze fingered the ring with the huge ruby Toulouse had given her. His fingers were long, and his nails neatly trimmed. "What if you give me your jewels, and I just disappear?"

They were playing verbal chess, and it was her move. "That's possible. Initially, I thought you were a robber, a highwayman."

Anduze smiled, leaning back and stretching out his legs. "Perhaps I am."

Ermengarde found his languorous posture distressing. Her brain flew, trying to come up with a parry. "The Viscount of Anduze, a robber?

"Isn't the Count of Toulouse a robber?"

He had her there. Certainly Toulouse's extortion and exploitation of her inheritance was a form of robbery. "If you are indeed a lord of dubious repute, this will provide the opportunity for you to restore your honor and be richly rewarded."

Anduze's face clouded. "What makes you think I care for honor or riches? Not every man wants the same things, just look at Abbot Stephen. He only wants the welfare of the abbey and to hunt once in a while."

Ermengarde sighed, not liking the direction their discussion had taken. "Don't fool yourself. He has honor and wealth, even if his wealth isn't of this world." Her words were more caustic than she intended, and she watched Anduze for his reaction.

His eyes narrowed. "Do you have an answer for everything?"

"Hardly. I'm just desperate." She bit her lip, struggling to control her rising frustration with their conversation. "Do you want me to throw myself at your feet and beg your help with tears?"

"It might work, but I can't imagine you doing it." He grinned. "Let me understand. You want me to go to Narbonne, raise an army, and come and liberate you and Lady Ermessende."

A lump grew in Ermengarde's chest at his mocking description of her plan. He must think her ridiculous. She was shocked to realize that she cared very much what this man, almost a complete stranger, thought of her. "Anduze, surely you must know desperate situations demand desperate measures." She paused to steady her voice. "But enough of this banter. Will you aid us or not?"

He hesitated for long moments, his face solemn. "My lady," he said with a deferential bob of his head. "I'm flattered by the trust you have put in me, even if I am the choice of last resort. I will do what I can."

Weak with relief, Ermengarde sat back in her chair and sent up a quick prayer of thanks to Saint Just and Saint Pastor. "When can you depart for Narbonne?"

Anduze walked to the window. When he turned to face her, his eyes were calculating, preoccupied. "I'm not sure your plan will work. As we speak, Toulouse is no doubt gathering support in Narbonne. I'll take your jewels, in case they are needed." With a swift motion of his tanned hand, he swept the jewels back into their velvet bag. "And there is one more thing. Since you have employed me, you'll have to trust me to work out the details."

His answer was evasive. He didn't say when he'd leave for Narbonne. She wrinkled her forehead. Even though he was going to help her, he would do things his own way and keep her in the dark. But as in the past, she had little choice but to accept his terms. Someday that would change.

Ermengarde went to his side. "May God be with you," she said, giving him the kiss of peace, her lips barely brushing the smooth cheeks that smelled of harsh soap.

Anduze didn't appear surprised at her gesture of friendship. She had surprised herself, and the sensation of his skin on her lips lingered.

He bowed slightly. "At your service, my lady."

She was at the door when she remembered Missee's request. "Missee is wondering if perhaps Nicholas could go by the stables and check on Hebe. She's worried about the mare."

"You may tell Missee that Nicholas checks on her little horse every day, and he's well on the way to spoiling Hebe with apples."

Ermengarde smiled. "She'll be happy to hear that Hebe is being coddled. Be sure to thank Nicholas."

Chapter 11

FROM THE NARROW, HIGH WINDOW of her cell, Ermengarde watched Anduze talk with two men dressed as pilgrims who had arrived to spend the night at the monastery. The rain had passed, but the sky was still overcast. To her distress and dismay, he was still at Fontfroide, and he chatted and laughed, as if he didn't have a care in the world. They had not spoken in days, and her anxiety grew with each one's passing. She let out a big sigh. People came to the monastery and left on a regular basis. If Anduze wasn't afraid of the armed men who waited without, he should have left before now. Her plans, her hope for escape to Narbonne, were coming to naught, and each day Toulouse would be able to garner more support in Narbonne.

Missee, her brow furrowed, came to Ermengarde's side. "I see Anduze hasn't left yet. What are we going to do?"

Ermengarde wanted to reassure her sister, but she couldn't find the words. "I don't know." She moved from the window to the hard cot. "But our sanctuary ends Sunday. My only recourse may be to beg for a few more days."

"The days hang as heavy as a coffer filled with lead, and each passes and nothing happens. There's nothing to do here but pray and worry."

Ermengarde was thoughtful for a moment. "Now that I've been here for a while, I understand Damian better. When he counseled me before my marriage, I felt he'd betrayed me. Yet I see now that it was difficult, if not impossible, for him to set aside a whole life of quiet prayer and learning for me. If only I had the benefit of his learning now. There may be some provision in canon law about sanctuary, something that would compel Abbot Stephen to keep us here longer."

Unable to contain her nervous energy, she got up from the cot and returned to the window. Anduze and the pilgrims were no longer in view. She breathed deeply through her nose, fighting to suppress her frustration. "It seems everywhere I turn I'm thwarted by my lack of power and my own ignorance."

Missee came to her side. "It's not your fault. You've done wonderfully to get us this far."

"This far may not be far enough. Toulouse's lackeys are still camped outside, guarding every egress from the monastery."

* * *

Anduze paced the cloister at Fontfroide. Red squirrels chased each other from tree to tree and sparrows flitted about, but he paid little attention to them. No doubt Ermengarde was growing more and more anxious as the days of her sanctuary slipped away. God's bones, he was worried, too. He had hoped that once he delivered the runaways to Fontfroide that would be the end of it, and he would be free to continue his hunt. But he had not counted on Abbot Stephen limiting their sanctuary. Yet his friend was right. A sennight, a fortnight, or six months, whenever the viscountess left the monastery, Toulouse's knights would be waiting for her. And the abbey was dependent on the largesse of whoever was in control of Narbonne, and at present it was most likely Toulouse would retain his claim to the city. Abbot Stephen had to be careful.

One of the stone carvings on the capital of a pillar in the cloister caught Anduze's eye. He stopped and looked up at the depiction of the biblical story of Judith and Holofernes. In one hand she held a knife, and in the other, Holofernes' head. Anduze should have known better than to involve himself in a dispute in which emotions ran high. He needed to come up with a ruse, something that would fool Toulouse's men. He wished he'd paid more attention to the troubadours' tales. In them, someone was always in disguise. Usually a woman donned male attire and fooled everyone. Ermessende and Ermengarde might pass as young boys, but the sight of two slight young fellows leaving the monastery would fool no one.

Disguises were still on Anduze's mind later when he entered the commoners' hall of the guest quarters for dinner.

Three pilgrims had arrived that day, and now they sat at a long table, waiting for monks to bring them trenchers and potage for the midafternoon meal. One pilgrim was a matronly, thickly built woman; another was a portly man, probably her husband; and the third was a wizened old woman of seventy or more years.

Anduze smiled as a plan began to form in his mind. "The peace of the Lord be with you," he said, taking a seat at the long table next to the matronly woman. Nicholas and Gilles, seated at the other end of the table, looked at him questioningly, but said nothing.

"And with you," the woman answered.

"I see by your scallop shells you have been to the shrine of Saint James at Compostela."

"Yes, we have seen and touched the silver reliquary." The woman sighed. "It was wonderful. We are shriven and on our way home to Nîmes."

Anduze thought quickly. "I am headed to Compostela myself."

"We have met many pilgrims these many months," the man said. "And we have found them, with few exceptions, to be good people. But, sir, you don't wear a pilgrim's garb."

"Therein lies a story." Anduze's eyes danced.

Before he could say more, a monk arrived with a heavy kettle that he placed on the table. Another followed with a basket full of bread trenchers and a jug of wine. Anduze and the pilgrims helped themselves to the food. Making the sign of the cross over his food, he began to eat heartily. "Have you had good weather?" He knew that a good storyteller made his audience wait before he told his tale. He gave the woman his most charming smile.

The matron answered between mouthfuls of stew. "We nearly drowned a few days back. It was quite a downpour, and we were out in it."

"Yes, it was a nasty storm," the man agreed. "But tell us your tale. Our way is long, and a good story helps to pass the time."

"I don't know that my story's entertaining since I don't yet know its ending." Anduze shook his head.

"Oh please," the older woman spoke for the first time, displaying a toothless mouth, "I do love a tale."

Anduze filled the pilgrims' cups with wine and then took a drink himself. "You do not find me dressed as a pilgrim because I had not planned on going to Compostela. But I serve a noble lady. She and her sister are upstairs in the guest quarters. When the sister was ill unto death, my lady swore an oath that if her sister were spared she'd make the pilgrimage to the shrine of Saint James. But alas, her husband is a hard man. He refused to let her go. So she begged me to accompany her on her pilgrimage."

With a sigh, Anduze shook his head. "I didn't know what I was getting myself into." He smiled to himself. At least that part of his tale was true. "My lady had to flee her husband in the middle of the night. She and her sister have only the finest clothes, totally unsuited to such a journey. We have made it this far, but her husband's men wait without, ready to fall upon her and drag her home. If only we had pilgrim garb, we might get by them unnoticed." He didn't like lying, but this was close enough to Ermengarde's actual situation that he didn't feel too bad about it.

He gave them a helpless look. "My Christian willingness to help my lady fulfill her sacred oath may cost me my life."

"Can't the lady stay here?" the old woman asked.

"The abbot has granted her only a sennight's sanctuary. And the seven days are almost up."

The man shifted in his seat. "What will you do?"

Anduze shook his head. "I prayed for an answer to our plight, but none has come. Good sir, experienced in the way of the pilgrim, what would you do?"

The man leaned forward, his brow furrowed, but he said nothing.

The matron, her eyes bright, spoke up. "You say they have fine clothes?"

Anduze brightened. "My lady has a blue mantle of the finest wool and a gown of the latest fashion especially for riding. Her sister's mantle and gown are fine, too."

The matron harrumphed. "I've got an idea. In the spirit of the pilgrimage, we could exchange clothes. Then perhaps, you could dupe her pursuers."

Anduze raised his hands in protest. "Do you mean the three of us could don your clothes so that we would look like pilgrims? How clever of you to think of such a ruse, but it's too much to ask."

"Not at all," the man agreed, stealing a look at Anduze's fine leather tunic.

Anduze remained silent, pretending reluctance.

The matron's eyes glinted. "We are nearly home, and in truth our pilgrim clothes are old and worn. If it would serve fellow pilgrims, we'll part with them gladly."

"You would have to bide here an extra day until we are well away," Anduze said. "Would that be a problem?"

"We are tired and would welcome a day of rest," the matron said hastily.

Anduze slowly nodded in agreement. "Then let it be done, and may Saint James and all the saints bless you for your generosity. When it is time for you to retire for the night, leave your clothes beside your pallets. I'll collect them and leave our clothing for you."

A look of doubt passed over the matron's face, and Anduze smiled reassuringly. "'Twill all be done quietly, and in only the time it takes for me to go up the stairs and return here." He inclined his head. "Until this evening."

Only when he was out of the hall did Anduze break into a wide smile. Now all that remained was to tell the rest of his party his plans and to convince Ermengarde and Missee to give up their fine clothing.

* * *

Toulouse walked with Archbishop Arnold into the busy courtyard of the archbishop's palace in Narbonne. The courtyard abutted the cathedral where construction was underway on a new nave. Workmen stirred a vat of mortar, preliminary to hoisting it up to men on scaffolding. Yesterday, his mail had arrived from Toulouse with a contingent of his knights and Ranulf from Lagrasse. And today, the courtyard was astir with knights, squires, men-at-arms, and horses.

The archbishop shaded his eyes with his thin, blue-veined hand. "I see you've managed to assemble quite a force. I take it you'll not have need of my personal knights."

Toulouse surveyed his men as he spoke. "It's enough that your knights have occupied the towers of those knights that have gone off with that slippery Minerve. And it's important for them to keep an eye on things here. I'm leaving twenty of my knights in case they are needed."

The archbishop visibly paled. "Do you think Narbonne will be attacked?"

"I don't think it likely. However, it doesn't hurt to be prepared. Minerve didn't find much support for the viscountess here. If he goes on to Montpellier, it will be a different matter altogether. I doubt Minerve will find much support elsewhere."

"I take it Montpellier's still smarting from the support you gave to the town consuls when they rebelled against him."

"Montpellier's been loath to support my plans to unify the south. He's as obstinate as his old ally, Viscount Aymeri." Toulouse glowered. "I'm sick to death of their ilk. To think my years of planning may come to naught because of one willful, stubborn woman. I intend to go after that traitor, Minerve, and the rebellious knights of Narbonne as soon as the situation with Ermengarde is resolved. They'll pay for their disloyalty with their lives."

The deep voice of the cathedral bells sounded. "Won't you join us at vespers?" the archbishop asked.

In spite of the archbishop's lavish hospitality, Toulouse had grown impatient with the man's haughty demeanor and pretentious piety. "I've too much to do. We leave tomorrow at first light for Fontfroide. The sennight Abbot Stephen granted my lady wife is almost over. It's in both our interests to bring this matter to a close."

The archbishop gave a small bow of acknowledgement. "Of course. If you'll excuse me." He made the sign of the cross. "May the Lord be with you." He hurried off in the direction of the cathedral.

Toulouse watched him disappear into a small door at the side of the cathedral. He would bring the archbishop to heel after he dealt with Ermengarde and Minerve.

* * *

Just before compline, the last canonical hours before retiring, the oblate came to the gloomy cell where Ermengarde and Missee had spent a very long day. "My lady, Anduze wishes to see you both in the parlor," he said, before hurrying away.

"At last," Ermengarde said. "I am out of patience with Anduze. Perhaps we'll learn the cause for his delay, for the reason he has been avoiding us."

In the parlor, they found him sprawled on the long, oak bench. He got to his feet as they entered, and yet his manner was casual. Ermengarde felt her cheeks heat with anger she found difficult to contain. She would let him have his say, before she confronted him.

He looked pleased, expectant. "My lady, all is in readiness."

Taken aback, she frowned. "I don't know what you mean. I thought we had agreed that you'd go to Narbonne and return with knights who support my cause."

He gave her a curious look. "Did I agree to that? I don't think so."

She took a deep breath, trying to control her impatience. "Explain yourself, sir."

His mouth curved ever so slightly, as if he was going to smile. "We'll leave here tomorrow at daybreak."

"And just how will we do that? Shall we fly over Toulouse's guards hanging about the gates like vultures?" She had heard people say their blood boiled, and she'd never experienced it until now, dealing with this man.

Anduze raised his hands in a helpless gesture, and the suppressed smile emerged in a grin. "A small band of pilgrims en route from Compostela are in the monastery seeking shelter for the night. A woman, a tiny old woman, and a middle-aged man. Tomorrow, we'll put on their garb and leave through the front gate. It's all arranged, if you can part with your finery. I think my plan will work, and it's much simpler than raising an army on short notice. They'll need your clothes in exchange for theirs."

Ermengarde struggled to digest what he had planned. "But what will we do when we get to Narbonne? Toulouse is there."

"One step at a time, my lady."

Missee had turned pale. "What if we're discovered?" she asked, timidly.

Anduze gave her a reassuring smile. "My lady, we'll deal with that, if and when the time comes."

Ermengarde's anger at Anduze passed, and she had the curious sensation of relief and apprehension at the same time. Still, it was a good plan, better than the wild scheme she had devised. "I don't know what to say," she ventured.

"That's all right," he said. "You can thank me when it is a success."

She glared at him.

He went to the table on which was stacked a pile of clothing she hadn't noticed before. "You're to dress in these. There are also ashes to make what little of your hair might show, gray. You'll find a pillow to stuff the front of your tunic. If you can think of anything else to make you look middle aged, I recommend you do it. I know most women are expert in the arts of delusion."

"I know little of those arts," Ermengarde said tartly, surprising herself with the defensiveness of her tone of voice.

Anduze looked at her appraisingly. "Try to make yourself look less like a landed lady and more like a woman of good burgher stock."

"How should I look?" Missee asked, her eyes bright with interest.

He studied her for a moment. "Perhaps a few pimples or a blackened tooth?"

Missee gasped. "Will they examine us that closely?"

"I hope not. Abbot Stephen has granted permission for you both to visit the infirmary. The monk in charge knows much about berries and herbs. Perhaps he can suggest things to help you look different."

Missee's face was troubled. "What about our horses? I don't want to leave Hebe here."

"Once we're safely away, I've arranged for our horses to be brought to us. 'Tis best we travel fast," Anduze said.

"Does Abbot Stephen know of your plan?" Ermengarde asked, her voice tight with anxiety.

"No one knows except those who absolutely must know," Anduze answered evasively. "The oblate will take you to the infirmary. And I'll come for you at first light. Be ready."

* * *

It was still dark when Ermengarde got out of bed. The only light came from a gibbous moon. Shivering from the cold, she awkwardly gathered her pilgrim clothes in one arm and went next door to Missee's cell.

Her sister was already dressed in the simple brown robe of a pilgrim. "I didn't sleep much." Her voice was shaking. "I've been awake for hours."

Ermengarde tried not to betray her own misgivings. "Neither did I. But 'tis common knowledge that sleeplessness is often the case before traveling, and this is more fraught with dangers than the usual journey."

Missee helped Ermengarde on with the coarse robe that smelled of sweat and damp wool. Then Missee stuffed a pillow in the front of the robe and secured it with the sturdy wide belt. Finally, she helped her put on the scratchy woolen stocking and heavy leather shoes with wooden soles. "How uncomfortable burgher women must be!" She stepped back to admire her handiwork.

"*Ma petite soeur*, let me put some of this on your tooth." Ermengarde blackened Missee's front tooth with a little of the black paste that the infirmarian had given them.

"I'll powder your hair." Missee dipped her hand into the bowl of ashes. "And then cover most of it with this gray linen coif."

Ermengarde leaned toward Missee, closed her eyes, and coughed as Missee dusted her hair with fine ashes. When she finished, Ermengarde put on the broad hat with its scallop shell, the unmistakable symbol of the pilgrim.

"I have been in need of a change of clothes, but not these." Missee indicated her unattractive, but serviceable, old lady's gown, heavy woolen stockings and sturdy, worn shoes. "I wish we had a mirror. I'd like to see how I look."

"It's probably just as well we don't, if I look anything like you." Ermengarde managed a smile in spite of the butterflies in her stomach. Toulouse's knights might not be fooled by their disguises, and she tried not to think about what would happen if they were captured.

They finished dressing and went to the parlor where Anduze was waiting. In his pilgrim garb and pillow, he looked very much like a substantial burger with a big stomach. He helped Ermengarde on with the heavy woolen, pilgrim cape under which she concealed her injured arm.

"Follow me," Anduze whispered. He didn't need to whisper, but perhaps he was as anxious as she was.

He led them down the stairway of the guesthouse, their footsteps echoing on the paving stones. They followed him into a stable that smelled of manure, where a saddled donkey munched hay. Missee wrinkled her nose in distaste.

"You're to ride with our saddlebag," he said to Ermengarde, throwing a pack over the animal's withers and securing it with a girth. Her first inclination was to protest. Riding a donkey was beneath the dignity of a viscountess. Yet the woman whose place she was taking must have ridden to the monastery on the smelly donkey.

Missee looked relieved. She clearly wasn't interested in riding. Anduze helped Ermengarde up on the donkey that smelled like a wet dog. She flinched from a dagger of pain in her groin. There was no saddle or stirrups. Her gown bunched up, and her feet dangled uncomfortably.

Anduze handed Missee a pilgrim staff and picked up one himself. They left the stable, waiting with two real pilgrims for the abbey drawbridge to be opened. They sleepily looked at Ermengarde and her companions, perhaps wondering if they were the same people they had seen yesterday.

THE VISCOUNT'S DAUGHTER

The sun appeared over the rim of the distant hills. Two monks removed the heavy bar that secured the drawbridge and, with ropes and pulleys, lowered it across the vallum. The rumbling of the drawbridge must have woken one of Toulouse's men. He emerged from a makeshift shelter, rubbing his eyes. Ermengarde held her breath and turned her face away.

Her little donkey and the walkers made slow progress. The grass along the path was stiff with frost, and puddles had frozen during the night. Slowly they advanced to the road that lay five or six furlongs from the monastery. As they neared the road, it became fully light.

Suddenly, a brown blur—a polecat—bounded across their path. The donkey shied, braying loudly. Ermengarde struggled to keep her seat, and the cape covering her sling slid off her shoulder.

A loud shout pierced the quiet of the morning. "It's them!" Toulouse's guard alerted the other knights who rushed from their makeshift shelter. The knights strapped on their swords and ran to where their horses were tethered. Another knight came around the monastery wall from where he had been guarding the postern gate.

Anduze rushed to Ermengarde's side, grabbing the donkey's bridle. In the time it took him to steady the lurching donkey, Toulouse's knights mounted their unsaddled horses and were charging toward them. Hopelessness swept over her. There was no way they could escape horsemen.

She frantically turned to look back at the monastery. The drawbridge was closed again, and the approaching horsemen were between them and the postern gate. Why had she agreed to this ridiculous plan?

Chapter 12

ANDUZE STILL HELD ONTO THE donkey's bridle. "Stay calm," he said evenly, taking in Ermengarde and Missee with a glance. "All is not yet lost." He raised his free arm with two fingers extended.

Ermengarde's mouth fell open as Nicholas stepped from behind a tree and loosed an arrow. It hit the lead man in the back of his neck, and he fell from his horse. The horse galloped off. Gilles appeared at a run from around the side of the monastery, aimed, and fired his bow. A second horseman fell. The two other knights pulled up their horses. Another arrow from Nicholas' bow found its mark, wounding one in the arm. Gilles' second arrow whizzed by, only inches from a knight's head. Toulouse's startled men spurred away from them and reached the cover of the woods. They didn't reappear. Only then did Nicholas and Gilles lower their bows.

Missee's face was as white as newly bleached linen. Ermengarde exhaled, letting the tension of the last moments drain from her. Like a condemned criminal who received a last-minute pardon, her spirit soared. Her gaze fell on Anduze. He had done well. Her instincts about him had been right. He was worthy of her trust. Perhaps in future, she'd give more credence to her feelings. He acknowledged her appreciative look with a grin and a slight bow. "What now?" she asked.

"We're going to continue as pilgrims for a while."

"What if those knights return?" Missee asked.

"Those knights are but lackeys, willing to accept Toulouse's silver, but not loyal enough to him to risk their lives. We'll be on our guard." Anduze's deep voice was gentle, calming and at the same time confident, very much in charge of the situation.

The heavy drawbridge of the monastery opened again with its loud creak. The infirmarian, accompanied by another monk, rushed to the aid of the fallen men. Blood darkened one's surcoat. The other writhed in pain. A lump rose in Ermengarde's throat. Like her, these men had little choice; they had to do their lord's bidding. Her rebellion might result in the death of these men, and if war came, even more lives would be lost.

She stiffened as one of the pilgrims Anduze had spoken with yesterday, a strapping young man, approached, his face set in hard lines. "What's going on?" He was blunt. "It's unusual for pilgrims to be attacked."

"Some men fear neither God nor man, and they'll burn in hell for it," Anduze said in the comfortable language of the region. "Yon lady's husband has forbidden her to go on pilgrimage, and I have promised to conduct her safely to Compostela. You and the others are in no danger. But we'll not travel with you in case the ruffians return."

The pilgrim frowned. Anduze's story was thin, but the man accepted it. Ermengarde was impressed. Anduze had thought up a plausible reason for the attack on them.

"May Saint James protect you," the pilgrim said with reverence, before walking back to his companions shaking his head. If the man was unconvinced by Anduze's explanation, he was shrewd enough not to press further for details.

Brother Gervais, the young monk who had been gardening when they arrived, came out leading their horses. Anduze helped Ermengarde down from the donkey and then handed its reins to the monk.

"I am glad to exchange the uneven lope of the donkey for the predictability of the bay," she said as Anduze handed her and then Missee into their saddles.

Nicholas and Gilles joined them.

"Well done!" Anduze inclined his head to Nicholas and slapped Gilles on the back.

"We are in your debt," Ermengarde said. "A debt I will gratefully discharge at the first opportunity."

Nicholas grinned. "My lady, he who fears danger shouldn't go to sea."

Gilles shifted uneasily from one foot to the other, and he mumbled, "At your service, my lady."

She took a deep breath, savoring the moment. They'd been blessed to stumble across three such stalwart allies. She offered a prayer of thanksgiving to the Virgin in Majesty.

"'Tis best we not tarry," Anduze said, looking in the direction the knights had fled. "I don't think the men will return, but there's no telling what Toulouse has gotten up to. I suspect he's on his way here since your sanctuary ends today."

Anduze's reminder that they still were in danger tempered Ermengarde's euphoria at their deliverance. At least for the moment, they were safe from her pursuers, but Toulouse was a formidable enemy.

They rode away from the abbey, the pilgrims, and the fallen men. "Good way," the pilgrims called out to them as they left. Anduze returned the traditional pilgrim farewell.

With a last glance over her shoulder at the Abbey of Fontfroide, Ermengarde squinted in the bright sun of early morning as they headed east toward Narbonne. They made their way to the main road and, crossing it, took a narrow road. They passed through the gray and brown countryside and met a peasant, his back bent under a heavy a load of sticks.

"Greetings," he called, as if he knew them. "Safe journey." Perhaps the man recognized Anduze, even wearing a disguise.

A little way farther on, they met an old woman leading a small boy by the hand. Because she was so frail, it was unclear who was leading whom. "Pray for us," the woman called from a toothless mouth.

It dawned on Ermengarde that people were responding to them as pilgrims. Their disguise was successful. As pilgrims, they were not threatening. Pilgrims might be strangers, but pilgrims would not harm others. In Toulouse, she had always been treated deferentially, but this kind of warm response was new to her. It gave her a queer, unsettled feeling. Perhaps she should consider going on a pilgrimage someday.

She leaned toward Anduze. "What will we do when we get to Narbonne?"

"My lady, you and Lady Ermessende are not going into Narbonne. Not yet. Toulouse's men who escaped the little surprise we had for them must be on their way there. Although our pilgrim garb may fool others, it won't fool Toulouse if his men reach him. "

Her breath caught in her throat. "But—"

"But nothing. Remember you left the details to me." His tone was preemptory, curt.

Blood heated her face. How dare he speak to her in that tone of voice and tell her what to do? She'd had more than enough of others controlling her. She bit her tongue to keep from speaking. He was right, of course; they were not yet out of danger. And it was unlike Anduze, who was usually so mild-mannered, to speak so harshly. Perhaps, like her, his initial exhilaration at their narrow escape had given way to worries about the future.

* * *

Toulouse and his knights headed in the direction of Fontfroide. It was not long after daybreak, and he rode next to the Templar. Crows cawed overhead, and the road was damp with morning dew. He congratulated himself for waiting in Narbonne until he had a substantial force at his command and his fine coat of mail. This unfortunate turn of events would soon be settled. Once he captured Ermengarde, he'd exile her to one of the nunneries he generously supported. It would be an expense to keep her under guard, but he wanted to be rid of her. The very thought of her out of the way brought a smile to his face.

The smile disappeared as two horsemen, riding fast, approached. Wulfrid, who he had left in charge at Fontfroide, was in the lead. Something was dreadfully wrong.

Wulfrid pulled his destrier to a halt in front of Toulouse. "Lady Ermengarde has escaped! The others are wounded or dead."

"Damn it all to hell! How did it happen?"

"We were taken unawares. They were disguised as pilgrims."

"And you couldn't stop them?"

"It was a trap. Archers were waiting for us."

"God's teeth, must I oversee everything myself! I'm surrounded by fools and incompetents! Can I trust no one to do my bidding?" He spat on the ground. "Where in God's name are they headed?"

"I didn't stay around to see," Wulfrid said. "I thought it more important to reach you."

Toulouse glared at Wulfrid. "Get out of my sight."

Chastened, Wulfrid skulked away.

Toulouse turned to the Templar. "Ranulf, take half my knights and search everything to the north and east of the Roman road. I'll search the south and west with the remainder. I don't dare divide our force any further. 'Tis possible Ermengarde has met that traitor Minerve and the knights from Narbonne."

The Templar's face was impassive. "We'll find them. They can't have gone far."

"We'll turn over every stone if necessary. That is how you find snakes, under stones."

"With or without them, we'll meet back at the archbishop's palace at nightfall."

* * *

The pilgrims drew close to Narbonne. Ermengarde saw the spires of several churches in the distance and the towers of the knights. She remembered living there, but that had been years ago, and her memories were mostly of her father, stepmother, and Missee. She couldn't make out the stately massiveness of the viscount's palace at this distance, but just being near to it made her long to live there again.

To her disappointment, Anduze led them on another narrow road that wound away from the city.

"Where are we going?" she asked anxiously.

"To a farm belonging to friends," he said, his equanimity seemingly restored. "It's not far now."

Ermengarde grasped the bay's reins more tightly. They took yet another road, filled with potholes and tree roots. A short while later, they arrived at a large stone-and-timber framed farmhouse with a tiled roof, the home of a well-to-do farmer. Several barns and other outbuildings were off to one side. They passed a pigpen, and she almost gagged at the acrid smell. An indignant gray and white goose waddled toward them and began to honk loudly as they drew nearer. That set three briards—black and brown, shaggy sheepdogs—to barking, and a woman in a starched white coif emerged from the farmhouse and gave them a welcoming wave.

"Peace be with you, Anduze," she called. "At least I think it's you." The woman harrumphed.

A man with broad shoulders and a sunburned face came out of the barn with a rake in one hand. "I see you've made it." He strode up to them and clapped Anduze on the shoulder. "Well done, *mon ami*!"

Anduze introduced the man, Odo, and his wife, Bette. He only introduced Ermengarde and her sister by their first names, but it was clear from the deference they were shown that the couple knew, or at least suspected, their true identities. Ermengarde's hand went to her mouth. This new situation, like unexplained noises in the night, unsettled her.

Bette immediately took charge. "Come along. You'll probably want to get out of those clothes, to wash, and to have something to eat."

Missee and Ermengarde followed her into a large room with smoke-darkened, oak beams from which hung sprigs of rosemary and lavender. Ermengarde inhaled the sweet smells with a twinge of heartache. Her stepmother had loved rosemary, and she never smelled it without thinking of her. In a life where she'd had little affection, her stepmother made an effort to love her, even though she wasn't of her blood.

A fire blazed brightly in the stone fireplace at one end of the room. From a kettle on a spit came a wonderful, meaty smell of some kind of soup or stew. Bette led them through the large room to a smaller one, with a bed, a cradle, and a chest. Odo and Bette had clearly surrendered their only bedchamber to them.

"I've done the best I could with the clothes." Bette indicated two clean looking, but worn, homespun gowns spread on the bed along with linen aprons. "Anduze has his strong points, but he wasn't helpful with your sizes." She smiled and made a gesture with her hand, holding it to an approximation of Ermengarde's height and then lowering it to Missee's. "And he didn't tell me you were both were in need of fattening up a bit. I'll find you something to cinch in the gowns."

"I'm sure they will be fine," Ermengarde said, again surprised and intrigued by how thoroughly Anduze had thought this through. She'd need to do some thinking too, to keep up with him.

"I'll leave you to change. There's fresh water to wash in and soap I made myself. When you're through changing, we'll have our midday meal. You must be hungry."

Ermengarde wasn't sure how to appropriately respond to Bette. She had plenty of experience with servants, but none with a well-to-do peasant. She would rely on her best courtly manners. Surely good manners were always appropriate. "Thank you. You're very kind."

Bette smiled again, nodded her head, and left, closing the door behind her. She seemed to be enjoying her role as hostess.

Missee examined the small bowl and the ewer of water on the chest. "Do you suppose we'll ever again have a real bath?"

"We'll have to make do with what we have." At the prospect of washing the ashes from her hair the small basin, Ermengarde rolled her eyes. But wash it she must.

Missee picked up the smaller of the two gowns. "We're going to wear another costume." She giggled. "We shall have stories to tell of our adventures for the rest of our lives."

"Yes, if the stories end happily." Ermengarde examined the larger gown. "From the look of these, we are going to be peasants instead of pilgrims."

It didn't take them long to change out of the pilgrim garb, but washing was another matter. It took a long time. They scrubbed their hands and faces with the caustic black soap. Missee washed the ashes from Ermengarde's hair and then braided it, still wet. The gown Missee put on was dun-colored and drab, while Ermengarde's was a faded, dark blue. Over these they tied the white aprons Bette had provided. There were also white coifs to cover their hair. When they finally emerged from the bedchamber, they looked like two peasants.

THE VISCOUNT'S DAUGHTER

The main room was crowded with people. At the long table near the fireplace, Anduze sat with a small, chubby boy about three years old in his lap. He entertained the child by mysteriously producing a coin from the boy's nose. The boy giggled in delight as the coin miraculously disappeared. Again, Anduze surprised Ermengarde. She couldn't recall knowing any man who paid attention to small children.

Odo sat beside him, and two older children were across from them. Five young, deeply tanned men and an older man, all dressed in farm workers' short tunics and braies, had found places at the far end of the table. Bette, balancing a baby on one hip, nodded to a servant girl.

"Please have a seat." Bette indicated a space left for them at the long table.

"It smells wonderful," Ermengarde said, slipping around the end of the bench to sit across from Anduze. Missee arranged herself beside her, and Anduze passed the small boy to an older girl, possibly a daughter of the house. She had a jutting chin like Odo's, and her gaze at Anduze was worshipful. There was an awkward moment of silence. No one moved.

He leaned across the table and whispered, "Ermengarde, you must begin the meal."

She felt her face flush. She hastily made the sign of the cross over the table. The others followed her lead. Bette filled wooden mazers with soup. She gave the first bowls to Missee and Ermengarde, and then passed the remaining mazers to the others. The girl who had taken away the little boy filled their cups with fragrant, spiced wine. Everyone ate in silence, broken only by the slurping of soup from bone spoons.

Next Bette passed the trenchers, before joining them at table. Ermengarde took one of the thick pieces of stale bread. The servant brought a steaming kettle to her side. Using her eating knife, she skewered a piece of meat and a turnip and placed it on the trencher. She was unused to having everyone stare at her while she served herself, and she breathed easier when the servant with the kettle moved along to stand next to Missee. Ermengarde glanced across the table at Anduze, who nodded his head slightly in approval. His small gesture pleased her, and she smiled.

After the others helped themselves, Bette sent the servant with trenchers heaped with stew to Gilles and Nicholas, who were guarding the road leading to the farm.

Ermengarde tasted the savory stew. "This is quite delicious. Did you make it?" she asked Bette, seeing no cook in evidence.

Bette's face reddened with pleasure. "Yes, my," she hesitated, "my lady. I like to cook because I like to eat."

"Is that rosemary I taste?" Ermengarde asked. Polite dinner conversation apparently wasn't the norm at midday on a working farm.

"Yes," Bette said proudly. "I have an herb garden. Everything we're eating is grown right here. We even make our own wine." She cast a loving look at her husband, and he grinned at her.

Ermengarde had never been in a peasant farmhouse before, let alone shared a meal with peasants. The food was simple, hearty, and remarkably flavorful. The thing that struck her the most was that without the luxuries of her station, Odo and Bette seemed happy, content. Ermengarde was not only in a farmhouse; she was in a home. No one would ever mistake the Château Comtal for a home, and no one would accuse its denizens of being happy. A window opened in her mind in the same way it did when Damian first introduced her to the wisdom contained in books. Seeing Bette and Odo gave her a glimpse of a world beyond that of politics and the endless jockeying for position at court, a world she'd only dimly perceived. Her heart ached with a longing she little understood. In her perilous position, happiness and contentment appeared to be more precious than gold.

Things happened quickly after the meal. Anduze politely thanked his host and hostess, and then he turned to her. "Ermengarde, I'm going in to Narbonne to try and locate Minerve." He spoke in his usual mild manner, but she detected urgency in his expression. "You'll be safe here with Nicholas and Gilles."

"Wait one minute, Anduze." She would not be put off so easily. "I want to go with you."

"You forget, my lady, your husband may still be in town and waiting for you. By now, the fellows who got away from Nicholas and Gilles certainly have conveyed the news of your escape to him. And where are you likely to go except to Narbonne? I'll have a look around and return this evening."

She bit her lip so hard she tasted blood. She didn't want to be left behind. As amenable as their host and hostess were, she was anxious to find out what, if anything, Minerve had accomplished. She had no choice. She had to trust Anduze. "I'll be most eager to find out what you learn."

He nodded and then left the farmhouse. Bette and the servant began clearing the table. Missee and Ermengarde were alone in the middle of nowhere in a strange place.

Odo and the farm workers returned to their tasks as silently as they had eaten. Bette's older children followed the men outside. At the door, the oldest boy, perhaps nine or ten, tow-headed and solidly built like his father, stopped. For a moment, he seemed tongue-tied. Then he blurted out to Missee. "My lady, would you like to come with us? We have six kittens in the barn."

Missee gave Ermengarde an inquiring look. She could tell by the eagerness of her sister's expression that she welcomed the opportunity to just be a child for a few moments.

"Go ahead," Ermengarde said.

With a bright smile, Missee left the farmhouse with the boy. As soon as they were gone, Bette sat at the table to nurse the baby. Like her, the baby was rosy-cheeked and fair-haired. A distant memory of her stepmother holding Missee in one arm, but extending the other arm to her brought Ermengarde a pang of loss, even sharper than when she'd smelled the rosemary. But she mustn't dwell on the past. Now was her chance to learn something from Bette about Anduze.

Ermengarde wasn't quite sure what to say, but she couldn't help but admire the infant. "She's a lovely, healthy babe."

Bette glowed at the praise. "I lost a babe to the pox before her, but this one is strong and bonny."

There was no easy way for Ermengarde to bring up what was on her mind. She could do nothing but plunge in. "How long have you known Anduze?"

"Oh, for years," Bette explained. "Abbot Stephen and Anduze hunt together each fall. We hold several of our fields from the abbey, and my Odo tends Abbot Stephen's hunting dogs." She conspiratorially inclined her head toward her guest. "I don't need to tell you it is hardly seemly for the abbot to keep hunting dogs at the monastery."

So Anduze and his party had been on their way to Fontfroide for a hunting expedition. That explained their dress and lack of military accoutrements. Ermengarde had heard much mention of how corrupt many monasteries had become. One of the common complaints was about worldly abbots, who hunted and enjoyed meat at every meal. She'd seen no signs of worldliness at Fontfroide, but she suspected Abbot Stephen was sensitive to the current criticism of monastic abuses.

She wasn't sure how to frame her next question. Anduze had said he was the Viscount of Anduze, but she'd never known a lord to have friends among the peasant class. She considered her words carefully before beginning. "Anduze hasn't been very forthcoming. And in our situation it didn't seem appropriate to ask, but I find it curious I've never seen him in Toulouse."

Bette didn't respond immediately. "Anduze is a very private person, never says much about his personal affairs. We never know when or if he'll appear here, but we usually see him at least once a year late each fall when he comes this way to hunt with the abbot. But as for not being known in Toulouse, perhaps it's because he doesn't much care for the city or its ruler."

Ermengarde raised an eyebrow. "He seems to get along well with everyone."

Bette grinned. "He can charm the birds out of the trees."

"He does have a way about him."

Bette put the infant over her shoulder and burped her before returning the baby to the breast. Seemingly unable to resist the chance to gossip, she continued. "I do know he recently has been to Toulouse. His wife was very ill for several years and died a while back. Nicholas told me she was no more than a bundle of sticks when she passed. Anduze stayed with her to the end, even though, according to Nicholas, they never got on very well. Her last wish was that masses be said for her in Rocamadour and at St. Sernin's in Toulouse. And Anduze honored that wish. He stopped here on the way back from the pilgrimage he made on her behalf. I don't know what got into him, but he wasn't himself."

Anduze was more complicated and interesting than Ermengarde had thought. And from what she'd just heard, he was loyal, too.

The sated baby's eyelids drooped. "It's time I changed this one and put her down for a nap." Bette righted her gown and, with adept movements, changed the diaper cloth before putting the baby into a cradle near the fireplace. She sat at the table again and then poured them another cup of wine.

"Do you often go to Narbonne?" Ermengarde asked.

A cloud came over Bette's face. "We don't go any more than we have to. In recent years, the fees to do business there have kept increasing. The fee to set up a market stall is so high it's hardly worth the effort. Then there is a fee to bring a wain into town and another to cross the bridge from the bourg into the city. The trip costs more than our profit. There was a time when honey from our hives was highly prized, not only in Narbonne, but it also graced tables all over the south," she said proudly. "Now we mostly trade it locally."

In the press of the last days, Ermengarde hadn't had time to consider that being viscountess of Narbonne in fact, rather than only in name, would entail considerable responsibilities. "I've been led to believe the city is rich, thriving," she said.

Bette huffed. "The city is only a means to line the coffers of Archbishop Arnold and the Count of Toulouse. And that's not the same thing as being a place where everyone benefits from the exchange of goods." Her ears grew red as if she was worried she had overstepped the bounds of acceptable conversation. She must have guessed Ermengarde's identity, even though Anduze probably had told them no more than was absolutely necessary.

Ermengarde couldn't resist asking, "Do you remember the times before Viscount Aymeri died in Hispania?"

Bette's face brightened. "When I was young, my family often went to the city, not only to trade, but for the festivities. One year at the Feast of Fools, Viscount Aymeri and Viscountess Ermessende personally gave all the children silver pennies. I remember it to this day. I vowed to keep the silver penny always, but before the day was out, I bought myself ribbons for my hair." She laughed, her face glowing. "Pennants flew from all the towers, and bonfires burned throughout the city. Huge cauldrons of stew filled the air with rich smells of meat, and we ate and drank our fill, compliments of the viscount. It was grand."

Ermengarde had a misty memory of riding pillion behind her father at this or a similar festival, her tiny hands firmly grasping his surcoat. One of the responsibilities of great lords was largesse, although she'd seen little of it in Toulouse. If she ever came into her own, she would continue the proud heritage of her family, and she would take steps to ensure the smooth flow of trade. She would rule fairly and justly, and the wellbeing of her city would be her highest priority.

Bette stirred. "My lady, I have chores that need seeing to, and I suspect you might like to rest."

"I am quite exhausted." Ermengarde smiled. For all her lack of sophistication, as skillfully as a courtier, Bette had brought their conversation to a close.

Ermengarde shook crumbs of the hard bread from her apron and returned to the chamber they'd been given. She stretched out on the lumpy straw mattress to rest. Closing her eyes, images of her wedding night crowded in on her. She shoved them aside and thought of Anduze, wishing she were with him.

* * *

Narbonne was an easy ride from Odo and Bette's farm and, still dressed as a pilgrim, Anduze attracted little notice as he rode through the countryside. The day was sunny with flocks of birds migrating and peasants gleaning in the fields after the harvest. Deep in thought, he paid little attention to the passing scene. What bizarre twist of fate had placed him in the role of rescuer? He wished he could extract himself and his followers from Ermengarde and her problems. However, until he ensured her safety, he didn't feel he could do that. She was depending on him, and he had agreed to help her. And there was something else, too. She attracted him in a way no woman had attracted him before. He didn't understand it. She was certainly not voluptuous, since she was as thin as a scarecrow. She was attractive, but it was her spirit rather than her body that drew him. He felt like a moth drawn to her flame and worried the fire would consume him. As soon as she and her sister were safe, he and his men would return to their hunt.

The stout walls of Narbonne came into view, and he entered the eastern gate into the bourg. Immediately he sensed tension, even in this, the part of the city filled with woolen mills, dyers, potters, coopers, and other business people. He spotted knights and men-at-arms wearing Toulouse's colors in line at a cookhouse and others drinking at a table in front of a tavern.

Dismounting, he led his horse to the bridge that led into the city. It cost him a coin to cross. The shops on the bridge were open, but not especially busy, as if people were staying inside their dwellings. On the other side of the bridge, to his right was the viscount's palace with Toulouse's pennon flying above it. To his left, he recognized the palace of the archbishop from the double budded cross on its banners.

The gate to the archbishop's palace was open, and Anduze glanced into the courtyard. Knights, wearing the archbishop's insignia, were practicing their jousting skills at a quintain, the familiar training post with its revolving crosspiece, target, and sandbag. Another group of knights wearing the twelve-budded cross of Toulouse stood waiting their turn.

A knight struck the quintain a resounding blow, and the others cheered. Anduze made a mental note of the number of knights, each probably accompanied by men-at-arms and squires. Toulouse and the archbishop were preparing for something. Surely, all these troops were not needed to capture two young women. They undoubtedly had found out about Minerve's mission and suspected that the viscountess might find allies.

Anduze moved on and spotted a seedy-looking tavern. Above the door was a dirty white sign. Rudely painted on it, were three black crows. It was a likely place to find out what was going on in the city. Tethering his horse, he went inside. The interior was dim, and the small room smelled of ale and sour wine. All the rough-hewn tables, except one, were occupied with workingmen and soldiers in quilted tunics, probably members of the city militia. He sat at the empty table and took out a bezant.

The barkeep came to his side, eyeing the small gold coin.

"A jug of your best wine." Anduze flipped the man the coin. He guessed the gold coin would soon bring him company.

It wasn't long before a pug-nosed man wearing a workman's leather apron came to his side. "Drinking alone, friend?" the man asked.

Anduze extended his hand, indicating the bench across the table from where he sat. He called to the barkeep, "And a cup for my new friend."

The man initiated the conversation. "I see you've been on pilgrimage."

Anduze nodded, knowing the less he said, the more inclined the other would be to talk. The barkeep brought the wine and cups. Anduze poured the drinks, raising his cup to the workman. "To Saint James."

"Saint James," the workman replied. "What brings you to Narbonne?"

"I'm on my way home." Anduze refilled the man's cup. "I've never seen so much excitement in Narbonne, what's going on?"

The man rubbed the spiky beard on his chin. "I guess you wouldn't have heard." He proceeded to tell Anduze about the runaway viscountess. "It's said she's a beauty," the man concluded, "and some say she's a witch, and she's bewitched her husband."

Anduze suppressed a smile. "So all these soldiers in town are to return a runaway wife? She must be quite a woman."

"The soldiers in town are only part of the Count of Toulouse's men. Most of them are out combing the countryside, trying to find the runaway wife." The man laughed. "I've heard tell she's as slippery as butter. She keeps getting away. And it's more complicated than just the wife. A nobleman, the Viscount of Minerve, came here and left with a handful of knights loyal to her."

"Why did they leave?" Anduze asked, giving the man his best innocent look and pouring them more wine.

"I'm chief woodcutter to the archbishop and, from time to time, I hear things." The man lowered his voice. "There's going to be a war."

"A war? How can a handful of knights and one noble fight the combined might of the Count of Toulouse and the Archbishop of Narbonne?"

The man took a long drink and then coughed as some of it went down the wrong way. "Not everyone in the region and in the city are happy with the way things have been going, and the archbishop and the count expect the lady to find willing allies.

"And who would those allies be?"

"Well, I've heard that the Viscount of Béziers had an alliance with Toulouse, but between you and me, I suspect the nobles are all afraid of Toulouse's growing power."

Anduze scratched his head and then retrieved the coins still on the table. "I guess Narbonne 'tisn't a place for me to tarry. I want no part in a war."

The man's face fell. "But you've yet to finish your wine."

"That's more for you, my friend." Anduze passed him the jug. "I really must be on my way."

* * *

Ermengarde heard Missee call her name, and she opened her eyes. She'd fallen asleep. Her sister's cheeks were glowing and her eyes bright. "Ermengarde, the kittens are lovely. May I have one?"

The sight of her sister so happy gave Ermengarde a feeling of lightness and hope. Perhaps someday they could have a normal life and a chance to enjoy simple pleasures. "Cats aren't commonly kept as pets, but as soon as we're settled," she said, rubbing her eyes, "you may have one, I promise."

"Anduze came into the barn when I was there," Missee announced. "And he asked me to fetch you."

Ermengarde got to her feet and then straightened her gown. Outside, the shadows were lengthening.

"This is really a nice place, in spite of the flies and the barnyard smells." Missee wrinkled her nose. "Bette is going to show me how to peel apples and make cider."

"Yes, this is a nice place." Ermengarde smiled at her sister. "Right now, I need to find out what Anduze has discovered in Narbonne." *Everything is going to be all right now. Minerve must have accomplished his mission and gathered together those people still loyal to my father.* She left Missee in the main room where Bette was already peeling apples.

Outside, Anduze stood near the rough, wooden bench beside the front door. One look at his stony face, however, told Ermengarde that something was wrong.

"My lady, please sit."

She sat on the bench. He pulled up a three-legged stool and sat across from her. "Toulouse has soldiers in Narbonne and he's out scouring the countryside for us. His banner is flying above the viscount's palace. I heard about Minerve's visit and learned he has left the city with a few knights loyal to you. And," he paused and let out a long breath, "Toulouse and the archbishop are preparing for war. I even heard the rumor you were a witch and had bewitched Toulouse."

Her bright hopes of moments ago plummeted. "Bewitched? What evidence is offered to support such a wild idea?"

"Toulouse doesn't need evidence. Innuendo and the fact you've been educated beyond what is considered the capacity of women, is enough."

Ermengarde shook her head in disbelief. "War?" Their brief sojourn in this idyllic place and a good rest had lulled her into the unfounded hope that her city would be ready to receive her. If not with open arms, at least with a show of support. Minerve had only been able to find a few nobles to rally to her cause, and now, Toulouse and the archbishop were preparing for war. How naïve she'd been. What should she do now? She rubbed her forehead, as if in doing so, she could find a solution to their predicament.

Anduze shifted uneasily on his stool. "Ermengarde, don't be hasty to predict the worst."

"I hope Minerve has more success in the region than he had in my city." She gave Anduze a wan smile. "I'm afraid you may have a long wait for your just reward." The hollowness of her words hung in the air for a moment.

The skin around his mouth relaxed into its usual amused expression. "I'm flattered that you are worrying about my reward," he said, "but let's focus on the prospect of war. Tell me again, who were your father's allies?"

She gave him a grateful look. The problems in Narbonne hadn't scared him off. He was still willing to help her and was already formulating plans to that end. She exhaled deeply, not realizing until that moment she'd been holding her breath. She concentrated on the political situation, as she understood it. "I was a mere child when my father fell at the battle of Fraga, but I've been told he was allied with Barcelona, Carcassonne, and Montpellier."

Anduze's eyes were thoughtful. "Those would be natural allies."

"I'm quite sure there must be others too, in spite of any crazy stories Toulouse may spread. If he deals with others as roughly as he has dealt with me, he must have enemies. It seems I have no option but to attempt to get to the nearest city, Béziers, and seek the viscount's help."

"I heard in Narbonne that Béziers had allied himself with Toulouse. So I'm not sure how safe you'd be there. It would be advisable for me to go to Béziers first on your behalf."

"No, that would never work," Ermengarde said impatiently. She didn't want to be left behind again. "If I'm to rule, to take control of my inheritance, then I must convince potential allies of my ability, my seriousness."

The lines around Anduze's eyes crinkled, and he laughed. "I guessed you wouldn't be content to stay behind, but I suggest that Lady Ermessende stay with Bette and Odo."

Ermengarde glared at him. "So you had figured this all out beforehand?"

His face grew serious again. "You don't have a lot of choices."

She shook her head. "I can't leave Missee, though I think she'd not mind staying here. If Toulouse seized her, it would go badly with your friends. To save her from harm would be the only reason I would return to him. Whatever happens, Missee and I will stay together."

"In spite of the peril of your situation, my lady, I'm impressed with your loyalty to your sister and that you consider the safety of those who have befriended you."

"I am loyal to those who have earned it as you have, my lord." This was the first time she had called Anduze *my lord*. "I assure you, Anduze, your reward will be great when I come into my viscounty."

"You speak as if I were a pauper and in this for gold. Land, I will accept, for Gilles."

She looked at him curiously and then felt a flush creep across her cheeks. Gilles must be Anduze's bastard. In that situation, he would want land so as not to alienate his patrimony. "Land you shall have."

"Speaking of rewards…" Anduze held out the pouch containing her jewels. "Keep these. I haven't needed them."

She took the jewels from his outstretched hand. Their hands touched briefly, and she smiled. He continued to amaze her. She lowered her voice. "I'd like to reward your friends."

"I have taken care of it." He made a dismissive movement with one hand. She realized she was not to question him. When she came into her own, she'd handsomely reward Bette and Odo. "Thank you. Thank you for everything."

Anduze sniffed. "Your thanks are premature. We are a long way from securing your position in Narbonne. We'll head for Béziers tomorrow. If we are welcomed there, I'm still not sure we can trust the viscount. He is, after all, allied with Toulouse."

Chapter 13

MORNING FOUND ERMENGARDE AND HER party
headed towards Béziers. For their protection,
Gilles scouted ahead while Nicholas rode behind.
The bitter wind whipped through Ermengarde's worn, woolen
mantle and thin gown. She rode hunched over on her horse,
favoring her arm, still in the sling.

Missee spurred her little horse and came to her side.
Ermengarde sat up straight.

"I hated leaving the farm," Missee confessed. "Bette and
Odo are very nice. I felt safe there."

"We'll see them again," Ermengarde assured her, "and
thank them properly for their help."

Missee's eyes lit with concern. "Are you still hurting?"

Ermengarde smiled. "After riding the donkey even for a
brief time, Titan's stride is almost comfortable," she lied.

They rode in silence past vineyards and fields, and through a small village composed of a handful of gray stone houses and a graceful little church. Few people were out and about, probably because of the biting wind. If anyone studied them from the inside of their houses, they must have found them peculiar. They were dressed as peasants yet riding fine horses.

They rode on. The sun was well up when Gilles galloped toward them.

"Horsemen," he shouted, "Dozens of them, traveling fast and heading in the direction of Narbonne."

Anduze spurred his horse. "Follow me," he ordered.

No one questioned his order. They urged their horses into a gallop, followed by Nicholas who had quickly grasped the situation.

Ermengarde's heart sunk with this new threat. Would Toulouse pursue her to the very ends of the earth? The answer was yes. Narbonne was too valuable to let it slip through his greedy fingers. And as Anduze had astutely pointed out, her defiance offended his pride.

Their horses strained and lathered, their sides heaving as they kept pushing them forward. Ermengarde breathed in the gritty dust from the pounding hooves. They couldn't keep driving their mounts like this, but neither could their pursuers. They'd ridden perhaps two Roman miles when Anduze reined in his horse at a narrow passageway between two large outcroppings of rock.

Dismounting, he grabbed the bay's reins. "We'll wait for them here."

He led Titan behind one of the boulders. Missee followed. Nicholas and Gilles joined them, readying their bows.

"Nicholas, I'm placing you on the other side." Anduze pointed directly across from them.

Moments later the first horseman, in a black-and-yellow surcoat, came into view. He slowed at the place where the road narrowed. Other horsemen pulled up beside him. One held a lance with a black, yellow, and white pennant fluttering from the end of it. The first horseman directed some of his men to go around them on either side. Soon they would be surrounded.

Anduze's brow furrowed. "I recognize the black arrows on the banner. It's Béziers, but is he friend or foe?"

A shiver went down Ermengarde's spine. Perhaps Béziers was searching for her to turn her over to Toulouse. She took out her eating knife. Someday she'd own a sword and know how to use it.

Anduze laughed at the sight of Ermengarde with her knife, the worry lines in his face easing. "Our pursuers don't know what they are in for."

Anduze must think me ridiculous. He doesn't know, can't know, what I endured at Toulouse's hands.

His face grew serious again. He put an arrow into his bow and then crouched in readiness.

They waited, but an attack didn't come. Time passed slowly, and Ermengarde couldn't gauge how long they hid behind the rocks. Hearing someone approach, Anduze poked out his head, and she followed his lead. A knight rode slowly forward with a white strip of cloth affixed to a lance, fluttering and flapping in the brisk wind.

Cautiously, Anduze stepped from behind the rock where they were concealed. He disarmed his bow and placed it and the arrow at his feet, a signal he was ready to talk.

The knight came closer, and Gilles and Nicholas lowered their bows. The knight dismounted, threw down his lance, and pushed up the visor on his helmet, revealing the battle-hardened face of a man of middle years. He was less than average height and stood very tall as if compensating for it.

"May the peace of the Lord be with you," he said.

"And with you," said Anduze.

"You must be Anduze. I heard Lady Ermengarde is traveling with you. Please tell my lady that Raymond Trencavel, Viscount of Béziers, wishes to speak with her."

Ermengarde scowled, unsure what was going on. She hurriedly put away her eating knife and then, at Anduze's nod, stepped forward, her palms sweating in spite of the cold day.

"My lady." Béziers bowed and gave her a benevolent look. "I can understand that you run from your enemies, but not from your friends."

Ermengarde cleared her throat. "Friends, like rare jewels, have been few. I have not known whom I could count on." She surprised herself by speaking evenly as her anxiety gave way to a cautious hope.

Béziers looked appraisingly at her. "Minerve has sought my friendship on your behalf."

She raised an eyebrow. "And where is Minerve?"

"My lady, he left Béziers for Montpellier to rally Viscount William to your cause. And I have sent a letter to my brother, Roger at Carcassonne. I am quite sure you will be able to count on his support."

Anduze smiled and opened his mouth to speak, but Ermengarde cut him off. She was through letting others speak for her. "Toulouse and his men may well be on their way here, seeking to capture me. We thought you might be in league with him. We have heard you were allies."

Béziers shook his head. "It has been expedient for me and others to seek accommodation with Toulouse. But we've been only biding our time until something or someone could unite us. It appears that someone is you. Everyone in the south knows that to side with you will mean war."

"Yet you offer your friendship?" She stared at this man, wondering and hoping that since his family, the Trencavels, had been her father's allies he could be trusted.

"I've already proven my friendship, my lady. If you will stay your men's arrows, I'll show you."

"Tell us what proof you offer," Anduze said.

"I have captured four of Toulouse's men. Unfortunately, a handful of others escaped, and they are now probably informing Toulouse of your whereabouts. With your indulgence, I will bring the captives forward. Surely since they are from Toulouse, Lady Ermengarde will recognize them."

The captives might be part of a ruse to get her to surrender. Yet something told Ermengarde to trust Béziers. "That will not be necessary, Béziers," she said with a sense of diplomacy she didn't know she possessed. "If we are to be allies, there must be trust between us. I accept your offer of friendship and offer mine in return."

A smile flitted across Raymond of Béziers' narrow face. "My lady, Minerve told me of your plight, but not your courage."

"Courage is found in many places and within many people, my lord. Courage certainly is not in short supply in Béziers."

"Perhaps you and your entourage will accept the hospitality of my city."

Ermengarde almost laughed at the idea that Anduze, his men, and Missee were her entourage. She looked at Anduze. "What say you, Anduze?"

He inclined his head. "As you will, my lady."

Ermengarde had a moment's worry that she hadn't consulted Anduze about the advisability of accepting Raymond of Béziers' offer of friendship. Anduze had more than proven his loyalty. However, the moment passed, and her doubts with it. She wasn't the same young woman who had sought his help in the woods only days ago. She was beginning to trust her instincts and had found strength she didn't know she possessed.

Béziers mounted his horse. "My lady, it will be our pleasure to escort you to our fair city."

Anduze called to Nicolas and Gilles. "Unstring your bows. We are among friends." Then he helped Ermengarde and Missee to mount, and they rode to where Béziers' knights waited.

Ermengarde noted Toulouse's men, bound and heavily guarded, but didn't let her gaze linger on them. Once again hope stirred in her. Her spirits lifted, as if she had just received the Holy Sacrament. Perhaps she'd someday be viscountess in more than just name.

* * *

Toulouse and his men had been searching a wide area around Narbonne for any sight or signs of Ermengarde and those aiding her. The sun disappeared behind the hills and he led his men to the Via Aquitania. He didn't want to return to Narbonne, but the gathering darkness made going on impossible. God's body, that woman had eluded him again. He was about to order his men to return to the city when several of his knights appeared.

They drew near. "We've been searching for you," one said. "The Viscount of Béziers, with a sizeable force, captured four of our number."

Toulouse threw up his hands in the air. "Fools! I'm surrounded by fools. Why did you engage them? Why didn't you return and tell me of Béziers' betrayal?"

The man visibly quailed. "We had no choice. They were upon us before we knew it."

Toulouse grunted and, with a dismissive gestured, waved the knights away. "See if you can make it back to Narbonne with us without further mishap."

The shamed knights went to the back of Toulouse's men. Ranulf came to his side. "I guess you heard," Toulouse yelled, unable to control his anger. "Béziers has turned traitor. And no doubt Ermengarde is now with him. He must have found her before we were able to."

The Templar nodded his head. "As you feared, my lord, this matter is getting out of hand. I thought Béziers had sought your alliance."

Disgust disfigured Toulouse's face. "I thought he was to be trusted."

"Minerve?"

"Whatever he told Béziers must have fallen on willing ears."

Ranulf shifted in his saddle. "What will we do now?"

Toulouse thought for a moment. "We'll return to Toulouse and prepare for war."

Ranulf's face, usually impassive, betrayed his surprise. "You'll undertake a campaign this late in the fall?"

"I will crush this rebellion before Ermengarde finds more allies and the whole south gets involved."

"Does that mean you'll besiege the city of Béziers?"

"Since you have come from Outremer, you surely know of the newest, most effective siege engine, a counterweighted trebuchet. When I learned of it, I sent all the way to Jerusalem for a builder. He has since built me two massive trebuchets: Avenger and Ballbreaker. I happen to know there are Roman ruins near the city, a ready supply of boulders to feed the trebuchets. Béziers will be unable to withstand an assault with such weapons." Toulouse clenched his fist. "I'll crush the city. It will surely fall."

* * *

It was growing dark when Ermengarde, riding beside Raymond of Béziers, crested a hill. Before her was the city of Béziers, situated on a bluff above the Orb River. She remembered the river's name from the maps she'd studied with Damian. How valuable his lessons had been. The small city, with its stout walls interspersed with sturdy towers, looked unassailable. At least for now, she'd found refuge.

They made their way down the hill and then up the bluff, passing through a gate into the narrow, twisting streets of the city. A carter stopped, removed his hat in deference to Viscount Raymond, and stared as they passed. A peasant woman, carrying a squawking chicken in a wooden pen, curiously eyed them. They must have made an unusual sight. Béziers' knights were a handsome escort for two women in peasant garb, a man dressed as a pilgrim, and two woodsmen. Ermengarde glanced at Anduze, who wore a particularly jaunty look, as if he was enjoying the spectacle they were making.

The cobbled street became so narrow they had to ride in single file. She anxiously looked around. Such tight quarters might be a trap. Yet she'd made the decision to believe in Béziers' sincerity. She took a deep breath. They passed under the overhanging buildings and emerged on another wider street. At the end of the street, the viscount's palace rose in splendor above the houses and shops of the townspeople. With its paired mullioned windows and a semi-circular arch over the main entry, it wasn't ominous like the Château Comtal in Toulouse. They dismounted in the courtyard. There was something familiar about the palace. "Viscount Raymond, have I been here before?" she asked.

Béziers smiled with his lips, but not with his eyes. "I remember you and your stepmother and infant sister visiting here when you were just a child of perhaps four or five years old. Your father and I had our disagreements, but there is a long history of cooperation between your house and mine."

"So this is not our first meeting," she said, heartened by his words. "I wish to talk with you about my father and his rule in Narbonne while I am here, at you convenience. I long to know more about him."

"My lady, I'll be glad to tell you what I can." Before he could say more, a boy rushed from the stables to see to their horses.

Béziers offered Ermengarde his arm and led her inside to the great hall. As she looked around, the feeling of déjà vu returned. The handsomely appointed room was only half the size of the great hall in the Château Comtal, and less military in aspect with its linen wall hangings, many of them embroidered. Colorful, thick pillows cushioned the benches and chairs near the fireplace. Rushes, mixed with dried flowers and herbs, covered the floor, and their fragrance evoked a long-lost feeling of security, as if she were a small child again, protected by a strong father and an attentive stepmother. Béziers led her to a chair near the fire.

A petite woman, of perhaps thirty and five years, heavy with child, sat by the fire with three blond little girls. She passed the child on her lap to a servant and then came forward to receive them. Béziers greeted her with affection, suggesting to Ermengarde that the woman was his wife. She gave them a wide smile. "I'm Lady Saure. Welcome, Lady Ermengarde. I knew your mother. And this must be Lady Ermessende. I knew your mother, too. Two very fine women."

"Thank you for your hospitality," Ermengarde said. "It is more than I could have hoped for." She couldn't help feeling that her mother and father were here, present if only in memories, in a way they had never been in Toulouse.

"You must be half frozen," Saure said. "The day was bright, but there was a chill in the air. Please come with me. I'm sure you'll want to change out of those rough clothes and have hot baths. I see from your sling, Lady Ermengarde, that you've been injured."

"A bath would be lovely. We are in your debt," Ermengarde said. "And yes, my arm was broken, but it is mostly healed. I just use the sling to rest it." Possibly, Saure knew how she'd gotten the broken arm. When one was the source of gossip, one can only guess at what was being said.

"I am longing for a hot bath." Missee scratched her head. "I'm chilled to the bone, and even though we washed at the farmhouse where we stayed, it was only in a basin."

Ermengarde glanced at her sister. Missee was pale with dark circles under her eyes. They followed Saure to a spacious upstairs room.

"This is our best chamber. Your parents once stayed here," Saure said. A fire blazed in a brazier, and a large wooden tub, resembling half a barrel, had been placed directly in front of it. "I kept the fire going for your arrival." She took one of the cushioned seats and indicated for them to take the others.

Ermengarde gave her a curious look. "You knew we were coming?"

"The whole south is abuzz with your story. For a long time, the leading nobles have been afraid to challenge Toulouse. They complained of his bullying interference and his financial exactions, but they have been unwilling to alienate him. In fact, my husband found it expedient to make an alliance with him. Then you, a woman, little more than a girl, defy him. It is a challenge not only to Toulouse, but also to the manhood of our leaders. Well done, Lady Ermengarde!"

Ermengarde felt her face redden, embarrassed, but pleased, at Saure's enthusiastic appraisal of her actions. "I had no choice."

Saure shifted on her cushions to find a more comfortable position. "We heard you sought sanctuary at Fontfroide and guessed you might seek shelter here. When we learned you were in the company of Anduze, we were somewhat perplexed. We know of him, of course, but he has kept aloof from the political squabbles in the south. He is a stranger to us and has a reputation for a certain inconsistency." She paused, perhaps wondering if she had said too much.

"What do you mean?"

"He has long been allied to Raymond's family, but he hasn't supported our interests in any substantial way. In any case, you were very fortunate to meet him and his men. What a chance you two took, going into the unknown without an escort. Most noble women won't even venture to the shops without someone to accompany them. I'm even more impressed after meeting you. I thought you might be like the hearty women I've met who are men in all but name, but I find instead you both to be lovely."

"I was terrified," Missee confessed. "I've heard blood-curdling tales of women traveling alone."

Lady Saure gave Missee a reassuring pat on the arm. "I am glad Anduze found you before Toulouse or some other miscreants managed to. You're safe now." She gave Ermengarde a sympathetic look. "I'm sorry for your troubles, my dear, but it is time Toulouse's tyranny is challenged and, I hope, put to an end. We've been waiting for something or someone that would bring together an alliance against him. No one ever thought it would be you."

Ermengarde found Saure's words arresting. If she was the means of uniting Toulouse's unhappy neighbors against him, so be it. Their conversation was interrupted when servants appeared at the door, carrying pails of hot water.

"I'll leave you, my dears." Saure placed her hand on her belly. "My time is drawing nigh. I'm sure we'll have a healthy boy this time."

"May God grant you a safe delivery," Ermengarde said.

Saure spontaneously hugged her, and then Missee. "Now that I've been able to take your measure, I'll find you more suitable clothing."

When she had left, Ermengarde turned to Missee. "*Ma petite soeur*, do you want the first bath?"

"Please go first," Missee demurred. "I'm content to sit next to the fire. I don't know if I've ever been more tired."

As soon as the servants left, Ermengarde removed her sling, took off the scratchy peasant dress and soiled chainse, and climbed into the steaming tub. She closed her eyes for a moment and let the hot water ease the persistent ache in her groin. Then she washed off the grime with fragrant Castile soap, marveling at the turn of fortune that had brought her to Béziers, Saure, and the bath. Their hostess's ready smile, gentle manner, and motherly concern reminded Ermengarde of her stepmother. She had bathed Missee and Ermengarde in the same tub and sung the whole time. The songs were usually silly children's songs, and she hadn't known if her stepmother made them up or if other mothers knew them, too.

"Missee, can you please help me with my hair? I don't think I'm yet able to manage on my own."

Her sister came to the side of the tub and dropped onto a small, three-legged stool. Her fingers massaged soap into Ermengarde's hair and scalp, getting out any remnants of the ashes they'd used for disguise. Then she rinsed out the soap with warm water from a stoneware ewer.

Ermengarde didn't allow herself to linger in the steamy, relaxing bath so it would still be warm for Missee. "Your turn," she said, getting out of the bath and drying herself with the blue-and-white towel Lady Saure had provided.

Missee moved from the stool to sit again close to the brazier. "I'm not going to bathe. I'm too tired."

Ermengarde looked at her questioningly. "But you've wanted a bath for days." She wrapped herself in a blanket and went to Missee's side, noticing again the circles under her eyes. "Are you feeling all right?"

"Yes, I just need rest."

Ermengarde put a hand on Missee's forehead. Her hand was warm from the bath, but she could still tell Missee was burning with fever. "*Ma petite soeur*, I'm afraid you are coming down with something. I'm sure Saure won't mind if you get into bed without a bath."

"Could I?" Missee's eagerness was somehow pathetic, and it alarmed Ermengarde.

"I'm sure it won't be a problem. Strip to your chainse. I'll turn down the bed."

Missee had just settled in the bed when Saure returned. "I've found you these." She put an assortment of chainses and gowns on the chair. "Take your pick. I've also included articles for your toilet."

"Thank you," Ermengarde said. "It's lovely to be clean, and it will be grand to have fresh clothing." She gestured toward her sister. "Missee's feverish. I'm concerned. I've put her to bed without bathing. I hope you don't mind."

"Of course I don't mind." Saure walked to the side of the bed. "Can I bring you anything, my dear? Soup? Hot cider?"

Missee stifled a yawn. "I just want to sleep."

Saure sat on the bed next to Missee and gently put a hand on her forehead. She shook her head and turned to Ermengarde. "Please join us downstairs. I've ordered a hot meal for you in the great hall. I'll send in a servant to stay with Missee. If she worsens, I'll call in my herb woman." Saure bustled away.

Ermengarde selected a clean chainse with flowers embroidered around the neck and at the sleeves and a lilac gown of soft wool from the ones Saure had brought. It was too large for her, but her hostess had provided a girdle, and Ermengarde cinched in the gown between her waist and hips so it didn't look like she wore a tent. What luxury to again wear fine clothing! She brushed, combed, and parted her damp hair. She was unable to braid it with only one hand, so she coiled it at both sides of her head, fastening it with hairpins Saure had thoughtfully provided. After a quick glance in Saure's small hand mirror, Ermengarde was ready and eager to talk business with Raymond of Béziers.

Missee was already asleep.

"I won't be long," Ermengarde whispered and then tiptoed from the room. A servant, a capable-looking woman with gray hair, waited outside the door and went inside to keep an eye on Missee.

Ermengarde returned to the great hall where Béziers and Saure sat at the head table, awaiting her arrival. The knights and men-at-arms, who had accompanied Béziers this day, occupied other tables. From their loud chatter, she gathered their meal, with ample servings of wine, was already well underway. She glanced around. She didn't see Anduze and his men.

Béziers escorted her to his table. "We are pleased to have you here. We have much to talk over."

"Anduze should join us also," she said. "I wouldn't have made it here if it hadn't have been for him."

Béziers hesitated. "Anduze has left with his apologies. He was about to undertake a hunting expedition when he met you and your sister. He is returning to Fontfroide and his plans now that you have found refuge."

"Left?" Ermengarde thoughtfully covered her mouth with her fingers. She hoped she hadn't inadvertently neglected Anduze once they joined forces with Béziers. Perhaps he was angry with her. What did it portend that her first supporter, outside of Minerve, had already deserted her? In the short time of their acquaintance, she had begun to depend upon his counsel and his presence.

A slight smile appeared on Saure's lips. Ermengarde felt blood rush to her cheeks. She was concerned about Anduze and sorry he had left without a word, but not for the reasons Saure's smile suggested. Ermengarde gave her hostess an innocent look. "I am surprised. He said nothing to me of his departure."

Béziers appeared not to notice her reaction. Servants brought in hot platters of lamb and bowls of potage, placing them on the table. While they ate the thick soup, Ermengarde recounted their adventures since their escape from Toulouse.

Only when a servant produced the delicious subtleties, the sweets, signaling an end to their meal, did Béziers bring up what was most on her mind. He sat back in his chair and pursed his lips. "When Toulouse learns you are here, he'll raise an army. I've already begun preparations to defend the city."

Her stomach lurched at his blunt words. She took only a small portion of an elegant almond confection and then turned toward him. "Isn't it common for wars to be waged mostly in the spring when the weather fairs? I thought I'd have several months to gather supporters."

"That's exactly what Toulouse doesn't want you to do."

"I had no idea he would act so quickly. Will the city be able to hold out against him?"

Béziers' face was sober. "I hope so."

"Is there no possibility of negotiations?"

He laughed. "Some things dividing the nobles in the lands of the southern Franks can be negotiated, but a runaway wife isn't one of them. You have wounded Toulouse's honor and deprived him of your wealthy inheritance. If I read him rightly, he will go to whatever lengths are called for in order to get it and you back. "

Saure helped herself to a pastry. "*Certes*, husband, these things can be discussed on the morrow. Ermengarde must be exhausted. Missee has fallen ill from it all, and we must take care Ermengarde doesn't get sick as well."

"I am sorry, Ermengarde, to bring all this up before you have had a chance to catch your breath. We'll talk more after you've rested. My impatience sometimes knows no bounds, as my lady wife too often has to remind me. I hope Missee is not seriously ill. But if she is, my Saure is an excellent nurse."

Saure acknowledged her husband's praise with a loving look, and he smiled at her in return. Ermengarde envied the easy camaraderie and mutual regard that seemed to exist between them. She had much to learn about relationships between men and women.

They finished their meal, and Saure called to a woman servant who was beginning to clear the tables. "See that hot broth is brought to Lady Ermengarde's room."

The serving woman nodded deferentially and hurried off.

With weary steps, Ermengarde followed Saure up the stairs to their chamber. Her brief feeling of wellbeing had passed when she'd heard Béziers was already preparing for an attack. It was as if she had seen the sun for a few moments only to have it covered with dark, threatening clouds. She shook her head. Could the small city of Béziers hold out against Toulouse?

In their chamber, Missee tossed and turned in bed. Little beads of moisture had formed on her upper lip. Ermengarde's chest tightened. She lightly touched her sister's burning forehead and then glanced at Saure. Without speaking, Saure poured water into a bowl, sat on the other side of the bed and, taking a cloth, put a cool compress on Missee's head.

"Let me help," Ermengarde said.

"No, I've had a lot of experience with fevers. Sit and rest so you don't become ill, too."

Overcome with the events of the day, Ermengarde moved to a chair beside the bed. Worry over Missee sapped what was left of her strength and confident in Saure's abilities, she closed her eyes for a few moments, as if by doing so she could shut out her fears. The next thing she knew, Saure was shaking her awake. "Help me. Your sister's fever is worse. We have to cool her down."

Missee was awake, but her eyes were glazed.

"We are going to get you into the bathtub," Saure said.

"I don't want a bath," Missee protested weakly, as if speaking to them from a distant room.

Together they removed her chainse and then guided her to the bathtub, which hadn't yet been emptied. She was too weak to resist.

"The water's cold," Missee complained, as they maneuvered her into the water.

"That's the idea," Saure said soothingly.

They sponged down Missee until her body cooled. Then they dried her, wrapped her in a warm blanket, and put her back in bed. Now that she was cooler, she fell into a fitful sleep.

Saure's face grew long, and she sighed. "I'm afraid for her."

"What of the herb woman you mentioned?"

Saure was thoughtful for a moment. "I had no idea Missee would take such a bad turn and need her so soon."

"Can you ask her to attend us immediately?"

"I'll go to fetch her myself. She's an independent old crone who will need assurances our need is real."

"Thank you, but are you sure you should?" Ermengarde indicated Saure's advanced pregnancy with a gesture of her hand.

Saure shrugged. "If I go myself, I'll be sure no one dallies. A servant will accompany me. The walk will do me good." She hurried from the room.

Ermengarde collapsed into the chair by the bedside and put her face in her hands. Her breath was squeezed, restricted, and the dinner she'd eaten rested uneasily in her stomach. She would never forgive herself if her rebellion cost Missee's life. Her illness was an even bigger threat than Toulouse. He had ravaged Ermengarde's body, but he hadn't touched her heart. Now her heart was breaking.

She knelt beside the bed on the cold, stone floor and prayed. *If you spare Missee and save us from Toulouse's wrath, I'll build a fine chapel for the monks at Fontfroide.*

Chapter 14

SHADOWS WERE LENGTHENING AS ANDUZE, Nicholas, and Gilles turned their horses in the direction of Fontfroide and the delayed hunting trip.

"Don't you think we should have said goodbye to the viscountess?" Nicholas asked when the walls of Béziers were no longer in view.

Anduze shifted uneasily in his saddle. It was churlish of him to leave Béziers without a word to Ermengarde. Their shared experience in the last days had created a bond between them, a bond he neither sought nor wanted. "If we had done so, we would have had to endure effusive expressions of thanks."

Nicholas laughed. "I'm not sure what the word *effusive* means, but my guess is, it doesn't describe Lady Ermengarde."

"You are probably right about that, Nicholas." Anduze laughed. "The real reason we left suddenly was I was quite sure

Ermengarde was going to ask us for our support in the coming war."

Gilles, who rode beside Nicholas, urged his horse closer. "And will we not support her?" he asked eagerly.

"I need to think on it," Anduze said. "It's not our fight, and since winter will be soon upon us, I'll not need to make a decision any time soon."

Nicholas gave him a long look. "Are you really sure it's not our fight?"

"Need I remind you, that it was you who taught me to turn the other cheek? To let sleeping dogs lie."

Nicholas' lined face softened. "That was a long time ago when your father was away fighting in Hispania. Things have changed. You are no longer a headstrong youngster, spoiling for a fight like Gilles here. There are times when turning the other cheek is the only viable alternative. I also taught you to choose your battles carefully."

Anduze thought fondly of all the things Nicholas had taught him. The older man had a rare wisdom, honed by enduring many personal losses.

"I'm not spoiling for a fight," Gilles protested. "But Lady Ermengarde's cause is just."

Anduze let out a long breath. "That may be the case, but I'm still not convinced I should commit my knights to a war against Toulouse. I have already put both of you in danger."

Nicholas shook his head. "It's a bit late to worry about us. When Toulouse learns of your part in the viscountess's escape, he'll want you, and perhaps us, drawn and quartered."

"That's reason enough to spend another night in the woods, avoiding the inns and taverns between here and Fontfroide."

"I thought you'd decide that," Nicholas said, "and took care to purchase a few provisions in Béziers."

Anduze smiled. "You know me pretty well."

"I know myself and this youngster here. A spot of wine goes a long way to comfort my old bones at night, and Gilles here is always as hungry as a bear."

Their banter ended. Anduze nudged his mount ahead of his companions. He was worried about Toulouse finding them, more worried than he wanted the others to know.

* * *

Days passed and Missee was no better. The herb woman had visited and left several concoctions, but none of them helped. In the long hours Ermengarde spent at her sister's side, Saure kept her company when her duties in the palace allowed.

One rainy afternoon, Missee slept peacefully, and Saure came into the sickroom and made herself comfortable on the settle.

"If you have a little while, I'd appreciate you telling me what you know of my parents," Ermengarde said.

"Today's a good day for it. Usually on Wednesdays, I visit the nuns at the hospital, but today because of the heavy rain, I sent servants in my stead with a basket of food. Besides, my ankles are badly swollen. What would you like to know?"

"Anything you can tell me about my family. I know only the barest outlines of my history."

Saure laughed. "I can tell you something I remember about you from one of our visits to Narbonne, and I didn't remember it until I heard about you fleeing from Toulouse. You were about three years old, and in the solar with your stepmother. You were playing on the floor with three wooden bowls. A nurse came for you to take you to your chamber for a nap. You shook your head and clearly said no. The nurse picked you up and placed you on your feet. You swatted at her, not hitting her, but coming close. Your stepmother reprimanded your unladylike behavior, but I could tell she was amused."

"I must have been a terrible child."

"Not at all. You apparently never actually hit anyone, and your mother told me later you soon grew out of the habit. I think it showed that, even then, you were spirited. The only other thing I remember is how upset your stepmother was when you tottered into a brazier and were burned."

"It wasn't her fault. I'd been repeatedly warned about going too near it. But I was cold and determined. I paid dearly for ignoring their warnings. Since that time, I've had a great fear of being burned."

Saure gave her a sisterly pat. "Let me see what I can tell you about your birth mother. I was only thirteen years old when I married Raymond and first met your mother. She was comely, poised, and fashionable, and I was in awe of her. She must have been seventeen or eighteen at the time. I hadn't yet

246

conceived a child, and it worried me that your mother had born two sons, neither of whom lived beyond the first few days. And my worries were not unfounded since I, too, lost my first child. When you were born strong and healthy, your parents rejoiced, but the joy vanished with the death of your mother from childbed fever six weeks later." Saure shook her head. "I only saw your mother a half-dozen times, but I remember the smallest things pleased her—the crunch of snow beneath one's feet, the tiny furry caterpillars that feasted on the parsley, a piece of boiled sugar."

For a moment, Ermengarde was silent, feeling closer than she ever had to her mother. "What do you remember of my father?"

"He was skilled in arms, handsome, and gallant. His arrival in Béziers caused great excitement among the ladies of the court, even when he arrived with your mother, and later, with your stepmother."

"Did he take advantage of the admiration of the ladies?"

"Not that I know of. But he was, after all, a man. And few are steadfast in matters of bedding. What I found charming about him was that he seemed oblivious to how attractive he was."

"I remember the day he left to fight the Moors, the last time I saw him. He was clad in shining mail, astride a magnificent white destrier, wearing a red, silk caparison decorated with the gold key of Narbonne. I thought him magnificent."

"You surely have heard the jongleurs singing the epic of your heroic ancestor Aymeri, who fought with Charlemagne. It's an ancient tale, but jongleurs embellished it with your father in mind."

A distant memory came to Ermengarde of the epic being sung in the palace in Narbonne. "It was never sung in the great hall in Toulouse." She scowled.

Saure gave her a surprised look. "Count Alfonse Jordan must have banned it from Toulouse. Perhaps he was jealous since no such tale of bravery exists for the house of Toulouse." She shook her head and smiled. "When I first heard you had run away from your husband, I thought surely courage was part of your inheritance."

Resentment at Toulouse and delight in this new knowledge of her heritage warred in Ermengarde. "Tell me more about it," she begged.

"Well I know the tale. It's one I've heard often. The Moors held your fair city. Seeing its wealth and power, Charlemagne determined to conquer it. He offered it in fief to each of twelve nobles, if they would undertake its conquest. Tired of fighting and eager to get home, they refused him. But your ancestor, Aymeri, agreed, and he and his followers captured the city. From that time on, your family ruled the city. Aymeri married Ermengarde, the daughter of the king of Pavia in Lombardy."

"Wait," Ermengarde interrupted. "Are you sure that was her name?"

"Yes, of course. 'Tis true. Her name was Ermengarde."

"Please go on." Ermengarde had never heard the history of the name she'd inherited from her mother.

"When Aymeri was away, the Moors attacked the city, and Ermengarde led an army to relieve the siege. Our jongleur knows the epic well, and I'll make sure you hear the whole story while you're in Béziers."

Ermengarde shook her head in wonderment for a moment, and then her anger flared. "It makes my blood boil to think Toulouse purposely denied me knowledge of my family's history. How could he be so petty?"

"Probably he didn't want you, or anyone else, to recall your close ties with the renowned Charlemagne, king of the Franks. *Certes*, he hates the tale, especially the part about the heroic Ermengarde."

Ermengarde took a deep breath and exhaled slowly. "I thought I was an individual, but I see now I'm more than that. I'm part of a long stream of courageous leaders. When I come into my inheritance, I'll be sure to honor the proud traditions of my ancestors."

Saure smiled warmly. "You already have."

Missee stirred and opened her eyes. They both turned to her. She gestured for the basin on the table. Saure rushed to her side, holding the basin while Missee retched with dry heaves.

"Look." Saure pointed to red pustules on her face and thin arms.

Ermengarde recoiled. "Saure, is it the Moorish pox?" The very word *pox* sent a chill through her. It was a disfiguring, often a fatal disease. Crusaders and pilgrims returning from the Outremer carried the plague with them, and if Missee survived, she might be scarred for life.

"I don't think it's the fearful Moorish pox. It's most likely a children's disease, a milder pox. That, however, doesn't make it any less serious. She probably was exposed to it at the farm where you stayed."

Missee finished retching and then sank back into the pillows. Saure took the basin to a servant, who waited just outside the door.

Ermengarde sat in the chair Saure had vacated. She took her sister's hand, struggling to put aside her fears that her sister's life might be in danger. "You poor dear."

Missee closed her eyes and drifted into a restless sleep.

Hours passed, and Ermengarde didn't dare leave her side. It was dark when Saure returned, bringing a steaming mazer. "I'll watch with her for a while. Eat a little soup and try to get some rest."

Ermengarde forced down a little of the oniony broth and then stretched out on the truckle bed, wheeled out from beneath Missee's. The narrow bed was designed for children or a servant, and she couldn't get comfortable. Even covered with a warm blanket, the chill of the coming winter seeped through to her bones. Dark thoughts crowded in like vultures she had seen feasting on a dead horse. She had brought Missee to this. Her sister wouldn't be sick if she hadn't brought her along. Ermengarde gave up trying to find a comfortable position and pondered making another bargain with God. If he would spare

Missee's life, what could she promise besides the endowment of the chapel at Fontfroide?

She had a flash of insight. Trying to control God was probably futile, as well as blasphemous. She would be lucky to control her own destiny. If her sister got better, and she ever came into her inheritance, she'd use what limited influence she had not only for the good of her viscounty, but also for all those who turned to her for leadership. However, she still needed to pray. Sometimes there was nothing left but prayer. Praying was different from bargaining. She'd often heard that in dire situations, it was common for even unbelievers to pray. Prayer was a form of asking for help. An image came to mind of the Virgin in Majesty in the hospital attached to Saint Sernin. Over and over, Ermengarde prayed: *Holy Virgin, the mother of motherless children, intercede for us.*

* * *

In the morning, Ermengarde got up stiffly from the truckle bed. Saure dozed in the chair beside Missee. When Ermengarde approached Missee's bed, Saure opened her eyes.

"Good news," Saure said, getting up. "I gave Missee another potion hours ago. Her fever is down, and she is sleeping peacefully. She's on the mend. I'm sure of it." Saure stifled a yawn. "It's time for me to look in on my children."

Seeing Missee's regular breathing, Ermengarde clasped her hands together, whispered a prayer of thanksgiving to the Virgin in Majesty, and took Saure's place at Missee's side.

Later that morning, Ermengarde's vigil at her sister's bedside was interrupted when Saure returned to their chamber. "My husband would like to see you," she said. "I'll stay with Missee. I see her spots are already beginning to fade."

Ermengarde had slept little since Missee had become ill, and the prospect of discussing politics and the possibility of war was daunting, even though these would determine whether or not she could claim her inheritance. "I'll be back as soon as I can."

She found Béziers in the great hall, sitting at a table full of knights. They quieted and stood as she approached. With a sweep of his arm, Béziers invited her to sit at his side. When they were all seated, he began in a somber voice. "Toulouse has called for his knights and is already on his way here."

"On his way here. So soon?" Her words came out strangled. A storm was coming with her directly in its path. "I thought he might possibly attack a number of your castles first, seeking to destroy the head by cutting off the limbs?" She took a deep breath and then continued in a stronger, more resolute voice. "I'm sorry to have brought the wrath of Toulouse on you and your city. Thank you for spearheading our defense. Missee and I would leave here immediately, if she were able to ride."

The viscount nodded his head. "Well said, Lady Ermengarde, but I did not lightly offer the hospitality of the Viscounty of Béziers. I knew full well what it would entail."

Because of Missee's sickness, Ermengarde hadn't paid much attention to the city's defenses. Now she longed to go to the nearest window to study the city walls. "Will the city be able to withstand Toulouse's assault?"

"We are doing everything we can to strengthen our defenses," the viscount said. "As for now, you can aid us best by continuing to care for your sister."

This was Ermengarde's cue to leave. She wished he would include her in the planning and preparations for the siege, but she had to accept her role as a guest with a dangerously ill sister, even though she didn't like it. "Thank you for keeping me informed. Toulouse must be very eager to get me back."

"I have not underestimated him or his determination to get you back." Béziers spoke confidently, but his eyes were worried.

Ermengarde left the great hall with no intention of going directly back to Missee's side. Instead, she went outside and ran a hand along the rough, stone surface of the walls surrounding the courtyard of the palace. Beyond them lay the stout city walls. Were they sufficient to protect them from the might of Toulouse and his army? She shuddered at the thought of him breaching them and dragging her back to the Château Comtal. She leaned against the nearest wall and closed her eyes. She must be strong, not only for Missee, but for those who risked everything for her.

Back inside, she climbed the steep stairs to their chamber. Saure greeted her. "I must be going. Missee seems to be resting comfortably, but you don't look very well yourself. What did my husband want?"

"Toulouse is on his way here," Ermengarde said in barely a whisper.

"My husband has no doubt heard from our spies in Toulouse that the count is headed directly here."

Ermengarde frowned. "Spies?" It had just occurred to her that someday she might need to employ spies.

"When you come into your inheritance, you will learn that in every city some of the town consuls, churchmen, or merchants are willing to play a double game for their own advantage. It's all about power."

Who were Béziers' spies in the Château Comtal? She'd paid little attention to the comings and goings at the castle. But that was the past. In future, she'd question more, be more suspicious. She forced a smile. "We're forever in your debt."

Hearing a commotion in the courtyard, they went to the window. Servants unloaded bags of flour, casks of wine, and vegetables from wains while men built a stockade to house the animals that would be brought in from the countryside. Ermengarde's pulse quickened at the sight of these preliminary preparations. War was coming as surely as thunder after a flash of lightning.

With a sigh, Saure turned away. "I have preparations of my own to see to, if you will pray excuse me."

Ermengarde reached out with her good arm and gave Saure a hug. "Thank you. I am sorry to have brought war to your family and city."

Saure gently pulled away. "You mustn't blame yourself. War with Toulouse was inevitable." Her words were kind, but her face had blanched, and she looked older than her years.

* * *

Anduze had cut the hunting trip short, and they were heading home. He'd heard from Abbot Stephen that there was talk of Toulouse attacking Béziers before winter and he hadn't been able to keep his mind off the prospect of war.

With Nicholas and Gilles following behind, Anduze urged his tired horse up the last long hill that led to Sandeyren. The day had been sunny and pleasant, but now the last rays of the sun turned the gray stones of the castle to gold. His chest swelled with pride, as it always did, when he approached his ancestral home. Perched high above the plains below, like a friendly giant, it guarded the passage into the Cevennes Mountains.

In the three days of the journey from Fontfroide, Anduze had pondered the coming war. His animosity toward Toulouse had smoldered for nineteen years. As they often did, his thoughts flew back to the day Toulouse had brutally raped Nicholas' only daughter, Helena. Anduze touched the scar on his face, a daily reminder of his failed attempt to rescue her. Later that same day, he had planned to challenge Toulouse to combat. But a devastated Nicholas begged him not to seek revenge. The older man hadn't said so, but in hand-to-hand combat, Toulouse had far greater prowess as a warrior. Since that time, Anduze had come to realize, what he hadn't at age twenty, that though his martial skills were considerable, his strength lay in his quick wits and charming manner. Back then his challenge to Toulouse would have proven fatal. Because of his respect and love for Nicholas, Anduze had acquiesced and promised not to seek revenge. Nonetheless, after all those years, his failure to right the wrong done to Nicholas's family, and to the girl he loved as a sister, still rankled.

Now the situation was different. Ermengarde was the spark that would set the whole south aflame. Béziers had allied himself with her cause, and his Trencavel brothers would offer assistance too. Perhaps now was the time to settle an old score.

The main gate of the castle opened, and Anduze and the others rode into the bailey. Storm emerged from the keep. He carried himself straighter and walked with the confidence of a man. Anduze gazed at him in surprise and admiration. His son had changed immensely in the short time they'd been away.

"Welcome Father, Nicholas, Gilles," Storm called. He seemed genuinely pleased they had returned earlier than they'd planned. "The castle guards saw you coming from afar and preparations for a homecoming feast are well underway."

"We didn't bring any game," Anduze said. "We killed a wild bore, but left it at the abbey." He dismounted and then handed the reins to his son.

"I see, and you are dressed like a pilgrim," Storm said with a puzzled look. "What happened?"

"It's a long story. Best told with a glass of mulled wine before a warm fire."

Storm gave the reins of his father's horse to a servant. "The fire is ready, as is the mulled wine."

"Join us at the fireside." Anduze motioned to Nicholas and Gilles. "The tale is yours also."

Anduze led the way to the benches, strewn with pillows, before the blazing hearth in the great hall. He eased into his favorite chair and pulled off his boots, stretching his feet toward the fire. The others found seats, and a servant brought them cups of steaming mulled wine. He told his son about their meeting with Viscountess Ermengarde and their subsequent adventures evading Toulouse. Nicholas and Gilles chimed in with details from time to time. Anduze concluded, "I heard rumors from Abbot Stephen that Toulouse is on his way to Béziers now."

Storm's eyes were bright. "And you've come home to gather your knights and return to Béziers. This time, I will not be left behind."

Anduze laughed. "Not so fast, my son." It was one thing for him to risk his own life, and he would do so willingly, but he didn't want to risk the lives of his son and Nicholas' grandson. "I know you and Gilles would like nothing better than to go to war, but I must think on it."

Storm rolled his eyes, and Nicholas chuckled. Anduze determined to have a long talk with him sometime soon. If the old man would release him from the promise he'd made so long ago, he'd surely return to Béziers. But he'd think long and hard before endangering those who depended upon him.

Chapter 15

*D*RESSED IN A HEAVY WOOLEN rust-colored mantle loaned to her by Saure, Ermengarde left the palace courtyard that was covered that morning with a thick layer of hoarfrost. Missee was better, and Ermengarde had borrowed money from Saure for a *Te Deum* to be sung in the cathedral after matins.

In the cathedral, she thanked God for Missee's life, even though she was still weak and clearly not strong enough to travel. At this early hour, the cathedral was cold and gray, but the somber surroundings didn't distract from the fact that her worst fears hadn't been realized. Missee was recovering. Ermengarde rejoiced at the sonorous voices of the cathedral canons as they intoned the familiar Latin hymn of praise to the Almighty. Long after the *Te Deum* ended, the words *we praise you Lord* echoed in her ears.

THE VISCOUNT'S DAUGHTER

Leaving the church, she walked about in the chilly air to assess the city's readiness for attack. For days, knights, their squires, and men-at-arms had been arriving at the palace. Now the courtyard was filled with men. A quintain had been set up and knights practiced jousting with their lances. Men-at-arms readied their arrows and sharpened their blades, while squires removed rust from the knights' mail and applied grease to leather grown stiff from lack of use.

Ermengarde had heard the unceasing clang of the blacksmith while in the sickroom. Now she followed the banging of his hammer until she found his workshop and watched as he repaired a helmet. A heap of other equipment needing repairs lay on his workbench.

The city gates were still open, and handcarts and wains continued to come into the city heavily laden with foodstuffs. The smell of fresh-cut timber, which carpenters were using to construct temporary parapets along parts of the city walls, permeated the air. In other places, masons were shoring up the walls with wet mortar. Everywhere, city dwellers began their day as usual. Yet an uneasy calm had settled over Béziers. Shops opened, but few shoppers were about. She guessed everyone was waiting for this situation, her fate, to be decided. Few people looked directly at her. They clearly knew who she was, but apparently didn't know whether to offer her support or curse her.

Her joy over Missee's recovery dimmed in the face of the preparations for war. Ermengarde hugged herself, thinking that if the city fell, she'd probably again be brutally raped either by

Toulouse or his men. She touched her eating knife. It was sharp, but small. She might be able to kill herself with it although she wouldn't have the heart to kill Missee, even to save her from rape. Her pulse quickened. If only they could flee the city. Yet her sister still wasn't strong enough to go anywhere.

Ermengarde took a deep breath to calm herself. Perhaps she could aid in the defense of city. She'd speak to Béziers about it. For now though, all she could do was pray. In the last days, she had begun to understand why people prayed. They prayed because there was nothing else for them to do. Prayer came from powerlessness. She implored Saint Nazaire, whose relics gave the city's cathedral its name, to deliver the city, and save them from danger.

Near the imposing, gray-stone Church of Saint James, she caught sight of a slender, black-robed monk. She blinked a few times before realizing it wasn't Damian. If he thought of her at all, he surely would disapprove of her deserting her husband. She threw back her shoulders. Whatever he thought of her didn't matter. What the citizens of Béziers thought didn't matter. From the moment she'd left Toulouse, she had gone against everything that was expected of a woman.

At that moment, the yelling began. Ermengarde flattened herself against a wall with a feeling of dread and flagged down a young squire rushing past. "What's going on?"

"The viscount's lookouts have spotted Toulouse's army drawing near the city." The young man hastened off in the direction of the palace.

THE VISCOUNT'S DAUGHTER

Hurrying to the ramparts and the nearest arrow loophole, Ermengarde looked in the direction of Toulouse. Her throat tightened at the sight of the approaching army. She had been expecting this, but the knowledge Toulouse was actually nearing Béziers made the world spin dizzily. She leaned against the cold stone of the rampart to steady herself. But she was also angry. Surely Viscount Raymond had known her enemy was close, and he hadn't shared that information with her.

Ermengarde found him at table with several of his knights. To her surprise, Anduze was there too, wearing mail and over it, a surcoat prominently displaying his family's badge, three gold stars on a field of green. His battledress made him look much larger, more formidable. Her steps faltered, and a smile rose unbidden to her lips. He met her gaze and slightly inclined his head in acknowledgment. He hadn't deserted her.

"Lady Ermengarde." Béziers showed her to the bench next to Anduze. Her gown brushed his thigh, and his nearness comforted her. Béziers poured a cup of wine and placed it before her. "As you have no doubt heard, Toulouse will arrive here soon with a sizeable army."

She opened her mouth to voice her displeasure at not being kept informed. But Béziers cut her off. "He has sent a message ahead, or should I say an ultimatum? He has agreed to spare the city if we turn you over to him. He has given me until nightfall to reply."

She willed her voice not to quaver. "And how will you answer him?"

Béziers leaned back in his chair. "I haven't yet replied. But be assured, my lady, I intend to inform him that you are my guest for as long as you like."

It was not the time to mention her distress at not being informed of the nearness of the army. She shot him a grateful look. "You are very kind, Béziers."

"I'll delay sending my reply until the last possible minute. But I fear Toulouse will not be put off. He knows time is on our side. Time will gain you allies and him enemies. The coming winter will be our ally also. The harvest was good this year, and the granaries and storerooms are full. I've seen ample firewood has been brought into the city. We should be able to withstand months of siege."

"I need all the allies I can get." Ermengarde turned to Anduze. "I am glad you have come to our aid, Anduze."

He gave her a bemused look, as if he was going to say something smart about her promise to reward him. Instead he spoke to the group. "I have brought all the knights I could raise on short notice, including my son, Storm." He indicated the handsome young man on his right.

Ermengarde didn't know if it was appropriate for her to speak, but she was determined to be a part of the things affecting her. She addressed Béziers. "Has there been any word from Minerve and the letters you sent on my behalf?"

"In fact, there has been a message for you. In the press of preparations for the siege, I'd forgotten it." He snapped his fingers to call a servant. "Have my scribe bring Lady Ermengarde the letter that arrived for her yesterday." He scowled. "I've not yet heard back from the letters I sent. My lady, these things take time."

"Thankfully, it didn't take you long, my lord, to come to my aid."

Béziers' manner seemed to soften. "A good answer, my lady. Let's hope others are of the same mind. In the meantime, I've ordered the city gates closed and called out the city militia."

A gaunt-faced monk came into the great hall and gave Béziers a letter. Without more than a glance at it, he handed to Ermengarde.

She broke the wax seal, unrolled the parchment, and read the brief letter.

> *Lady Ermengarde,*
>
> *I was happy to learn you are safe in Béziers. William, Viscount of Montpellier, as I suggested to you, is still smarting from the aid Toulouse gave to his town consulate when they rebelled against him. He has enthusiastically agreed to support your cause. I return to Minerve to summon my knights.*
>
> *Peter, Viscount of Minerve*

She passed the letter to Béziers, who read it quickly. "Minerve doesn't say when we'll receive the promised support."

"As you have said, these things take time." Ermengarde looked anxiously at Béziers. "I'm sorry to bring you to this, this impasse. What can I do to help in the coming battle?"

He leaned back in his chair and steepled his hands. "We are not at an impasse, not yet, and if you want to be involved, I'm quite sure Saure will need help caring for the wounded." He gave her a thin smile. "But if you will excuse us, many details for our defense need our attention. Also, there is a procession planned, and I must attend it. The holy relics of Saint Nazaire will be paraded through the streets, seeking the aid of the saint in our travail."

She was being dismissed again. It was frustrating, but she didn't want to interfere. "Of course." She stood, but before leaving, she turned again to Anduze. "Thank you for your support."

A hint of a smile passed over his face. "You do me a disservice, Ermengarde, if you think I would forget our agreement."

She had doubted his intentions. But she would not admit it. "Why, sir, I am only glad to see a friend in these dire times."

His eyes crinkled around the corners. She hurried off, her thoughts in disarray. She obviously still amused him. Yet before she was out of the great hall, she had to admit that as much as his insouciance maddened her, she was very glad he was back.

In her chamber, she tiptoed past the closed bed curtains. She went directly to a window and opened the shutters. A cold wind whistled into the room. Straining her eyes, she tried to make out what was going on. In the distance, Toulouse's army was setting up a village of tents just out of range of the archers on the battlements. The sounds of sawing and hammering suggested the army was already busy assembling siege engines and assault towers. Anger blazed in her like a fire out of control.

"Hellfire and damnation," she hissed, making a fist.

"Ermengarde?" Missee pushed back one of the bed curtains. "What's the matter? You look like you're ready to fight someone."

Taking a deep breath, Ermengarde unclenched her fist, closed the shutters, and went to sit beside her sister. She tried to speak calmly. "I'm sorry you heard me swearing, but what we have been dreading has happened. Toulouse is preparing to lay siege to the city. I was not told he was so near and my offer to help was rebuffed."

Missee's face became frighteningly pale. Ermengarde wanted to say something to reassure her, but she couldn't find the words.

* * *

Anduze wandered the great hall, wending his way among the dozens of knights and their men bedded down on the floor, trying to get what rest they could. The rush floor was cleaner than most, due to the careful supervision of Lady Saure, but nonetheless, the room was crowded and uncomfortable. He had refused the offer of one the chambers, preferring to stay with his men, but now as the darkness deepened, he regretted his decision. Storm and Gilles and the younger men were in the city, drinking and visiting the whores. Anduze located Nicholas watching a dice game, made his way there, and sat beside him.

"Why didn't you visit the town's taverns with the others?" Nicholas asked.

"I'm sure Storm and Gilles will have a better time without me watching their every move."

Nicholas laughed. "That's a certainty."

"I've been feeling like a mother hen lately."

"Storm and Gilles can take care of themselves."

Anduze sighed. "It's not them I'm worried about."

Nicholas raised an eyebrow. "Can it be that you're concerned about Lady Ermengarde?"

"And you think my worry is misplaced?"

"Not at all. She's headstrong, courageous. God only knows what she might get up to. And for all your talk about returning to Béziers to fight Toulouse, I'm guessing it's she who's really behind our expedition here."

Anduze exhaled and shook his head. "You know me very well, Nicholas. But I ask you what kind of a man would I be if my courage didn't match hers?"

"She's inspiring, I'll give you that. She has even inspired me, old as I am. And I fully understand being a mother hen. I felt that way about you when you were young and foolish. I feel that way now about Storm and Gilles. I couldn't stay at Sandeyren any more than you could."

"I'm not sure if I'll be able to protect her. I'm not sure why I feel I want to protect her."

THE VISCOUNT'S DAUGHTER

* * *

Three days passed and Toulouse still hadn't attacked. When Ermengarde could do so without alarming Missee, she watched the continued preparations for war from their high windows. The city militia now manned the battlements twenty-four hours a day while citizens collected rubble and dismembered derelict buildings to strengthen the walls. In the great hall, the knights checked and rechecked their equipment and donned their mail. The mood in the palace was as taut as a strung bow.

Early on the fourth morning, a loud crash awakened Ermengarde. She jumped out of bed and tore open the shutters. Under the cover of darkness two enormous siege engines had been brought within range of the city walls. She gaped at the machines. She had never seen trebuchets as potentially destructive as these before. She watched in horror as a massive boulder arced from one of them and hit somewhere nearby with a loud bang and crumbling of stone.

Toulouse's archers stepped from behind a moveable barricade and sent a volley of flaming arrows into the city. She stiffened and raced to another window in time to see several arrows lodge in the wooden houses huddled together along the narrow streets. They erupted in flames. She gasped and forced herself away from the window. "They're setting the town on fire!"

"Ermengarde!" Missee called out in alarm.

She hurried to her sister's side. Missee's small frame shook, and she had covered her ears with her hands.

Ermengarde sat on the bed and held her sister close. That was all she could do. Missee was traumatized, and the city was under siege. This was her fault. Lives would be lost, and she would have much to answer for. But what else could she do besides help with the wounded? Her fevered brain refused to come up with a plan.

Gradually Missee's shaking ceased. "I'm sorry I'm such a baby. I'm going to be brave, brave like you." She pulled away from Ermengarde and with a decided effort seemed to compose herself.

"You've given me an idea." Ermengarde weighed several courses of action. "I must be brave, set an example. If people are fighting and dying for me, the least I can do is show myself."

"You don't mean go outside? Oh, Ermengarde, you mustn't. It's too dangerous."

Ermengarde put on the red gown Saure had lent her. If she was to show herself, she must wear something bright.

Missee shook her head. "I don't understand. What are you going to do?"

"I'm going to the city wall. I'm the cause of all this trouble and I want people to see I'm not afraid, that I'm worth fighting for."

Missee struggled to sit up. Finding she was too weak to do so, she put her head back on the pillow with a defeated sigh. "Please don't leave me. You are very brave. You've already proven that by running away from Toulouse. Do you really need to risk your life?"

Ermengarde returned to Missee's bedside. "You can help me by being brave, too. The battle between Toulouse and Béziers and the other nobles of the area has been festering for a long time. My rebellion provides a convenient excuse for the nobles to break with Toulouse. Yet if I am the immediate cause of war, perhaps my presence will strengthen the resolve of the city's defenders."

"Oh, Ermengarde, where will all this end?"

"Hopefully, it will end with us in Narbonne. I'll be back soon." She gave her sister a long hug.

Ermengarde left the room without looking back. She scurried down the stairs and into the courtyard, where she barely avoided being knocked down by servants running to and fro with buckets of water from the well. No one paid her any attention as she found her way out of the main palace gate.

In the street, a militiaman shouted orders at men beating at a burning building with heavy wet cloths. Smoke filled the air, obscuring the morning sun. Ermengarde coughed and backed away from the crackle and heat of the fire. A young woman leading a cow by a rope bumped into her, knocking her aside. Shaken, she recovered in time to get out of the way of soldiers running toward the city walls. Bells tolled ominously somewhere nearby, and a woman screamed at her as she ran by. "Go to the church for shelter!"

Another stone from a trebuchet found its mark. A portion of the city wall near Ermengarde collapsed with a deafening roar. Flying rubble stung as it hit her leg. A cloud of choking dust rose from the devastated wall, and attackers swarmed through the breach. Toulouse's men were close enough for her to see their faces. Then from far above, city defenders spilled cauldrons of hot water and huge stones on them. Men screamed in pain, fell, and writhed about on the ground. She gasped and covered her mouth, unable to take her eyes from the attackers.

Hearing the sound of running feet, she moved out of the way as a squad of city bowmen arrived at the breach. They stopped just feet away and aimed; with a whoosh, a cascade of arrows stemmed the onslaught. More men fell, screaming. Ermengarde cowered in the doorway of a small stone church, relieved to see Toulouse's men fall back.

Knights, the city militia, and townspeople rushed to close the breach with rubble and anything that came to hand. To their left, a stairway led to one of the defensive towers. She elbowed her way through the melee and began to climb the steps. Her legs quivered and threatened to buckle under her. She stepped over a dead man with an arrow through one eye. Bile rose in her throat, and she swallowed hard to keep from retching.

Reaching the top of the rampart, she crouched beside the tower. The battle raged around her. Men inside the tower fired arrows down at a group of Toulouse's men sheltering behind a moveable wooden barricade. She wiped her eyes, still smarting from the smoke that billowed from the city below. The morning sun glinted off wave after wave of mail, helmets, and shields. Toulouse still had many men in reserve, arrayed behind the siege engines. In the distance, other soldiers pulled a massive battering ram toward the main gate of the city. Not far from where she cowered, his knights had thrown up a ladder along one stretch of the city wall.

She glanced back at the turmoil in the city, ablaze with several fires. She should have stayed with Missee or gone to the great hall to help Saure with the wounded. How had she thought that anything she might do in this maelstrom would make a difference?

Ermengarde shivered. If the city defenses didn't hold, tonight would find her once more in Toulouse's hands, facing his anger. She raised her head and, from somewhere deep inside, strength coursed through her. *I am Ermengarde, Viscountess of Narbonne, heiress to a proud tradition. My ancestors fought with Charlemagne and were immortalized in heroic chansons. I've escaped a hideous husband. I cannot fail my people or myself now. I am Ermengarde, Viscountess of Narbonne.*

The curtain wall came to just above her waist and offered little protection from the arrows flying in every direction. She ignored them and stepped from the shelter of the tower. *I am Ermengarde.* Taking a deep breath, she walked along the curtain wall, head held high, Saure's red gown bright in the rising sun.

In a heartbeat, a cry went up from the defenders. "Look! There on the walls!" They roared in support, and Ermengarde sensed they renewed their efforts.

Toulouse's archers saw her, too. They took aim, probably awaiting the count's command before releasing their arrows. She stiffened, her pulse racing as she imagined her husband weighing the odds. Was she better off to him dead, or would her death ignite the whole region in war?

Though the roar of combat continued, time seemed to stop. She should seek shelter, but she couldn't move. It was as if her legs had turned to lead. Heavy steps sounded behind her. One of Toulouse's men, surely he had spies inside Béziers, was about to capture her. Before she could turn to see who it was, arms sheathed in mail and leather pulled her down behind the rampart wall.

Panicked, she struggled to free herself, but she was no match for her assailant.

* * *

Toulouse pulled his fur-lined mantle closer about him. "You don't seem to mind the cold at all, Ranulf," he said to the Templar whom he had called into his tent.

"I much prefer the heat of Outremer."

Toulouse reached out his hands to warm them before the small brazier, the only heat in his pavilion. "I want to end this siege. My spies report relief armies are already assembling. Each day increases the probability they will take the field and come to the aid of Béziers."

"You can always try to parley."

"Exactly my thoughts. There's a chance Béziers is tired of the siege and will want to end it. I don't think he was prepared for Avenger and Ballbreaker. The trebuchets have done their work well. Have you noted the destruction to the city walls?"

"If we keep it up the walls can't hold for long. Do you suppose Béziers is putting pressure on Lady Ermengarde to come to an agreement?"

"He could and should. This is ridiculous. He must know we are near to taking the city."

"Convincing Lady Ermengarde is the key. If you can come to terms with her, you may end this war before it gets any bigger."

Toulouse threw up his hands in despair. "Believe me, I've tried several times to come to terms with that woman."

"Can you try one last time? It would be worth it to prevent further loss of life and keep her rebellion from getting totally out of hand."

Toulouse took a deep breath. "I'll try to arrange a parley. But if that fails, I swear to you the city will fall the same day."

Chapter 16

STOP IT, ERMENGARDE. YOU'LL GET us both killed."
She recognized the familiar deep voice of Anduze and
relaxed, inhaling his smell of greased leather and oiled
mail. His hold on her produced an unfamiliar, not unpleasant
sensation. It was as if he held her in a lover's embrace,
passionate yet caring.

"Stay down." He let go.

She turned to him and was surprised to see how angry he
looked.

Crouching above her, he took her hand and led her toward
the safety of the tower.

"You are determined to interfere where your help is not
needed," he hissed. "The game that Béziers is playing now is a
waiting game. Your appearance could have inspired an all-out
charge of Toulouse's men, the last thing we need at the
moment."

She didn't like being chastised and couldn't help feeling proud she'd dared to do something so brave. "How was I to know Béziers' plans if I am not a part of the laying of them?" she snapped.

"You know time is on our side. Come along," he said more mildly. "I'll return you to the palace. Promise me you'll not do something foolhardy like this again. Promise me you'll stay within the viscount's palace during the fighting."

She nodded.

"Say that you promise. I won't always be able to protect you."

"I promise," she said, but something in her rebelled.

They made their way down the steps through the chaos of the besieged city to the palace. Anduze's grip on her hand was steadying, protective. Thankfully, he said nothing more. Prickles of irritation at Béziers rose in her. Why hadn't he outlined his strategy to her? He was playing a game of chess with Toulouse and being cautious about each move. If she'd been party to the plan, she could have played her part better. As it was, she had only thought of rallying the citizens of Béziers, not of the effect of her actions on the attackers. She lifted her shoulders. She had a lot to learn. But learn she would, if given the chance. Even if her actions were unwise, she had been brave.

* * *

The next day was bitterly cold. Ermengarde had just finished feeding Missee chicken soup, and her sister had drifted to sleep when there was a loud knock. Ermengarde hastened to the door to shush whoever was so impolite to bang loudly on the sickroom. She stepped back in surprise. It was Anduze. She'd not seen him, except at a distance, since her impulsive heroics of the day before.

"My lady, please accompany me." His tone lacked his usual levity. "Béziers would like to speak with you."

She gave Anduze a questioning look, but he didn't respond. She quietly closed the door behind her and followed him to the great hall. A crackling fire blazed in the fireplace, but it still failed to dispel the chill and gloom of the large room. A shiver ran down her spine. Perhaps her cause was lost. Missee's life had been spared, but to what fate if they had to return to Toulouse?

Béziers sat at a table, conferring with several of his knights. He looked up as they approached. Dark circles under his eyes made his thin face look gaunt, haggard. "Lady Ermengarde," he said, "Anduze has insisted you be included in our discussions since this concerns you."

She flashed a grateful glance at Anduze. Perhaps it was her imagination, but she thought she noted the hint of a twinkle in his eyes.

One of the knights moved to make a place for her next to Béziers. Anduze found a seat at the other end of the table.

"Toulouse has asked for a parley," Béziers began, "and he insists it will be a meeting only between him and you."

Ermengarde gulped as the full import of his words came home to her. She never wanted to see Toulouse again, let alone parley with him. The memory of him looming over her with the poker flashed through her mind, and her stomach cramped. She shook her head. She didn't want to hear more.

Béziers continued. "We've been discussing the benefits and dangers of such a meeting. And we are of a mind that you should meet with him."

Her pulse began to pound in her temples at the thought they had already decided her fate. "Am I not to be consulted?"

Béziers let out a long breath. "You are here because we are consulting with you. But you need to know we are of the opinion that you should agree. The city is badly damaged, and even a brief letup in the bombardment will give us time to make needed repairs. However, we don't think you should meet with Toulouse alone. If you will agree to the meeting, we will ask that one man accompany you."

All eyes turned to her. What could Toulouse possibly say or offer that would bring this horrific siege to an end? Everyone was waiting. She had to respond, but her throbbing head and upset stomach made it hard to think. She knew she couldn't keep running. And if her participation in a parley would stop the killing, as much as she hated the thought, she had to meet with Toulouse. Sitting up straight, she addressed the assembled knights. "Yes, my lords, I'll meet him if someone accompanies me. But I have to know what such a meeting will accomplish."

"We are thinking," Béziers said, "Toulouse must have intelligence that an army is on its way to relieve the city, or he wouldn't be willing to talk. One way or another such a parley will gain us time, even if only a few hours."

Her head was still pounding, but she spoke calmly. "I know Peter of Minerve and William of Montpellier are coming to our aid with their knights. Yet, I can't imagine them fielding enough troops to lift the siege. Is there anyone else we are expecting?"

Béziers seemed impatient with her question. "My lady, I wrote to my brothers on your behalf. Nîmes and Carcassonne have agreed to support us. But, as I told you before, these things take time."

With a sigh, she turned to the matter at hand. "How will this parley be conducted?"

He stroked his clean-shaven chin. "You will meet with him and listen to him. I won't be the one who accompanies you. Whatever he offers, you must return here to confer with us. Our problems with him are greater than whatever is unsettled between you two. Again, remember that we are playing for time in the hope our allies will arrive before the city falls."

During her chess lessons, Damian had counseled her to think through her moves and not to respond emotionally. Now she struggled to quell her rising fear at the prospect of meeting with Toulouse. She had difficulty swallowing. Moments passed as she forced herself to think clearly. She glanced at the battle-weary faces of the assembled knights. Béziers trusted them all, but her gaze fell upon Anduze.

"If he will agree, I should like Anduze to come with me. He has served me well," she said.

Everyone looked at Anduze, who nodded his head. She guessed he had wanted to go with her and, for that reason, had personally summoned her to the meeting, instead of sending a page. For just a moment, he locked eyes with her. Her heart swelled. He was there for her.

"It's settled then," Béziers said, his voice betraying his weariness. "I'll send back Toulouse's messenger. We're fairly certain he'll agree to our terms for the meeting. So, my lady, it is best that you make yourself ready. We'll do everything in our power to ensure your safety."

His words signaled her dismissal. She left the hall and climbed the steep stairs to their chamber. Gradually, the pounding in her head subsided. She wanted an end to the siege and to control her own fate, but had never imagined this would entail meeting with the man she loathed more than anyone in the world. Yet she had said she would parley with Toulouse, and now she had to think about what to say to him.

By afternoon, all the arrangements for the meeting had been made. Ermengarde was determined to look strong and in control, not at all like the submissive, injured woman Toulouse had last seen. To that end, she dressed carefully in a fine worsted gown the burnished orange-rose color of bittersweet, and the complementary fur-lined amber mantle lent to her by Saure.

"You look like a lovely autumn leaf," Saure said when she came into their chamber. "And here is a headband to match your veil." She smiled as she handed Ermengarde the finely wrought gold circlet. It was as if Saure had intuited her need to look regal, powerful.

"Thank you. Strange you should mention leaves. I'm shaking inside like a leaf in a wind storm," she replied, securing her gauzy veil with the circlet.

Missee, who had been watching her dress, made a face. "Ermengarde, do you really have to meet him?"

Before she could answer, there was a knock on the door. Saure opened it.

"All is in readiness." A young page recited the words by rote as if he'd memorized them. "Béziers and Anduze await you in the courtyard. Toulouse has agreed to our terms, with one proviso. He demanded that whoever accompanied you not take part in the negotiations."

Ermengarde's throat constricted so much she found it difficult to speak. "How will that work?"

The page stuttered as if he were unsure of the answer. "If I understood correctly what was said, Anduze will remain just out of hearing."

Unsettled by this new information, she put a hand to her mouth. She didn't like the idea of a private discussion with Toulouse. But it appeared she had no choice, again.

Filled with misgivings and with hasty goodbyes to Missee and Saure, Ermengarde accompanied the page to the courtyard. Anduze was already mounted and wore his mail and, over it, his green-and-gold silk surcoat. His helmet glinted in the sun as he held the reins of her impatient bay.

Béziers stood near the mounting block and helped her onto Titan. A stab of pain shot through her loins, a reminder that no matter what happened, she wouldn't put herself at Toulouse's mercy again.

"God go with you," Béziers said, saluting them with a wave of his arm.

Anduze and Ermengarde rode out of the palace courtyard and into the city, now silent with the temporary cessation of hostilities. Titan shied nervously as if he sensed her fear. The fires had been put out, but the smell of smoke lingered. Citizens of Béziers gathered along the road and cheered as she passed. She didn't know, however, if they were applauding her earlier bravery or hoped she could bring the siege to an end. Militiamen drew the main city gate open with a loud groan, and she and Anduze passed outside. The cold wind blew through her mantle, tugging at her veil.

Anduze leaned over his destrier and whispered, his eyes alight with excitement, "Nicholas and Gilles will have their bows drawn. If Toulouse makes one move against you, he'll be dead."

She looked about, wondering where his men were hidden, but she didn't see them. Nicholas, Gilles, and Anduze, what would she do without them? She felt a rush of affection for them, but it was soon overshadowed by the precariousness of their situation. If Toulouse fell, his army would respond in kind. In moments, she and her trusted allies might all be dead.

The days were shorter now, and the cool sun was already sinking low on the horizon. Titan hadn't been exercised and was full of energy. Even though her broken arm had healed, it was still weak. It took all her strength to rein in his rambunctiousness. She sensed that in the city and Toulouse's camp, all eyes were on her. She must ride proudly. *I am Ermengarde, Viscountess of Narbonne.* She straightened her back and pulled on the reins, forcing the bay to step high.

They walked their horses toward the assembled army, stopping halfway to it. Toulouse's soldiers wore what mantles and furs they owned and, no doubt, they hated the cold wind as much as she did. Toulouse, on his big black stallion, also accompanied by one man, rode out to meet them.

Ermengarde began to tremble, and she struggled for self-control. *I am Ermengarde, Viscountess of Narbonne.* She must be strong. He, of all people, must not see her quake in fear before him. *I am Ermengarde, Viscount Aymeri's daughter.*

Anduze and the knight accompanying Toulouse edged their horses off to one side. Toulouse dismounted, and Ermengarde did the same, sliding from the bay with a jolt of pain. She strode toward him, halting before she got within arm's reach. He towered above her, and she stood taller, looking him in the eyes. His eyes, full of hate, told her he'd be happy to flay her alive. He had abused her on their wedding night, but he hadn't despised her then, as he did now.

Ermengarde, too, had changed since leaving him, and she wouldn't cower before him. She returned his hateful look with one of her own. "What do you have to say to me?" she demanded in a loud voice without even a perfunctory greeting.

"I've come to offer you terms." He seemed taken aback that she had seized the initiative. "If you return to Toulouse, you will remain countess." He paused. "And I will no longer demand payment of the marriage debt. I'll not touch you."

She smothered a sound between a nervous laugh and a gasp. "What other terms?" she managed to ask in an even voice. She longed to shout at him. *I am the Viscountess of Narbonne and that is more than enough for me. I never wanted to be Countess of Toulouse!* But she held her tongue.

"I'll end the siege. You have it in your power to resume your status, restore Béziers to my favor without punishment, and end the bloodshed."

"I'm not empowered to speak for Béziers." Ermengarde's own voice surprised her. It was cold and determined.

Toulouse scowled. "What say you for yourself to the first part of my terms?"

"I must think on what you offer," she said in the spirit of playing for time. Again, she longed to shout at him. How could he not realize she would rather die than remain his wife, even if only in name?

"You must do so quickly. If I don't receive an emissary from you and Béziers by sunset, the siege will continue."

"But, my lord, surely in such a weighty matter, you can give us until morning. Even I know you can't fight in the dark."

"No," he said, walking away and remounting his horse. "I'll wait no longer. I can and will fight in the dark. The blood of the citizens of Béziers will be on your head if you don't agree to my terms."

It was clear Toulouse planned to launch another all-out attack on the city if they refused. Ermengarde signaled to Anduze that the parley was over. He brought the bay to her. For a moment, she watched Toulouse's disappearing back. Her outward control belied the turmoil the meeting had caused.

Anduze gave her a hand up onto Titan. She sat straight in the saddle, her head held high, and with the sturdy familiarity of the bay beneath her, she recovered somewhat. Without a backward glance at the assaulting army, she galloped beside Anduze back to the city.

When they approached, the gate creaked open again. Ermengarde could feel anxious eyes on her as they made their way into the city and through the streets. A strange, unnatural quiet had settled over the city, and even the shrieks and yells of children who emerged to play whenever there was a lull in the battle were missing. She judged the city to be as taut as a newly strung drum.

At the palace, she dismounted. She leaned against Titan for moment, suddenly weak from her encounter.

Anduze gently touched her on the shoulder. "Ermengarde, are you all right? Béziers is waiting for us in the great hall."

She gave him a little smile. "Of course."

Together, they entered the great hall. Béziers greeted them with a thoughtful, questioning look. She told him the terms Toulouse had offered.

"And how do you feel, my lady, about going back to him?" Béziers asked when she finished.

The words that had been in her heart sprang to her lips. "I'd rather die."

"That is as I expected. Women don't go to such extremes to escape their husbands unless they've been ill treated." He spoke to her in a warm, consoling way, like a father to a daughter, and then turned to the gathered knights and men-at-arms. How few they were compared with the numbers of Toulouse's soldiers outside the walls.

Béziers spoke loudly. "I propose we reject the terms and continue to cast our lot with this brave woman, who will someday be our strong neighbor and ally."

The knights muttered their approval. But Ermengarde had doubts. They were outnumbered and the weakened city might not be able to withstand an all-out attack. Toulouse had said she'd be responsible for the deaths of the citizens of Béziers. Was she putting her interests above those of the decent people who had supported her?

Béziers seemed calm, as if he had never doubted the outcome of her meeting. "I don't intend to give Toulouse the courtesy of a reply. He will know of our decision when we don't send a messenger."

Servants brought wine, cheese, bread, and olives. It wasn't mealtime, but someone, probably Saure, had thought they'd be in need of sustenance. Ermengarde didn't have much appetite, but she drank a cup of wine and stayed in the great hall with the others, waiting for darkness.

The shadows deepened, and servants appeared to light the torches in the wall sconces and the candles in the chandelier.

As if the lighting of the great hall was the moment he was waiting for, Béziers ordered his knights to the walls. "Toulouse will throw everything he has at us. We must be ready."

Chapter 17

AFTER THE UNSATISFYING PARLEY, TOULOUSE summoned his leading knights to go over the battle plan. To get their attention, he rapped on the table in his pavilion. The knights grew quiet. "I'm confident we've weakened the city walls and outnumbered the city's defenders," Toulouse said. "I swear Béziers will fall this very night!"

"God is on our side! We will be victorious! The city will fall!" The knights erupted in a chorus of approval. They apparently were tired of fighting in the cold and eager to return to hearth and home for the coming winter.

Toulouse opened his purse. He poured bezants on the table. The gold coins glittered in the candlelight. "These will reward the man who brings me Raymond of Béziers, unharmed. Not only will his brothers Carcassonne and Nîmes cough up a huge reward, but his capture will ensure their loyalty to me."

A cheer arose from the knights. After they quieted, one asked, "What of the wenches?"

"You may have your will with them. Just save Lady Ermengarde for me."

"We'll sack the city!" another knight called out.

Toulouse was satisfied he had incited their greed and their lust. "Now, ready your men."

The knights left the tent in high spirits, everyone except the Templar.

"I'm glad you stayed behind, Ranulf. I heard from men I've posted strategically on the road. Minerve is on his way here with his knights and those few from Narbonne who have cast their lots in with the viscountess."

"Are you concerned, my lord? Does Minerve have enough men to lift to the siege?"

"I'd be surprised if he does. And I want his head. Can I depend on you to see to that?" Toulouse was close to making a favorite fantasy a reality. "I intend to put Ermengarde in a cage, suspended from my new tower where she can gaze all day at Minerve's severed head. That will be a lesson to anyone who thinks of rebelling against me."

The Templar's lips twitched, as if he might smile. "Whatever I can do to help, my lord."

* * *

Darkness came swiftly. With it a barrage of fiery missiles lit the city. Filled with misgivings, Ermengarde left the great hall to check on Missee. Their fate would be decided in the next several hours. Ermengarde silently prayed for strength.

Missee was sleeping with Saure by her side. A lone candle by the bed cast a flicking light on her sister's peaceful face. How she could sleep through the noise of the battle Ermengarde didn't know. She walked to a window where she could watch the progress of the siege. Saure came to stand beside her.

"I'm worried," Ermengarde whispered. "I can't stand the thought of being captured. I want to be doing something."

"You've already tried to do something with almost disastrous results." Saure's response was stern. "You can't do anything."

"If I can't do anything, it's because women have never been taught anything, except to sew, play games, have enough Latin to know a smattering of pious prayers, and be acquiescent." She had responded more sharply than she wished and continued in a milder tone. "If I ever come into my own, I assure you that will change, at least in my court."

They looked out into the night. Flaming arrows streamed over the city. "Not everyone treats women churlishly, the way Toulouse treated you."

"I have noted the easy rapport between you and Béziers."

Saure's face relaxed. "Yes, Raymond and I get on well. And there are rewards. My children have been my great joy and solace." She patted her belly. "It won't be long now."

"I'll not have children."

Saure put a consoling hand lightly on Ermengarde's uninjured arm. "But perhaps you'll be able to get an annulment from Toulouse and remarry."

"A man will never touch me again."

Saure removed her hand and sighed. "I'm sorry you've been badly treated. But you'll see. Time will heal your wounds."

"That may be the case, Saure, but until then, I'm going to have to learn to stand on my own two feet." The horrid memory of Toulouse picking her up and throwing her on the marriage bed flashed to mind.

Wood splintered with a loud crash. Missee awoke with a cry. They rushed to her side.

"You're all right," Ermengarde assured her.

"I fear the palace has been hit," Saure said, her voice tight. "I must see to my children." She hurried from the room.

Ermengarde smelled smoke, somewhere close, and heard the thunder of the siege engines. She took a deep breath and renewed her resolve to stay strong.

"I want to see what's going on." Missee struggled out of bed and made her way to the window. She shivered, and Ermengarde put an arm around her sister.

"I'm frightened," Missee said.

Ermengarde grabbed a blanket and then wrapped her sister in it. She was grateful they were together and yet worried that she'd caused more trouble for Missee than she'd be able to handle.

The flaming arrows had done their work and, in the eerie light of the fires, they watched the furious, hand-to-hand fighting on the ramparts.

"You must flee," Missee said, her voice shaking. "If Toulouse captures you, all will be lost."

A huge stone crashed against the palace directly over their heads. They backed away from the window as the stone cascaded to the ground, taking masonry with it.

Ermengarde made an effort to sound unruffled. "I've thought this through. I won't leave you."

"You've complained to me that you haven't been consulted in decisions affecting you. Well, you haven't consulted me. Your escape is our only hope. There must be a bolthole, a secret passageway out of the palace and the city. As long as Toulouse is married to you, he can't force me to marry him."

"I don't think you understand, Missee." She shook her head. "Toulouse can hold you for ransom." Her sister shivered even more. "That would bring me back to him without a fight."

Ermengarde pulled the blanket more closely about Missee before fetching the pair of the soft leather slippers Saure had given her. "Here, put these on. The floor's cold."

Missee stooped and put on the slippers. "I'm petrified of Toulouse. He might throw me in a dungeon or send me to a convent."

Ermengarde wanted to reassure Missee, but she couldn't. "He's capable of anything."

She sensed that in the weeks since their escape from Toulouse, Missee had changed. She wasn't the same innocent she had been before Ermengarde's wedding. Missee could now talk more openly about what bothered her, but her maturing was also a cause for concern. She might someday be mistreated as Ermengarde had been.

"You have told me that you want to determine your own life, to have choices. You should know by now that not all choices are easy. Is my falling into Toulouse's power worse than both of us doing so? I think not."

Missee's reasoned response surprised Ermengarde.

"Please," her sister begged. "Save yourself and once you have done that, come for me. I'm not as strong as you, but I'm learning, learning from your example. If you can be brave, I can be brave, too."

It took Ermengarde a moment before she could respond. "I won't go unless you come with me."

"I'm better, Ermengarde, but not well enough to travel. Please, please go. There must be a secret escape route. I've heard every stronghold has one. The very thought of you in Toulouse's hands would kill me, I'm sure of it."

"*Mon petite seour*, we've come this far together. I can't leave you." Ermengarde hugged Missee.

Her sister managed a wan smile and hugged Ermengarde in return.

Another barrage of flaming arrows arched into the city. A tremendous crash made them jump as a stone from a trebuchet struck somewhere nearby. One arrow landed on a thatched roof below them, and the thatch began burning furiously.

"The stables are on fire! My little mare! Your bay! Oh please, save Hebe and Titan!" Missee pleaded.

Ermengarde led a shaking Missee back to the bed. "You know how afraid I am of fire. And I promised Anduze I'd not leave the palace."

Missee burst into tears. "You must! Oh please! Just go and make sure someone is freeing the animals."

Never had her sister cried so piteously. Ermengarde was torn. She feared going near the fire and she had promised Anduze she'd not leave the palace, and yet the thought of their horses burning alive was terrible. Perhaps she could just check to see if someone was freeing the horses. She threw on her mantle. "I'll be right back."

* * *

On a slight rise, Toulouse watched the progress of the assault. His siege engines pounded away at the city, and he was poised for the crucial moment he would lead his knights into the fray. The Templar was at his side.

Toulouse had taken part in many sieges as both besieger and besieged, and he had been watching the telltale signs of Béziers' weakening. The stressed walls crumbled more frequently, and the citizens were less adept at hastily repairing them. The number of defenders on the ramparts was lessening.

The city couldn't withstand the impetus of his upcoming attack.

A well-aimed missile from Ballbreaker shattered a weakened portion of the wall. The defenders scrambled to repair it, but their numbers were few. Now was the time. Toulouse raised his hand to alert his knights. He took a deep breath, lowered his arm, and spurred his destrier forward.

At the same moment, horsemen approached on Toulouse's flank. Minerve and his knights! Toulouse signaled his force to confront them, annoyed, as if being pestered by a bothersome gnat.

Minerve's thin force broke with a shattering of lances. Casting aside his lance, Toulouse drew his sword, landing a blow on the nearest horsemen's shield. The knight's horse shied, and the man's right side was momentarily exposed. Toulouse's sword found the place, and the man crumpled, falling from his horse. The fighting was furious. Minerve's knights were outnumbered. It was only a matter of time before they were annihilated.

Looking around, Toulouse spotted Minerve and fought his way in that direction. Ranulf already engaged him. Toulouse felt his face arrange itself into a grimace-like grin. Minerve's decapitation would be a warning to traitors. Minerve, his tunic bloodstained, fell from his horse. Toulouse closed in for the kill.

Before he could reach Minerve, above the din of battle, Toulouse heard the groaning of the city's great drawbridge as it lowered. He turned in time to see a contingent of horsemen gallop from the city and the drawbridge rise. A half-laugh rose in Toulouse's throat. Béziers still had a few tricks up his sleeve. He was obviously deploying a last effort to save the city. Toulouse spurred his stallion to face this new threat.

This was the kind of fighting he excelled at. With a signal to his men, he turned the bulk of his force to meet the attack from the city. Their lances were already shattered, but they raised their shields and prepared to meet the lances of the attackers.

* * *

Ermengarde's breath came in short gasps as she hurried through the dark hallway of the palace and found her way down the stairs. Knights, men-at-arms, and servants ran frantically into the great hall, carrying the wounded, and reemerged moments later to return to the fray. She grabbed the tunic of one of the servants as he rushed past, only to have him escape her grasp.

Her heart beating fast, she glanced into the great hall, hoping to find someone she could collar to free the horses. Wounded lay on the trestle tables, and Saure, the other women of the palace, and the servants were busily doing what they could for them. Everyone was consumed with caring for the fallen. She'd have to look elsewhere. With uncertain steps, she went out into the courtyard.

The burning stables made the palace courtyard almost as bright as day. An old man led two blindfolded horses from the conflagration. Ermengarde covered her ears so she couldn't hear the screams of frightened horses and the thudding of their hooves as they kicked against their stalls. With burning eyes, she waited for the man to come back for the other horses, but he didn't return.

What should she do? She had told Missee she'd be right back, but no one was freeing the horses. She stared at the burning thatch of the stables, willing herself to move toward it. She had just started across the courtyard when the bombardment ceased. In the eerie silence that followed, she guessed a more furious attack was about to begin. A series of blood-chilling yells broke the silence, and one of Toulouse's men appeared where the palace wall abutted the city ramparts. Brandishing his sword, he stormed down the stairs, followed by a swarm of soldiers. Béziers' men rushed forward to drive back the attackers, and a furious battle began in the courtyard.

Men fought and fell only ells from Ermengarde, blocking her return to the safety of the palace. In the flickering light, one of the attackers spotted her and moved purposely in her direction.

She fled, running in the direction of the burning stables. Smoke poured out of the doorway. Caught between her fear of fire and her pursuer, she jerked to a stop. She pulled her eating knife from its sheath with a shaking hand and turned to face Toulouse's soldier. Her stomach lurched as he lunged at her with his raised sword. A flash of recognition passed over his face. He must have seen her somewhere and knew she was Lady Ermengarde. He hesitated.

His hesitation was just long enough for her to thrust her knife into his throat. Blood squirted. He fell backwards, his face contorted. He choked and grabbed at his neck.

Ermengarde couldn't move. She just stood there, looking in shock at her bloodied knife. What had she done? She let go of the knife and then fell to her knees, retching repeatedly, as if her whole insides were being expelled.

A contingent of militia from the city rushed into the palace courtyard and beat back Toulouse's men. The sounds of battle lessened, and she again became conscious of the screaming of the horses in the barn. The horses. She must save the horses. She struggled to her feet and looked around. A frightened servant, no more than a boy, ran by. She grabbed his arm.

"Come with me," she ordered, her voice coming out in a croak.

She paused for a moment, paralyzed by memories of her painful burns. She gathered her flagging resolve. *I am Ermengarde, Viscountess of Narbonne. Holy Virgin, protect me!* She took a deep breath and plunged into the burning building. The boy followed her through the stable door. A fiery timber cascaded to the floor, and Ermengarde jump backwards. She had descended into the furthermost reaches of hell. Smoke filled her lungs, and it was difficult to see. Yet the light from the burning thatch was enough for her to make her way to Missee's Hebe. The little horse's eyes were wild, and she thrashed about, trying to escape. Speaking quietly in a voice hoarse from the smoke, Ermengarde patted Hebe reassuringly. The mare calmed a little.

"Ride her out," Ermengarde ordered the boy.

He swung up onto Hebe's back, seemingly glad to be away. Ermengarde coughed, gasping for breath. The bay would be more trouble. She found Titan's stall. The gelding bucked and kicked so furiously that any moment the door of his stall might splinter. Standing out of the way, she forced open the heavy latch. The door swung open. Titan bolted out and, as she had hoped, followed the mare toward the door.

Flames surrounded Ermengarde. Sparks landed on her gown, and she swept them off. Covering her mouth and nose with one hand, she ran through burning hay to the next horse and opened the latch to the stall. The horse almost knocked her down in his frantic desire to escape. She struggled toward the stable door, freeing other horses along the way. A timber collapsed behind her with a loud swoosh. She reeled from the blast of heat and, as if directed by a mighty hand, stumbled into the courtyard.

Coughing and gasping for breath, she sank to her knees. She whispered a prayer of thanksgiving. She'd saved the horses and not been burned. Now she must get back to Missee. The thought of her sister, and how worried she must be, gave Ermengarde the strength to stand and head in the direction of the palace.

Out of nowhere, a man lunged at her. She whirled and raced through the open palace gate into the city. A moving mass of townspeople, searching for safety, careened through the narrow streets as if they were possessed. She was thrown against a woman carrying a wailing baby. The woman pushed her aside, and Ermengarde fell. She fought her way to her feet to avoid being trampled and surged forward with the others. She had caused all this. She would surely burn in hell. Perhaps she had already arrived there.

Everywhere was chaos.

The city was going to fall.

All was lost.

Above the din came shouts and the thunder of many horses' hooves. She wasn't sure what was happening. She tried to extract herself from the mob, but found she couldn't do so. The people moved forward as one body with one mind and one goal. They wanted to live.

Ermengarde staggered with the townspeople this way and that until she was cast onto the side of the street. She lost her footing and fell into heap, too exhausted to hide or flee. After a moment, she tried to stand. The earth spun wildly. The last thing she remembered was her head hitting the ground.

* * *

Fighting was near the palace now. The fury of the attack breached the city wall yet again, and the city's defenders rushed to repair the damage. Anduze held back his men, guessing that when everyone was distracted with repairing the walls, Toulouse's men would set up scaling ladders. He positioned Nicholas, Gilles, Storm, and his other men along a thinly defended section of the ramparts. A hand-to-hand fight was coming. The burning buildings lit the city with a hellish glow, and the yells of the advancing army could be heard over the crash of the great stones from the trebuchets.

Toulouse's knights came over the wall, and Anduze drew his sword. One of them lunged at him. Grasping his heavy sword with both hands, he swung at his attacker. The man fell backward into the courtyard with a scream. All around his men were fighting. Another soldier came at him. Their swords clanged as Anduze parried the man's blow. He struck his opponent's shield with such force it shattered. His next blow took off the man's hand. The man crumpled, grasping the bleeding stump. Without pausing, Anduze turned to face a man-at-arms swinging a broad ax. Anduze stepped aside in time to avoid a powerful blow that would have split his helmet and his skull. Panting, Storm raced to his aid and dispatched the man from behind. Above the sounds of the fighting on the ramparts, Anduze heard the distant thudding of a great number of warhorses followed by the clash of arms below the city walls. Help had arrived.

Freed for a moment, Anduze stepped back to take stock of the situation. Toulouse's men were retreating. Gilles and Storm fought side by side, their long training together making them a formidable fighting force. But where was Nicholas?

With eyes burning from the smoke, Anduze searched the place where he had last seen the old man. He was not in sight. Alarmed, he rushed in that direction. One of Toulouse's soldiers blocked his path, and Anduze barreled into him. The man lost his balance and fell from the rampart. Anduze stopped abruptly, seeing what he feared. Before him, Nicholas lay in a heap where he had fallen, blood oozing from his stomach.

* * *

Toulouse and his knights engaged Béziers' force that had emerged from the city. The battle was going well. A knight honed in on Toulouse, and he delivered the man a deadly blow to the head, splitting his helmet and sending him crashing from his mount. Toulouse confronted the next assailant, parrying a sword thrust with his own bloodied sword. Trusting his great strength, he landed a blow on the man's sword with so much force the knight swerved in his saddle. Before he could right himself Toulouse's sword found his exposed belly and ran him through.

Toulouse glanced about in time to see Ranulf fighting nearby. The Templar unhorsed a knight with a two-handed swipe of his sword and then Toulouse trampled the downed man with his horse. Everywhere his knights, inspired by thoughts of pillage and rape, overpowered Béziers' men, pushing them back toward the city walls. The city soon would be theirs.

Above the roar of the battle, Toulouse heard the thunder of many hooves. He turned his horse in the direction of the sound. An enormous force bore down on them. The fires in the burning city cast a reddish glow over the field and in the half light Toulouse made out the Virgin in Majesty, the blazon of Montpellier, flying from the end of a lance and alongside it another, probably that of Carcassonne. Hell and damnation! Toulouse's knights were outnumbered and would soon be surrounded.

Victory had been within his grasp, but now the worst had happened. The petty, independent nobles in the area had rallied to Ermengarde's cause. Damn them to hell! He'd see them all drawn and quartered! He was outnumbered, and if he were to save his knights, he'd have to flee like a dog with its tail between his legs. He had to save his men to fight another day.

He swerved to the south where the way was open. He grabbed his standard from his standard bearer. His men would know they must follow him. He spurred his stallion away from the attacking army. Toulouse righted himself in the saddle. It was humiliating enough to leave behind his pavilion, his stores, and more importantly his two prized trebuchets without bowing his head. *This isn't the end. I'll destroy them all! With God as my witness, I'll make the turbulent nobles of the south grovel. Someday I'll suspend Ermengarde from a cage for all to see the fate of those who rebel against me.*

* * *

Drawing off his gauntlets, Anduze dropped to one knee and felt for Nicholas' pulse. His fingers found a weak throb. Nicholas was alive. Buoyed by this knowledge, Anduze scooped up the old man. His inert form was heavy, but Anduze scarcely noticed the weight. Turning his back on the waning battle, he found the stairs leading down from the ramparts. He must get Nicholas to a place of safety.

Anduze forced his way through the defenders and citizens repairing yet another breach in the city wall. Men with buckets tried to quench the fires raging through the wooden buildings on the narrow streets. He almost tripped on a dead man. A frenzied woman, her dress on fire, ran past him. In the half-light he made out the bulk of the Cathedral of Saint Nazaire. He would go there.

Winding his way throughout the congested streets, Anduze reached the cathedral and entered the darkened building where a few candles flickered near the altar. Other wounded lay in the big nave. He carried Nicholas to the front of the church and put him on the stone floor. Anduze stripped off his surcoat to staunch the blood, knowing as he did so that the wound was a fatal one.

Nicholas' eyes fluttered open.

"I'm sorry," Anduze said, kneeling beside his friend. "'Tis my fault. We never should have gotten involved with the viscountess."

Nicholas shook his head. "No, 'twas meant to be." His voice was weak, and he already seemed far away. "It is enough. You and I have finally fought Toulouse."

"But he hasn't been vanquished."

"It's not a perfect world. I'll leave that to you."

Anduze breathed a deep sigh of relief. Their reckoning with Toulouse was as great a source of satisfaction to Nicholas as it was to him. Yet he couldn't bear the thought that his old friend was dying. "Is there something I can do for you?" he asked, his voice breaking.

"Yes." Nicholas' voice was labored and raspy. "Look after Gilles and don't be too hard on Storm. And I want to lie beside my women. Will you see to that?"

"Of course." Anduze thought sadly of Nicholas' wife, Sabina, and his daughter Helena, who lay side by side in the churchyard at Tornac. "Is there anything else?"

"Water."

Anduze looked around. An old nun with a cup and pail was passing among the wounded. He went to her and borrowed her cup. He spotted a holy water font near a side door of the cathedral. There, he filled the cup. Returning to Nicholas, he held him up and put the cup to his lips. "Holy water," he said, "for the best of men."

A weak smile came to Nicholas' lips. "You are the one, Anduze. How do you think of such things?"

Chapter 18

*I*T WAS BEGINNING TO GET light when Ermengarde returned to consciousness. The sounds of battle had disappeared, and a young soldier with a blond beard knelt beside where she lay. She stared at him, her eyes still blurred from the smoke, straining to identify him. Was he one of Béziers' men or one of Toulouse's? He didn't appear to wear insignias of either. A wave of weakness washed through her.

"What has happened? Who are you?" she murmured.

The soldier leaned back on his heels. "The battle's over. I'm with Carcassonne. We arrived in time to lift the siege."

"And Toulouse?" she asked, hardly believing her ears.

"He escaped, but his forces are badly beaten."

It took her a moment to fully take in what the soldier said. Toulouse had fled. Relief at their deliverance coursed through her, and she struggled to sit up.

The young man eyed her curiously. "Are you Lady Ermengarde?"

"Yes," she said without hesitation. "I am Ermengarde, Viscountess of Narbonne."

The soldier looked relieved. "Everyone is looking for you. I'll help you up."

He held out a hand. She got unsteadily to her feet, grateful for his firm grasp on her arm.

They made their way slowly through the devastated streets. Fires still burned throughout the city and soldiers and citizens rushed about dousing the flames with buckets of well water. Bodies lay scattered everywhere. She tried not to look at them. She had caused all this destruction, and even if it was over for today, her struggles with Toulouse weren't over for good.

A wounded man lying in the street stretched out a hand and moaned as they passed. She instinctively paused, but her rescuer steered her in the direction of the palace. "We can't stop here," he said. "I'll send someone to help him. It's important our leaders know you are unharmed."

They entered the palace, and Béziers rushed to her. "Thank heaven, you've been found!" He looked her over. "And it appears without serious injury. Whatever possessed you to leave the safety of the palace?"

"The horses," Ermengarde mumbled. "I must tell Missee that I'm all right."

"Yes, of course," Béziers said. "But first you must see Minerve. He's badly injured, and he's been asking for you."

She felt her face fall. "I'm so sorry." She glanced around the great hall. Wounded men lay on trestle tables and on the floor. Servants rushed hither and yon carrying water and hot food to those able to eat and drink. It was like one of the depictions of hell from church frescos. Only the suffering, the horrors were not imagined, but real. "Where's Saure? I don't see her."

A smile lit Béziers' haggard face. "She's in the great chamber, delivered of our healthy son, named in honor of Roger, my brother whose army lifted the siege. She is doing fine. She'll be happy to know you are safe."

"Blessed be God and all his saints!" Ermengarde closed her eyes for a moment in gratitude for Saure's wellbeing and that of the babe.

"Are you all right?" Béziers asked.

Ermengarde smiled. "Yes. Please take me to Minerve."

She followed Béziers past the wounded to a pallet in an alcove where Minerve lay, covered with a blanket. He opened his eyes as they approached and reached out his hand to her. As he did, the blanket slipped from his shoulders, revealing his chest, wrapped in a bloodstained compress.

"I'll leave you two to talk alone," Béziers said. "When you have seen your sister, I'd like to introduce you to our deliverers."

"*Certes*," Ermengarde said. She knelt beside Minerve and took his outstretched hand. "How can I ever thank you?"

"You might rather curse me."

She shook her head. "It's because of your efforts that I have allies and the siege was lifted."

307

"A little late."

She frowned. "I don't understand."

"I may not live to see another day, and I've a need to clear my conscience." He took a deep breath, winced with pain, and then continued. "At Fraga, your father's last wish was that I prevent you falling into Toulouse's hands. I swore if I survived, I'd honor his request."

Ermengarde felt a rush of love for her father. It was as if he were reaching out to her from the distant past. She swallowed before thinking of a reply. "But you were severely wounded."

Minerve's eyes were sad. He spoke slowly, as if it were taking him a great effort to find the words. "Yes, and when I returned from the crusade, you and your sister were already in Toulouse, and I was in no position to do anything about it. And my failure to act on your behalf made me feel worthless. I know Toulouse thought me so. When he asked me to encourage you to marry him, I thought it was for the best. I didn't realize you were so like your father, so strong, so brave, so defiant."

She thought for a moment. "I didn't trust your advice. I'm just glad that in spite of that I trusted you."

"Can you ever forgive me?"

She felt her face soften. She would never forget what Toulouse had done to her, but Minerve's confession and what he had undertaken on her behalf moved her. It was a moment before she could formulate her response.

"The girl you knew in Toulouse probably couldn't or wouldn't. But I've learned a lot since then. I once saw things in absolutes. Now I've come to think that most men are not all good or all bad, heroic or cowardly. Rather they can be both. It's in the final accounting they differ. I can't blame you for the way Toulouse treated me. And I did listen to your advice, although I knew I shouldn't marry him. From here on, I'll trust my own judgment, but you have more than redeemed yourself."

Minerve closed his eyes and didn't stir for several moments. "I guess that will have to do," he murmured. "If I'm to meet my maker today, at long last my conscience is clear."

She stood. "You better not meet your maker today, or any day soon. I'm still in need of your support."

He managed a weak smile. "I'll do my best."

"That's all anyone can ask." She retreated toward the stairway that led to the chamber she shared with Missee. Her legs shook as she climbed the stairs. Much made sense to her now that she'd heard Minerve's confession. Did she really believe, as she had told him, that all men were both good and bad? If so, did that include Toulouse? She smiled at the unlikely possibility. She turned instead to think about what Minerve had said about her being like her father. There could be no higher praise. He had left her a proud inheritance.

Missee turned in the bed at the sound of the door opening and her face lit up in a relieved smile. "Oh Ermengarde," she said, holding out her arms. "I've never been so glad to see anyone. I feared... No matter. You're here."

Ermengarde rushed into her sister's embrace. "We'll be all right now."

When she pulled herself away, Missee's eyes were stained with tears of joy. "I'll tell you all about it, "Ermengarde said, "after I meet the nobles who came to our aid."

She returned to the great hall and stepped carefully through the wounded to join Béziers, who sat at a table with several knights at the far end of the hall. They rose to greet her with the clank of mail and weapons. The sight of allies, in heraldic surcoats, now stained and grimy from the fighting, brought home to her the full realization of her deliverance. Like the sudden appearance of the sun after days of rain, they made the future look brighter, more hopeful.

Béziers took her arm and led her to the nearest man, who towered above her. He was solidly built, balding with a fringe of reddish hair and an open, pleasant face. "I'd like you to meet my brother, Roger, Viscount of Carcassonne," Béziers said. "It was he and his knights who turned the tide of battle."

"At your service, my lady." Carcassonne bent to kiss her on both cheeks.

"Thank you for coming to our aid," she said with a smile.

Béziers then led her to another nobleman with a shock of white hair, prominent dark eyebrows, and a commanding presence. "And this is William, Viscount of Montpellier. He arrived with Carcassonne. Together, they are responsible for lifting the siege."

Montpellier bent to offer her the kiss of peace. "And I am at your service, my lady, as well. Your faithful friend Minerve informed us of your plight."

"Thank you for hastening to help us." She gave them all a grateful look.

"Perhaps you will join us for a glass of wine and some nourishment," Béziers said, directing her to a seat at the table.

Determined to set the course for her relationship with those who had come to her aid, Ermengarde addressed them. "Please accept my gratitude and that of my sister, Ermessende, for delivering us from the Count of Toulouse. Know that from this day forward, I am in your debt and your interests will be my interests, your battles, my battles. I ask that you continue to help me secure my inheritance."

Montpellier, who had returned to his seat, untangled his long legs, and stood. He raised a flagon in her direction and spoke in deep, sonorous voice. "Lady Ermengarde, I think I speak for us all. We are bound to your family by ancient ties, and we will do all in our power to restore you to your rightful place at our side."

She raised a wine goblet in return. "To the timely arrival of our most noble allies Montpellier, Carcassonne, and Minerve and to Béziers, his men, and the citizens of the city who are worthy of my everlasting gratitude." Her gaze took in her rescuers, and she didn't see Anduze among them. Her joy drained from her like water from a broken bucket. Was he among the fallen?

They sat and as soon as she got the chance, she leaned close to Béziers and whispered urgently, "Where is Anduze? What has happened to him?"

"I don't know," he replied, frowning. "I'll send someone to find out." He summoned a servant, gave him instructions, and the man scurried off.

Servants appeared carrying steaming platters of roasted capons, meat-filled pies, and rabbit in a spiced sauce that smelled of cinnamon and ginger. Then others brought in bowls of turnips and baskets of round loaves of white bread for trenchers. Since the end of the siege, the cooks had somehow managed to put together an impressive feast. Ermengarde's stomach growled. It had been many hours since she had eaten.

She took a trencher from the basket and reached for her eating knife. It was missing! The distorted face of the man she had stabbed flashed to mind, and she blinked to try and dispel the terrible memory. She had to focus on the present moment. Snagging a bone spoon from one of the bowls, she used it to fill the trencher with dishes that could be easily eaten with only a spoon. At the first bite of the hardy stew, her stomach cramped. How could she eat when Anduze might be lying somewhere dead?

The others had just finishing eating when the servant sent to inquire about Anduze returned. He leaned close, spoke to Béziers, and took his leave.

Béziers whispered to Ermengarde, "One of Anduze's men is seriously wounded. He has been taken to the Cathedral of Saint Nazaire."

Her immediate relief that Anduze was unharmed gave way to distress, and she abruptly stood. For him to stay with the man, it must be Storm, Nicholas, or Gilles. Concern quickened her pulse, and she felt it throb in her temple. She had to find out what happened. Carcassonne stopped talking to William of Montpellier and looked inquiringly in her direction.

"My lords, if you will excuse me, I most go," she said.

Béziers stood also. "My lady, it has been a trying day. I'm sure our guests will pardon you if you retire." He took her elbow to see her to the stairs that led to the great hall.

"I must go to Anduze," she said.

Béziers stopped a servant. "Lady Ermengarde needs blankets, bandages, and a basket of food and wine. She'll also need someone to accompany her."

The servant hurried off, and Béziers returned to his guests. She kept out of the way of the women tending the wounded, clasping and unclasping her hands until the servant returned with a basket and a hunchback manservant who was to be her escort.

Ermengarde took the basket, leaving the man to carry the bandages and blankets. She left the palace, her steps heavy. In the courtyard, palace servants were passing out bread and ladling out potage to a throng of exhausted-looking citizens. The townspeople hadn't been forgotten. They paid no attention to her as she passed.

The hunchback led the way through the crowded streets to the cathedral. Ermengarde didn't look to left or right, fearing what she would see. On entering the dimly lit church, filled with the dead and dying, her stomach roiled. The acrid smells of urine, sweat and blood, combined with the lingering aroma of incense and candle wax, assaulted her nostrils. She stopped to compose herself, fighting down waves of nausea, before searching for Anduze.

In the flickering light of the candles, she spotted his broad back near the altar. He and Gilles knelt beside Nicholas. Storm stood off to one side with a long face. She hurried to where Nicholas lay without a blanket on the cold, stone floor. All color had drained from the old man's face, and his breathing came in the short rasping gasps of the death rattle. She was too late. The clothes and blankets, the food and wine, and her intended ministrations were to no avail.

Without a word to Anduze, she took a blanket from the hunchback and tenderly covered Nicholas before kneeling beside him. A makeshift, bloodstained cloth covered a wound in his chest. His gambeson was torn, dirty. She took his hand, already beginning to grow cold, and squeezed it, as if doing so could somehow restore him to life. Anduze's trusted Nicholas put a face on all the horrible suffering she had caused. Hot tears leaked from her eyes and rolled down her face. "Thank you," she murmured, "for all you have sacrificed for Missee and me."

If Nicholas understood he gave no sign. In a moment his hand grew cold, and his ragged breathing stopped. She carefully placed his hand on his chest and gently closed his eyes. Overwhelmed with a feeling of loss, she made the sign of the cross over the body and silently said the *Pater Noster*, the only words that came to her.

Then she turned to Anduze, who stood close behind her. His face was a mask, but she could read the grief behind it.

Without thinking, she reached out and put her arms around him. For just a moment, he let her hold him before gently pushing her away.

She struggled to think of something to say. The loss of a friend was new to her experience. But she'd learned to trust her instincts. "I'm sorry about Nicholas."

Anduze stared down at Nicholas' body. "He was more than a friend. He was a father to me. After my mother died, Nicholas and his wife cared for me during the years my father was fighting the Moors in Hispania."

"I didn't know."

"There's much you don't know and need to learn." His words were more regretful than unkind. "Now we must see to his body. I promised I'd take him home to Sandeyren."

Gilles rose from where he knelt beside Nicholas, sniffling and wiping furiously at his wet eyes. Anduze walked to his side and put one arm around the young man's shoulder. "We must do the only thing we can do now for Nicholas. Gilles, find our horses and bring them here." His voice was firm. He took coins from his purse and turned to Storm, who was hanging back, visibly shaken. "We also need salt and a skin to wrap the body in. If we wrap the body well and the cold continues, we may be able to get Nicolas to Sandeyren without problems. We'll have to travel slowly, but perhaps we can make it in three or four days."

The two young men seemed relieved to have something to do and for the chance to grieve in private. They hurried off.

"Won't you have food? Wine?" Ermengarde indicated the basket that the hunchback still carried.

"There are plenty here who need it more than I," Anduze said, with a nod of his head toward the wounded in the nave.

"I'll see what I can do to help. But there's one more thing." Ermengarde lowered her eyes. "I broke my promise to you. I left the palace to save the horses."

He gently placed his hands on her arms and solemnly looked at her. "On our brief acquaintance, I had no right to bind you with a promise. I know, better than most, the constraints of the promises we make. The day may come when I do have that right, but even then, I'd expect you to use your judgment."

She looked up at him. "I want always to keep my word, especially to you."

"I appreciate your honesty. It's a rare trait, especially in women." He smiled, lightening the moment.

She turned away, shaking her head, and moved in the direction of the nearest wounded man.

Anduze lightly touched her shoulder. She turned back to him. His eyes seemed to contain all the sadness in the world.

He leaned down, smelling of sweat, blood, and smoke, and kissed her gently on each cheek. The slight roughness around his lips from his unshaven face made her face tingle. "Peace be with you, Ermengarde. Thank you for coming,"

In the time she had known Anduze, this was the first time he had offered her the kiss of peace. It was more like a caress than a perfunctory obligation. She didn't know if it meant anything more, but she'd not forget the affection with which it was given. Tears again burned her eyes, and she returned the kiss, her lips lingering for just moments on his grimy cheeks. "Thank you for everything. I'm so sorry. God protect you on your journey."

She pulled away from him, her heart heavy. Stunned and shattered by the immensity of all that had happened this day, she knelt beside a man moaning in pain. He was bleeding profusely from a leg wound. Her hands shook as she uncorked the wine bottle, raised his head and held it to his lips. When she glanced in Anduze's direction a few moments later, he was sitting quietly beside Nicholas' body.

Ermengarde had barely known Nicholas, and yet he and Gilles had been integral to her escape from Toulouse and Fontfroide. She'd never had close companions in Toulouse so she didn't know much about friendship, but she sensed she'd lost a friend in Nicholas. Three friends really, since Anduze and Gilles were leaving and would be lost now to her too. It was as if her right hand had lost three fingers.

Sick at heart and trying to disregard the stink of blood and urine, she went among the wounded. It took all her self-control to keep from bolting from the cathedral, the injured men, and the presence of death. She offered what little comfort she could until her supplies ran out.

When the hunchback finally escorted her from the cathedral, each step was an enormous effort, as if she trudged through thick mud. Outside, huge, wet snowflakes drifted lazily down. It was time for the snows. There would be no more fighting until spring.

Fires still burned in the city. A clerk held a crucifix and prayed over a fallen young man. An older woman, probably his mother, tore her hair and wailed piteously. Beyond them, two men unceremoniously lifted a screaming man onto a stretcher. To avoid them, she swerved and almost stumbled over the swollen body of a horse, scaring away a mongrel gnawing furtively on its entrails. She lurched in the other direction. The smoke was still thick, and tears rose in her smarting eyes. She couldn't go on. She leaned against a house they were passing, resting her pounding head against its cold stones. She closed her eyes for a few moments to gather her depleted strength.

Someone approached, and a gentle voice asked, "My lady, is there something I can do for you?"

Ermengarde turned. An old monk with an angelic face stood before her. She wiped her eyes with the sleeve of her mantle. "It's been a trying day. I'll be fine in a moment." She glanced around for the hunchback, who stood uneasily nearby. She indicated him with a nod of her head. "This man is seeing me to the palace."

The monk made the sign of the cross over her. "Remember whatever our trials and failings, Christ, our savior, has redeemed us, and his love will sustain us. Go with God's blessing."

The monk disappeared into the darkness, and his few words made her thoughts whirl. There had been redemption this day. Minerve had redeemed himself, and Nicholas had given his life on her behalf. She had faced her fear of fire, and that was a kind of redemption, too. Love had sustained her in her trials, but it had been her love for Missee and the love of her new friends. Surely, there was no greater love than Nicholas laying down his life for her. And in spite of her failure to keep her promise and the loss of Nicholas, Anduze's kiss had been tender, caring. Whether or not human love was a living expression of God's love, she didn't know, but she put her hand to heart to hold their love close for a few moments longer.

Ermengarde took a deep breath. The future held problems she must solve. Toulouse was temporarily defeated, but he had many knights and huge resources at his disposal. The battle for her inheritance was far from won, and he would renew his campaign against her in the spring. She had seen from the hatred in his eyes that the confrontation between them would not end until one of them was defeated. She would fight with her last breath to be free of him, to control her destiny. She had allies now, and she must assure their continued support. Toulouse would probably find allies, too. And Anduze. His aid had been invaluable. Surely she'd ask him to return.

One move at a time, she said to herself, thinking of her chess games. She was tired now, but the winter months would provide a respite, a time for her to meet with her allies and plan. Whatever the future held, from now on, she'd trust her own judgment and insist on taking a real part in the coming war for her viscounty. There were difficulties ahead, but she was ready and able to face them.

Ermengarde pulled her mantle more tightly about her and headed toward the palace—and to her uncertain future—with strong, determined steps.

The End

COMING SOON:

VOLUME TWO OF THE NARBONNE
INHERITANCE

The Viscountess

Main Characters

Aymeri, Viscount of Narbonne, Ermengarde's father. He died at the Battle of Fraga in 1134.

Peter, Viscount of Minerve, Aymeri's friend and Ermengarde's ally.

Ermengarde, Viscountess of Narbonne, inherits her city in 1134.

Ermessende, Ermengarde's younger sister, called **Missee**.

Alfonse Jordan, Count of Toulouse, Ermengarde's overlord and husband. **Jordana** is his daughter and **Raymond**, his young son. His mistress is named **Mahalt**.

Father Damian, Ermengarde's tutor, a priest and canon of the Basilica of Saint Sernin in Toulouse.

Father Hugh, Ermengarde's chaplain in Toulouse.

Ranulf, the Templar, The Knights Templars were warrior monks, founded in 1129 to protect Jerusalem. They became leading financiers in Europe. The Templar is Toulouse's advisor.

Bernard, Viscount of Anduze, a noble with lands north of Nîmes. He has two companions, a commoner **Nicholas** and Nicholas' grandson **Gilles**. Anduze's son is also named

Bernard and is called **Storm**. Anduze's friends are the farmer **Odo** and his wife **Bette**.

Arnold of Levezou, Archbishop of Narbonne. He controls half of Ermengarde's city.

Abbot Stephen, abbot of Fontfroide Abbey.

Louis le Jeune, Louis VII King of the Franks. At this time, he is married to Eleanor of Aquitaine.

William, Viscount of Montpellier, one of Ermengarde's important allies. His viscounty centers in the city of Montpellier.

Raymond, Viscount of Béziers, offers Ermengarde shelter. He controls a city and territory near Narbonne. His wife is **Saure**.

Roger, Viscount of Carcassonne, is the brother of Raymond of Béziers and controls a city and lands north and east of Narbonne. He becomes Ermengarde's ally.

Author's Note

The Viscount's Daughter is a work of fiction. My interest in Ermengarde of Narbonne (1126?-1196) dates from 1967 at the University of Illinois where I did a master's paper on her life and historical contribution. This resulted in my first academic publication. I am indebted to the professors who encouraged my work on Ermengarde: Bennett D. Hill, Walter Wakefield, Richard Emory, and Joseph F. O'Callaghan. I enrolled at Columbia University, where in 1975, I received my Ph.D. in history. I intended to pursue my research on Ermengarde but, due to a number of unforeseen factors, I wasn't able to work with the professor whose specialty was medieval southern France.

A number of historians have subsequently written about Ermengarde, and I'm grateful for their careful research, especially that of Professor Frederic Cheyette. His book, *Ermengard of Narbonne and the World of the Troubadours,* is a valuable source of information.

Unfortunately historians do not agree about the details of Ermengarde's life. In telling her story, I have adopted what I felt were the most likely scenarios based on the documentary evidence. However, the documents are silent on key information, and in those cases I used my imagination, based as it is, on years of interest in the history of the area.

I was initially attracted to Ermengarde because she was an exception to what I had learned about the status of women in the medieval world and because her story destroyed many of the generalizations about her times I had learned in my graduate studies. More than that, her story enthralled me because she was a survivor against tremendous odds and as such her story goes beyond being an action-adventure tale set in a distant time.

Since I first encountered Ermengarde, a great number of books have been written about strong, heroic medieval women. Many of these are modern projections of what women are like today onto a past time. These should enhance interest in Ermengarde as a real example of what we wish for women of the past.

To accurately recreate Ermengarde's story, I traveled to the key sites in the story, seeking the remains of the twelfth century in Narbonne, Toulouse, Anduze, Fontfroide, and other places mentioned in the novel. Little did I realize when I began this project that Ermengarde's story would necessitate a trilogy. In this, and in the forthcoming volumes, it is my hope that I have captured her spirit and that of her times.

In June of 2013, the James River Writers selected *The Viscount's Daughter* as one of two finalists in their Best Unpublished Novel Contest.

About the Author

Readers often ask where I get my ideas. My answer is always one word: history. Much of my life has been devoted to the study of the rich mélange of fact, opinion, memory, and anecdote that is history. I love the "story" that is an integral part of the word history. My interest led to a Ph.D. in history, college teaching, and writing and it's no accident that I live in Williamsburg, Virginia, one of the most historic towns in the United States.

It is long been my desire to share my love of history with others. To that end, I have written a number of popular articles, six books of children's historical fiction, a book of nonfiction for the general reader, and now the first volume of my trilogy about Ermengarde of Narbonne.

When I'm not bent over my computer at a local coffee shop where I meet with other writers five days a week, I am walking. My husband and I are avid walkers, having trekked six times on the medieval pilgrimage route, the Camino de Santiago in France and Spain.

I have a grown son, Alex, who shares my love of writing, and a grandson Xander who is just beginning to learn the magic of words.

THE VISCOUNT'S DAUGHTER

Check out my website:
http://thegraceofironclothing.wordpress.com

Or contact me at:
Phyllis.haislip@gmail.com

CPSIA information can be obtained at www.ICGtesting.com
Printed in the USA
BVOW05s1708160315

391905BV00001B/17/P